TM

## BY RAE CARSON

*Star Wars: Most Wanted*
*Star Wars: Canto Bight*

*The Girl of Fire and Thorns*
*The Crown of Embers*
*The Bitter Kingdom*
*The Girl of Fire and Thorns Stories*
*The Empire of Dreams*

*Walk on Earth a Stranger*
*Like a River Glorious*
*Into the Bright Unknown*

STAR WARS
THE RISE OF SKYWALKER

Based on Characters Created by George Lucas
Screenplay by Chris Terrio & J. J. Abrams
Based on a Story by Derek Connolly & Colin Trevorrow
and Chris Terrio & J. J. Abrams

RAE CARSON

DEL REY
NEW YORK

Published in the United States by Del Rey,
an imprint of Random House, a division of
Penguin Random House LLC, New York.

Del Rey and the House colophon are registered
trademarks of Penguin Random House LLC.

ISBN 978-0-593-12840-4
International edition ISBN 978-0-593-15841-8
ebook ISBN 978-0-593-12841-1

Printed in the United States of America on acid-free paper

randomhousebooks.com

2 4 6 8 9 7 5 3 1

First Edition

*Book design by Elizabeth A. D. Eno*

THE DEL REY

# STAR WARS

TIMELINE

DOOKU: JEDI LOST
MASTER & APPRENTICE

I THE PHANTOM MENACE

II ATTACK OF THE CLONES

THE CLONE WARS (TV SERIES)

DARK DISCIPLE

III REVENGE OF THE SITH

CATALYST: A ROGUE ONE NOVEL
LORDS OF THE SITH
TARKIN

SOLO

THRAWN
A NEW DAWN
THRAWN: ALLIANCES
THRAWN: TREASON

REBELS (TV SERIES)

ROGUE ONE

THE DEL REY

# STAR WARS™

TIMELINE

## IV A NEW HOPE

BATTLEFRONT II: INFERNO SQUAD
HEIR TO THE JEDI
BATTLEFRONT: TWILIGHT COMPANY

## V THE EMPIRE STRIKES BACK

## VI RETURN OF THE JEDI

ALPHABET SQUADRON
AFTERMATH
AFTERMATH: LIFE DEBT
AFTERMATH: EMPIRE'S END
LAST SHOT
BLOODLINE
PHASMA
CANTO BIGHT

## VII THE FORCE AWAKENS

## VIII THE LAST JEDI

RESISTANCE REBORN
GALAXY'S EDGE: BLACK SPIRE

## IX THE RISE OF SKYWALKER

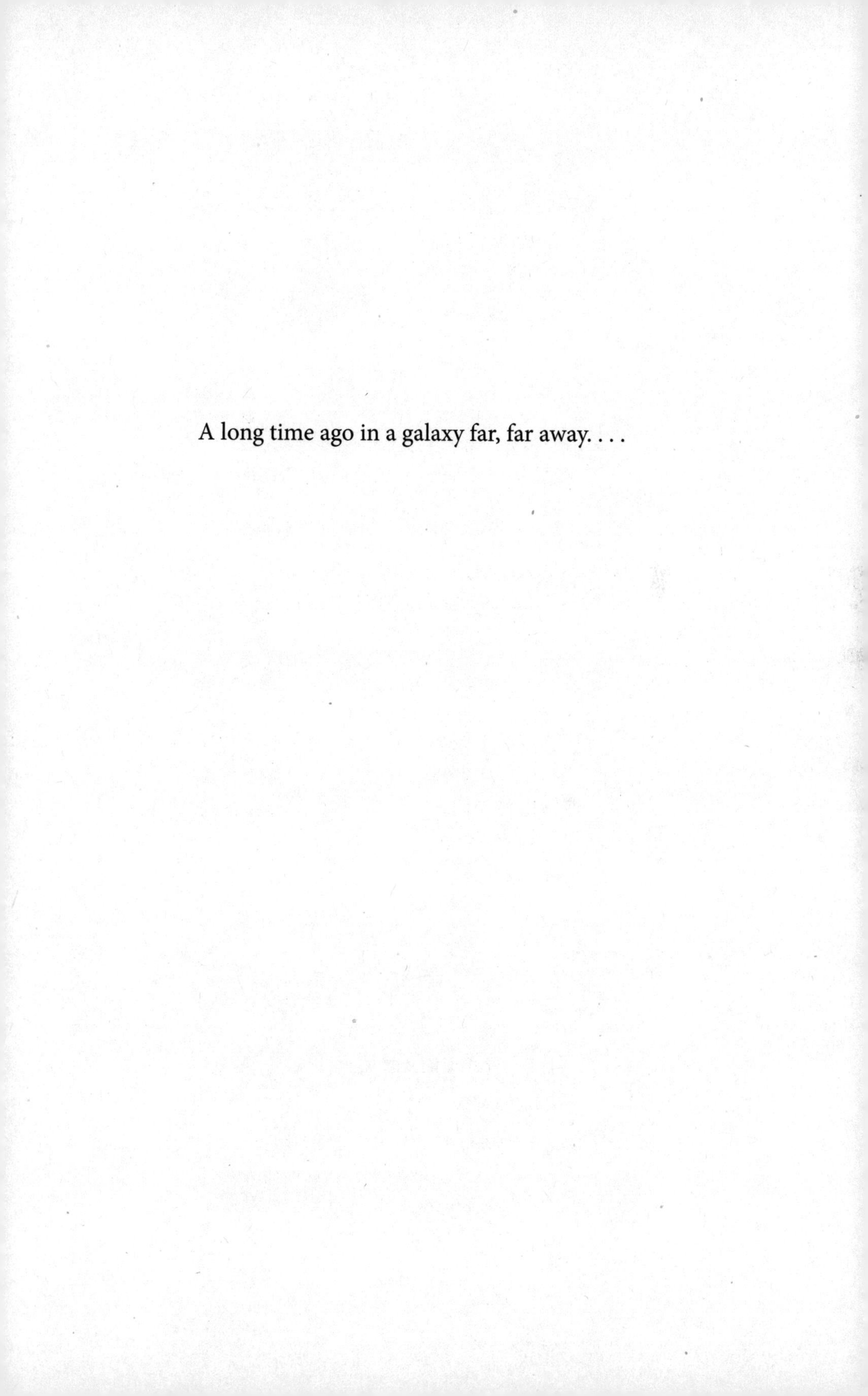

A long time ago in a galaxy far, far away. . . .

STAR
THE RISE OF SKYWALKER
WARS™

The dead speak! The galaxy has
heard a mysterious broadcast,
a threat of REVENGE in the
sinister voice of the late
EMPEROR PALPATINE.

GENERAL LEIA ORGANA
dispatches secret agents to
gather intelligence, while REY,
the last hope of the Jedi, trains
for battle against the diabolical
FIRST ORDER.

Meanwhile, Supreme Leader
KYLO REN rages in search
of the phantom Emperor,
determined to destroy any
threat to his power. . . .

# CHAPTER 1

Rey sat cross-legged, eyes closed. She didn't remember rising off the ground, but she was vaguely aware that somehow she'd ended up floating. Pebbles and small boulders hovered around her, like a field of asteroids orbiting their sun. The Force flowed through her, buoyed her, connected her to everything. The lush rain forest moon of Ajan Kloss was teeming with life. She could feel every tree and fern, every reptile and insect. A few strides away in a hidden den, a small furry creature groomed its litter of four kits.

"That's it, Rey," came Leia's voice, deep and soothing as always. "Very good. Your connection becomes stronger every day. Can you feel it?"

"Yes."

"Now reach out. If your mind is ready, you'll be able to hear those who have come before."

Rey inhaled through her nose and sent her awareness into the void. Peace and calm were key, Leia always said. She reached, she searched, she felt the breeze on her cheeks, she smelled loamy soil, damp from the recent rain.

"Be with me, be with me, be with me," she murmured. But she heard . . . nothing except wind in the trees and chirruping insects.

"Rey?"

She didn't want to admit that she was failing, so instead she said, "Why did *you* stop training with Luke?" Her words came out too harsh, almost like a challenge.

Leia took it in stride. "Another life called to me."

Eyes still closed, Rey asked, "How did you know?"

"A feeling. Visions. Of serving the galaxy in different ways."

"But how did you know those visions were true?" Rey pressed.

"I knew." She heard the smile in Leia's voice.

Rey didn't understand how Leia could be so sure. Of anything.

"I treasured each moment I spent with my brother," Leia added. "The things he taught me . . . I use them every day. Once you touch the Force, it's part of you always. Over the years, I continued to learn, to grow. There were times on the Senate floor when the meditations I'd practiced with Luke were the only thing that kept me from causing a galactic incident."

Rey frowned. Leia didn't need patience. She could have made anyone do anything she wanted, with the power of the Force. Surely she'd been tempted?

"Was Luke angry? When you quit?" She hoped Leia noticed that she could talk *and* float at the same time now. That was progress, right?

Leia paused to consider. "He was disappointed. But he understood. I think he held out hope that I'd return to it someday."

Rey almost laughed. "He should have known better." Once Leia made a decision, it was for keeps.

"I gave him my lightsaber to convince him otherwise. Told him to pass it on to a promising student someday." But Leia's voice had grown tight. Rey sensed she was holding something back.

"Where's your lightsaber now?"

"No idea. Now stop trying to distract me," Leia said. "Reach out."

Rey refocused and emptied her mind of worries, just as Leia had taught her. She cast out her awareness. Opened herself to anything the Force might want to tell her. Tentatively, she called for him: *Master Skywalker?*

Nothing, nothing, and more nothing.

"Master Leia, I don't hear anyone."

"Let go of all thought. Let go of fear. Reach out. Invite the Jedi of the past to be with you."

"Be with me . . . be with me . . ." She waited all of a second, maybe two. "They're not with me." Rey made a noise of exasperation, then flipped herself neatly to land on the ground. Rocks toppled around her.

"Rey," Leia said. The general could put so much into a single word: chastisement, acceptance, amusement, fondness. Maybe that's why she'd become such a powerful leader. "Be patient."

"I'm starting to think it's impossible. To hear the voices of the Jedi who came before," Rey said, striding toward Leia.

Her Master always managed to look neat and tidy, no matter how muddy their makeshift base got. Her hair was pulled back into a circlet of braids, and she wore a quilted vest over a brown tunic. Alderaanian jewelry always dangled from her earlobes, wrapped her wrists and fingers. Her eyes were bright and knowing, as always, but Rey had noticed that her movements had slowed recently, as though her bones ached.

Leia's face held a hint of a smile. "Nothing's impossible."

Rey grabbed her blast helmet and leapt to her feet. "Nothing's impossible . . ." she echoed, trying to believe it. "I'm going to run the training course. That I can do." Rey *needed* to run. Or maybe hit something.

Leia handed her Luke's lightsaber. Rey took it reverently. Then she dashed into the jungle. BB-8 rolling after her.

Leia watched Rey sprint away, a hint of a smile on her lips. Training the girl always filled her with pride, but also misgiving. Rey was both a wonderful and an exasperating student. Frustrated with anything she didn't pick up quickly, completely unaware how fast she did pick things up.

She wasn't one to judge, though. Leia had exasperated Luke just as much. Besides, there was something about growing old that made her connection with the Force even stronger. When the body began to fail, the mind reached out, unencumbered by physical ability. The truth was, Leia couldn't run through the jungle if she wanted to. Peace and calm came easily because her body craved them.

Then again, perhaps Leia had never been young. By the time she'd reached the age Rey was now, she was leading a rebellion.

Rey could be a great leader someday, and she would be, if Leia had anything to do with it. The girl had darkness inside her, just like Ben. But Leia would not make the same mistakes she had with her son. She would not give in to fear—neither of the darkness rising within her pupil nor of her own questionable qualifications as a teacher. Most important, she would never send Rey away.

Leia turned and began walking back toward the base. She reached out a hand and let her fingers trail through the ferns and broad-leafed creepers that lined her path. Ajan Kloss held so many good memories. Years ago, she'd trained here with Luke, who had declared it "Nice Dagobah." He'd claimed it was as wet, warm, green, and overflowing with life as the planet where he'd trained with Yoda—except it didn't smell bad.

She stepped into a clearing. To her right, a large tree with a massive trunk reached for sunlight, spreading a canopy of branches that shaded the clearing, keeping anything else from growing except ground creeping ferns and low, sparse grass. Leia had trained right here, in this very spot. She reached out and touched the tree trunk reverently. A large bole of bark had formed around an old wound. It was almost sealed shut.

Leia had been the one to damage the tree. She'd swung for Luke with her lightsaber and missed, slashing into the tree trunk instead. This tree had been healing itself for more than two decades.

*Oh, Luke, I hope I'm doing this right,* she thought. Leia was no Jedi Master, but she had learned from the best. And not just from Luke; over the years she'd occasionally heard the voice of Obi-Wan Kenobi through the Force, and even more rarely, that of Yoda. Some days it had felt as though she'd learned from the Force itself. She was first and foremost a politician and a general, but she had accepted her Jedi legacy and embraced it as best she could.

And maybe that's exactly what Rey needed: training in the Force *not* from a formal Master, but rather someone grounded in the everyday minutiae of life and survival. Obi-Wan had failed to keep Vader from the dark side. Luke had failed the same way with Ben. She could not fail Rey.

Insects sang as she walked. Birds warbled overhead, and tiny amphibians trilled their mating calls. Odd how such a raucous place could be so peaceful. The noise was so loud, so ever-present, and so soothing, it was almost as perfect as silence.

Many years ago, not long after the Battle of Endor, she'd discovered the meditative power of sound. She and Luke had stolen away for some training, and somehow she'd ended up standing on her hands while Luke slung good-natured taunts her way. Even with help from the Force, her shoulders had started to burn, her arms wobble. They'd already spent the last hour sparring with their lightsabers, and her body was exhausted.

"You know," Luke had said, his voice smug, "when I did this on Dagobah, Yoda was sitting on my feet."

He said that a lot back then. *When I did this on Dagobah . . .* It was obnoxious and completely unhelpful. So Leia reminded him, "You're being obnoxious and completely unhelpful."

"I also did it one-handed," he added

He was trying to provoke her, to teach her a lesson about anger and impatience, and all that nonsense. Luke had forgotten that his student was a superb strategist who'd already benefited from a royal education. Leia would not be provoked.

Instead, she considered. She reached out to the Force, let it flow through her like blood in her veins. A tiny insect began rubbing its mandibles together, whistling a sweet, high song.

Some instinct guided her, and Leia focused on the sound. It was beautiful, pure, ethereal—completely untethered to the worries of leadership and teaching, failure and learning.

With focus, and with *delight,* Leia raised herself off the ground.

She floated upside down, feet pointed to the sky. After a moment, she lifted her arms and held them parallel to the ground.

But she *was* just a student, new to the ways of the Force, and when she came back to herself, fully realized what she'd done, she whipped her hands back down lest she fall.

She did it just in time. Her form collapsed, and she found herself kneeling in mud. No matter. She'd do better next time.

Leia looked up to find Luke staring at her, mouth open.

"Did you ever do *that* with Yoda?" she couldn't resist asking.

He shook his head wordlessly.

"I can do better," she insisted. "Float longer."

Luke found his voice. "You're going to make me a better teacher," he said.

Not the response she'd expected. "What do you mean?"

He reached down, helped her up. "Your footwork is terrible," he said. "Don't get me wrong, your lightsaber craft is coming along, but . . . you do other things. Naturally." His face turned apologetic. "What I mean is, you're exceptional. Just . . . different."

Then he had smiled, with that wide farm-boy grin that had stayed with him all the way up until the night of Ben's betrayal.

Leia shook off the memory with effort. Memories were coming fast and vivid these days.

She was glad for this one, though. It would be the key to training Rey. Leia and Rey were different, the last remnants of a dead Order, and together, they would carve a *new* path.

Thick green foliage whipped past Rey as she ran, the flag in her hand flashing red with each pump of her arms. She bounded over tangled ferns, dodged hanging vines. Sweat soaked her collar, and her thighs burned with effort.

Even so, running through the jungle was not harder than running ankle-deep in desert sand. She could do this all day.

Rey had already taken out the first two training remotes and captured the flags they guarded. She had leapt a massive gorge, fought blindly over a ravine while balanced on a tightrope made of vines, traversed a thin ridge high above the jungle canopy. Now the course had her doubling back, where she encountered BB-8. He warbled at her.

"One to go," she said. "C'mon!"

The final remote eluded her because it was faster. Trickier. More droid than remote. She'd told Leia she wanted a challenge today, and Leia had delivered.

BB-8 sped after her, beeping complaints every time he had to dodge a tree root. Rey hid a smile. She was continually impressed by how well the little droid kept up with her, whether they were running the sands of Jakku, the rocky trails of Takodana, or the jungles of Ajan Kloss. His maneuverability made him the perfect training companion.

He bleated a warning.

"I see it, Beebee-Ate." She slid to a halt.

The spherical remote had stopped and now hovered midair as if waiting for her, or maybe taunting her. It was different from the other two she'd taken out, a wicked red shell surrounding shining metal firing ports. It hummed dark and low; she felt that hum deep in her chest.

Rey unhooked Luke's reforged lightsaber from her utility belt. Ignited it. Bluish light glowed against the leaves around her as she stared the remote down. She was going to *destroy* this thing.

Suddenly a blast shot out from one of the ports. Stinging pain exploded in her upper arm. Rey resisted the urge to clutch her arm or even grunt in pain. She deserved it, after all. She hadn't been ready. *Determination is not the same as readiness,* Leia would say.

Well, she wasn't one to make the same mistake twice. The next time it fired, she whipped up her lightsaber to deflect the blast and sent it flying into the trees.

She didn't even have a chance to congratulate herself before another blast hit her in the chest. *Of course* multiple ports meant multiple blasts. She had to *focus.*

She breathed deep through her nose. Reached out to the Force.

The training remote started to buzz around her, flashing angry red as it slung stinging darts in a dizzying array, but she let instinct take over and whirled her lightsaber with equally dizzying speed, deflecting every single attack.

Connecting to the Force came easily these days. So easily it was like breathing. But the peace, the calm that Leia was always going on about eluded her. So even though she could counter the remote's every move, she couldn't find her opening for attack. *Patience,* she imagined Leia saying. *Wait for your moment . . .*

The remote was behind her, then in front of her, then high above her head, darting through the air like a buzzing fly, and if she could just smash it . . .

The remote sped away and she tore after it. It stopped again, fired a few bolts to goad her. Teeth gritted, she swung her lightsaber. The remote dodged, and her blade missed, slicing through a tree trunk; sparks and leaves and bark splinters rained down as the tree toppled, smashing jungle foliage on its way down.

She leapt over the downed trunk after the remote. Swung again. The remote swooped around as if anticipating the arc of her blade, barely evading when the lightsaber slid through another tree as if it were made of butter.

A roiling dark cloud of frustration grew inside her.

She hardly realized what she was doing as raw instinct took over. Rey threw her lightsaber, winging it like a propeller through the air at the red remote. It dodged, and the lightsaber sliced through yet another tree. The remote screamed as it dived for her head, but this time she was ready.

She reached with the Force for a downed branch. It flew into her hand. She anticipated the exact angle of attack, and she whipped up the branch and thrust it into the remote, spearing it against a nearby tree trunk.

Her lightsaber returned to her hand with a satisfying smack.

The crushed red remote twitched and sparked against the tree.

She glared at it as triumph filled her. Maybe patience was overrat—

Whispers filled her ears. No, her very mind. She whirled, seeking their source even as the realization dawned: It was happening again.

The jungle around her faded. All went deathly silent as sweltering darkness closed in, threatening to smother her. An image sprang to mind, and she flinched away, though there was no avoiding the horrible sight: Kylo Ren, black-clad and ferocious, his crackling red lightsaber slicing mercilessly through robed figures. She heard their screams, smelled their blood, watched as they tried in vain to flee or beg for their lives. Nothing slowed him. He was a juggernaut of destruction, monstrous and unstoppable.

Relief flooded her like a wave when the vision shifted, but it quickly changed to utter desolation as she saw herself, wind-whipped and alone, standing in a forsaken landscape of endlessly fractured ground. The hair on her arms stood on end, for the air crackled with electricity. Before her, a massive monolith jutted upward, scraping the sky. It was black and shimmery, casting a huge shadow.

The monolith shifted. Became a giant face of stone, cloaked in evil . . .

No, not a stone at all. A form of something, part human, part machine, with tubes stretching away from it like tentacles, all filled with a strange liquid. Was this creature alive? Or was it—

Flashes of Luke's face. Then Kylo's. Han Solo, his hand against Kylo's cheek. A young woman in a hood. A freighter flying away from Jakku . . .

Finally, a burning voice in her head, as clear and unbearable as a desert sun: *"Exegol."*

She whispered the word back, her voice shaking: "Exegol . . . ?"

And suddenly she was standing before yet another giant stone structure, this one shaped like a huge claw, its thick, bent fingers grasping ever upward. Her legs twitched as if to flee, even as something about it beckoned to her, invited her. She found herself wanting to approach the massive claw-thing, wanting to know what it would feel like to run her fingers along its rough black surface.

The black claw-thing was a throne; she could see it now.

She took a step forward, but something beeped at her, and she hesitated. The beeping continued, grew more insistent. Clarity hit her like a quarterstaff to the jaw. Of course she couldn't touch that throne. It belonged to darkness and evil. She had already chosen a different path, hadn't she?

More beeping. Something appeared on the throne. A familiar figure. Rey blinked in shock and dismay.

Quick as it appeared, the vision evaporated like morning mist, and she was left gasping in the jungle. Rey was so relieved to sense the life and light and humid green around her that it took her a moment to come fully back to herself, to trace the sound of beeping to a felled tree, and beneath it a very indignant BB-8.

Rey dashed over to him, pushed some branches away. "I'm so sorry!" she said.

He babbled at her while she extricated him from the fallen trunk—it took a little help from the Force to free him completely.

One of the orange discs that protected his modular tool bay had popped off, exposing a dark channel to his motive system.

She'd hurt her friend. Poe was going to be livid with her, but not more livid than she was with herself.

The little droid warbled at her.

"Yes, Beebee-Ate, it happened to me again."

He whirred at her, part question, part empathy.

"No, I still don't know what the Force was trying to show me, but this time was . . . worse." So much worse. Unspeakably worse. She stared off into the trees. Some of the flashes had been memories. Hers, and . . . Kylo Ren's? "Let's get back."

Maybe she should tell Leia what had happened. Or maybe not. The general had enough things to worry about, and Rey needed Leia to believe in her, to trust her. What would the general say if she knew how Rey's frustration and anger were triggering visions of death and dark power?

She just needed more training. More time meditating in the Force, more time seeking the peace Leia was trying to teach her. She could do it. She *had* to.

If only she could hear voices through the Force, like Leia could. Surely Luke could provide some guidance. As Rey and BB-8 neared the camp, she decided to try again. *Nothing's impossible,* Leia had said.

"Master Luke," she said. "I'm afraid." Rey glanced around, making sure only BB-8 was there to observe her speaking to no one. Rey reached out to the Force and said, "Before *I* felt it, you saw it. I'm drawn to the dark side. Or maybe it's drawn to me. I don't know. Whatever it is, it's stronger now, and I can't push it away, hard as I try . . . I don't understand it."

BB-8 beeped.

"Shh, don't interrupt. Master Luke? I think you can hear me, I need your—"

BB-8 beeped again, more insistently.

They had reached the edge of camp. "Seriously, you're being annoying, go over there," Rey said, indicating a large flight case.

He did as asked, but he warbled his indignation.

"It *is* how it works," Rey countered. "There are Force spirits; Luke wrote about them in the Jedi texts. They come when you need them the most."

The droid remained loudly skeptical.

Rey ignored him. "Master Luke," she tried again. "I have visions of things that frighten me. I don't want to lose this . . . Leia is how I dreamed a mother would be . . . and my friends . . . I don't want to let them down."

There it was. Her greatest fear. That these people she'd come to care for so much would be disappointed in her. Maybe even hurt by her. She'd been alone for so long . . . she couldn't bear the thought of losing any of them.

"But no one here understands . . . except Kylo Ren. If the son of Han and Leia can be turned, can't any of us?"

A twig cracked, and Rey looked up. Snap Wexley and Rose Tico were walking toward her, questions writ all over their faces.

"How much of that did you hear?" Rey said.

"Of what?" Snap said, failing to look innocent.

"Nothing," Rey mumbled.

Rose's expression softened with empathy. The commander of the Engineering Corps had a disarming quality about her. Whenever she spoke to Rey, it was all Rey could do to keep from spilling all her fears and worries to her friend. "You okay?" Rose asked.

"Yes, of course, I was just doing . . . "

"Jedi stuff," Rose finished for her.

"Yeah."

Thankfully, Rose chose not to press her. She said, "The general asked for you."

Rey took a deep breath. It was decision time. Should she tell Leia about her dark vision or keep it to herself?

# CHAPTER 2

General Armitage Hux watched—from a safe distance—as Supreme Leader Kylo Ren and a squad of stormtroopers cut a swath of blood and destruction through the pathetic Mustafarian colonists. They battled through the gloomy woods of Corvax Fen, one of the few patches on this hellscape of a lava planet that was cool enough to support native growth, if you could call this "growth." Barren trees grew out of a noxious marsh, and the air was hazy with mist. The barbarian colonists were failing to put up a decent fight; their archaic halberds and broadswords were no match for the technical superiority of a good blaster, or even, Hux had to admit, a lightsaber.

Ren was a blunt instrument, a mindless dog, whose current obsession was putting all the First Order's plans behind schedule. The general was half tempted to wade into the fight himself to hurry things along—just so they could leave this awful planet. Or at least he would be half tempted if his skills were not better used elsewhere. Best if Ren did all the dirty work; Hux was too valuable to risk.

"He's almost beautiful to watch," mused Allegiant General Pryde, standing tall beside him. The older man had arrogant blue eyes and a high hairline that seemed immune to perspiration, even in a hell-climate like this. "Don't you think?"

Hux refused to gratify that with a response, because true beauty came from discipline, from *order.* So it was almost against his will that he found himself mesmerized as Ren met a barbarian's charge head-on, cloak flowing, mist swirling around him. The glow of his lightsaber occasionally snagged on his cheek scar, making it appear as though a crack of glowing lava slashed his face. It was like something out of a dream, or maybe a nightmare, as the Supreme Leader plunged his fiery crossguard into his attacker's abdomen, lifted him from the ground, and sent him toppling onto his back. Kylo Ren did not spare his fallen foe a single glance, simply rushed forward into the woods seeking his next kill.

But there was no one left. Corpses littered the ground, barely more than lumps of shadow in the gloom. The air smelled of ozone and scorched vegetation. All was eerily silent as Ren looked around, catching his breath. Even from a distance, Hux could sense his disappointment that the killing was over, that no outlet for his rage remained.

Kylo Ren gathered himself and strode away into the woods, shoulders set with determination, lightsaber still ablaze. The mysterious object he had come for—dragged all of them across the galaxy for—was nearly within his grasp.

"He's gone mad," General Hux said, and the contempt in his voice was obvious even to his own ears. "Flames of rebellion burn across the galaxy, and Ren chases a *ghost.*"

"No," Allegiant General Pryde responded, softly but firmly. "*Someone* was behind that transmission. And Leader Ren will answer to no one."

Hux narrowed his eyes. Ren would definitely answer to someone, someday. He just didn't realize it yet.

Kylo Ren showed mercy to nothing and no one, but he had a grudging appreciation for things that struggled to survive. Even though the nearest lava flow was many klicks away, it seemed as though the air ought to be too hot, too chemical, for life to truly thrive here. As they'd landed, Hux had proclaimed the planet a "desolate hell-scape," and Kylo hadn't bothered to correct him. The truth was, Mustafar was teeming with life—all connected through the Force. Like those hapless cultists he'd just killed, who'd been obsessed with protecting Vader's legacy. Or this forest of twisted irontrees they endeavored to cultivate. Or even the extremophile organisms that swarmed the lava flows. All fragile but determined, mutilated but indomitable.

It was no wonder his grandfather has chosen this place for a home.

Kylo strode through the trees, lightsaber still ignited. Malevolence lay ahead, along with a darkness that had nothing to do with the planet's day–night cycle. But that's not why he kept his weapon ready. He refused to put it away because for the briefest moment, as he was hacking away at Mustafarians, he had sensed *her.* Watching him. Now his guard was up, and it would stay up until he got what he came for.

By silent mutual agreement, the stormtroopers who'd accompanied him had declined to follow him through the woods, which suited him fine. He preferred to be alone for this.

A few more steps and the ground became soggy. The mist thickened. A small splash indicated that his presence had been noticed. Finally, the trees broke open onto a small lake with brackish water, bordered on all sides by forest and large black lumps like boulders, jutting out of the ground at odd angles. No, not boulders, he noted upon closer look, but rather fallen remnants of Darth Vader's castle.

An oily film slicked across the lake's still surface. But as Kylo approached, the water bubbled up in the center, sending tiny waves to lap at his boots.

A giant emerged, a hairless creature sheening with wetness, bits of lake detritus clinging to its pasty skin. Its eyes were squeezed shut, but it could still see after a fashion, because draped over its massive bald head and across one shoulder was a second creature with long spidery tentacles. The two were locked in symbiosis. Kylo sensed the giant's pain, as though it were a slave to the spidery being that clung to it. Yet neither could it survive alone.

The spider creature spoke. "I am the Eye of Webbish Bog. I know what you seek."

"You will give it to me," Kylo said.

The Eye cocked its head, making an eerie squealing noise. It took a moment for Kylo to realize the creature was laughing at him. "No need for that," the Eye said. "Do you really think my lord would have left it in the guardianship of one who could be swayed by a trick of the Force?"

No, he supposed not.

"You've been seeking it for a while, yes? I must warn you, our fiery planet burns away deception. If you proceed down this path, you will encounter your true self."

Kylo was growing impatient. He glared in silence.

"Fine," the creature said, as though disappointed that Kylo would not indulge him in ceremony. "In accordance with Lord Vader's wishes, you have defeated my protectors and earned it. His wayfinder."

The blind giant beneath the Eye raised its enormous hand from the water and pointed toward a small island in the lake. On it was a stone structure, like an altar.

Kylo turned off his lightsaber and hooked it to his belt. He waded into the shallow lake, soaking his boots and cloak. The water was warm, and the ground beneath the water a sludge that sucked at his feet. He ignored it all, reaching for a pyramidal object. It fit satisfyingly in his hand, heavy and hot, and he stared at it a moment, lost in its red glow. The sides were etched glass framed in deep-gray resin. The crimson light within seemed to pulse faintly. Ren had come a long way for this, and yet he hesitated, eyeing the pyramid with distrust.

"It will guide you through the Unknown Regions," the Eye said. "To the hidden world of Exegol. To *him*."

Whoever *he* was. The transmission purporting to be from Palpatine had reached the far corners of the galaxy. Kylo had it memorized:

*At last the work of generations is complete. The great error is corrected. They day of victory is at hand. The day of revenge. The day of the Sith.*

He wasn't sure what to believe about it, but it was a fair guess that Kylo wasn't the only one seeking answers. Others would follow the same path and come to Mustafar sooner or later, looking for this exact object.

So surely his grandfather would have made it harder than this? Those cultists were too easy to kill. This creature too easy to convince. Then again, he was Vader's heir. The object belonged to him.

Now that he had it up close, the etchings in the glass clarified into patterns. Star charts. Alignment markers. Something stirred deep within him, suggesting ancient knowledge and power, and he felt a rush of triumph. It had all been worth it—diverting ships, sending out spies, tracing old records, enduring the smug disapproval of that idiot Hux—all to find this.

Kylo looked up, and was startled to discover that the Eye of Webbish Bog was gone, slipped back beneath the surface of a lake so still it was as though nothing lived within it at all.

How long had he been staring at the pyramid?

Kylo Ren wasted no more time. Dried blood made the skin of his face itch, and his boots and cloak were soggy with lake water, but instead of returning to his command ship, the *Steadfast,* he dismissed everyone back to their regular duties and jumped into his modified TIE whisper to make the next part of the journey alone.

No one protested.

He connected the pyramid to his navicomputer, attaching ports where indicated by the glass etchings. The nav interface lit up with new information, but it also blared a warning.

For these coordinates would take him beyond the Western

Reaches into the Unknown Regions. Kylo overrode the warning and jumped his TIE to lightspeed. The stars turned to streams of matter.

The Unknown Regions remained uncharted because a chaotic web of anomalies had created a near-impenetrable barrier to exploration; only the most foolhardy or desperate ventured there—criminals, refugees, and, if the reports were true, remnants of the old Imperial fleet who had refused to accept New Republic rule.

A few planets had been discovered, but their populations remained small, and their trade with the rest of the galaxy had been throttled by the navigational risk. The Sith and the Jedi had found paths through to even more dangerous, more hidden worlds—or so legends said—and the specific, carefully stepped coordinate jumps required to safely navigate the anomalies were among their most closely guarded secrets.

The trip would be worth the risk. Someone was out there, claiming to be the Emperor himself, and Kylo could already sense ripples of doubt in the First Order. After all he'd done, after all he'd sacrificed to become Supreme Leader . . . who would *dare* to challenge him now?

But what filled him with absolutely incandescent rage was the thought that Snoke—his master, the one to guide him away from the duplicitous light, the one he'd looked up to above all others—has been someone's puppet all along.

Kylo was done with masters. He would be no one's lackey. He would destroy whoever—whatever—he found in the Unknown Regions. No one would question his right to rule supreme.

And Vader had left him a guide, a compass.

The TIE bumped out of lightspeed into rough space; it felt as though he were flying through gravel. He double-checked the nav—the TIE was on course. He had to have faith that Vader's wayfinder would steer him true.

That, and the Force. Kylo Ren drew on all the rage and frustration of the last few days and gripped the controls in cold focus. Once his flight steadied, he sent his TIE to the next set of coordinates.

This time, instead of the streaming stars of hyperspace, his ship entered a glowing red mesh of hexes. He'd heard tales of the Red Honeycomb Zone of exotic space—some called it the Blood Net, others called it the Ship Eater—but until now he hadn't been sure he believed any of them. It was one of the only known safe passages through the anomalies of the Unknown Regions, but it seemed malevolent and angry, and the sensor indicators on his console flashed wildly, unsure what to make of it.

Most pilots, when traveling faster-than-light for a while, used the time to stretch, do some interior checks and maintenance, or even sleep. But Kylo didn't dare let his guard down. He had to be ready for anything. Besides, while tracking down Vader's wayfinder, he'd heard whispers that time and distance became near meaningless in exotic space. He had no idea exactly when he'd revert to realspace or what would be waiting for him when he did.

It seemed as though only a short time had passed before his TIE lurched out of red zone and slowed. Kylo was prepared to attack or evade, but found himself on a perfectly normal approach, the planet Exegol looming before him.

From space, it seemed dead and gray, shrouded in massive dark storm systems. As he neared, the clouds burst with jagged light. It would be a rough ride down.

Kylo Ren strode away from his TIE whisper, across boundless cracked ground. The entry had been difficult, but the landing easy. The planet's entire surface was a landing pad—flat and empty. Reaching out with the Force, he could detect a moderate amount of life nearby—most of it deep below the surface—but this planet made Mustafar seem like a lush garden by comparison.

The air was hazy and hot and dry, and lightning split the sky in unending rage. His boot knocked over a small silica tree, where lightning had turned grit and sand into a branching tumor of glass. He spared a concerned thought for his TIE, exposed against the barren landscape, and realized he had to get undercover fast.

The planet's atmosphere didn't afford much visibility, so he didn't see the citadel until he was almost upon it; it hovered over the barren ground, a brutal edifice of stone towering high enough that its peak was nearly lost in haze. He ignited his lightsaber.

Kylo didn't need to see the entrance to know where it was, because he could feel it beckoning him, welcoming him. It was not the soft, warm welcoming of home or safety but rather one of conquest and need. His skin prickled. The Force was strong here, but it was different. Twisted, rotten, as though filtered through a miasma of decay.

He reminded himself that new things grew out of old decay.

Lightning crackled in the gap between ground and edifice. The space was just high enough for him to stride comfortably. He felt the weight of the massive structure as he walked beneath, trusting it to not fall and crush him.

It took power to create something so awe inspiring. That power would be his.

Kylo's footsteps echoed, and the bare stone ceiling seemed reddish in the light of his blade. Something clanged, like a gigantic gear moving into place. Suddenly the area he stood upon separated itself from the floor, becoming a floating disk that lowered him into the depths of the citadel.

As he descended, he found himself captivated by the wall before him, which was carved with colossal stone faces, all rendered in exquisite detail. Massive iron chains trailed down from the ceiling, as if mooring the statues in place. Something dark and inescapable moved within him, and he understood that he was viewing a monument. So much history and memory all in one place, and he was caught between reverence and rage. This was his inheritance; he knew it like he knew the feel of a lightsaber in his grip. But monuments preserved the past, and if he had learned anything recently it was that the past needed to die.

The disk came to a gentle halt in a vast space that brought to mind a cathedral. The stone faces were high above him now, crowning enormous statues of ancient lords. At his feet, dark chasms jagged through the floor, and Kylo could not gauge their depths. The chasms crackled with lightning, searing his vision, as though a bit of the planet's sky had been trapped within its crust.

He was not alone. Figures moved in the shadows, slight and stooped. Not dangerous—not yet, anyway—as they went about whatever work they were doing. They wore black, threadbare robes, and bandages shrouded their faces.

"At last," came a voice, and Ren whirled, seeking its source. It was raspy and half mechanized, straining as though in pain, and yet the sound reverberated within his very being. "Snoke trained you well," the voice said. Kylo *knew* that voice. He'd heard it his whole life. As a young man it had been like the wisp of a dream, one he couldn't quite grasp. Then the Emperor's transmission had flooded the galaxy, and Kylo had begun to dread that Palpatine had somehow survived, that his had been the whispering voice that had comforted, guided, *tormented* him for so many years.

"I killed Snoke," Kylo said. "I'll kill you."

"My boy, I *made* Snoke. I have been every voice you have ever heard inside your head." He spoke slowly, deliberately, the timbre of his voice morphing, becoming first Snoke, then Vader, and settling on Palpatine. "I have been your Master all along."

A figure began to materialize before him, still cloaked in shadow, silhouetted against the angry lightning flashes of the chasms around them. It moved oddly, as though with a mechanical gait. If not for the power emanating from the creature, Kylo Ren would not have been certain it was alive.

A flash of lightning illuminated a huge glass tank, containing three creatures, liquid life being pumped into them through mechanical umbilicals. They were all the same creature, he realized with a start, with wrinkled skin and an oversized bald head and features caught in a state of everlasting anguish. They were all Snoke.

Snoke came from this place. Yet Kylo's former teacher had told him nothing about it. What else had he kept from him?

When Kylo didn't respond, the robed creature added, "Do you

know who I am?" He leaned forward, which disturbed his sleeve enough that Kylo caught a glimpse of his hand, half rotted away, leaving only a few fingers covered with skin like melting candle wax.

Kylo's grip on his lightsaber tightened. He said, "I know you built the First Order. That I will not be your servant as Snoke was."

"Snoke." The voice filled with glee. "He was nothing but your *test.* You did well to destroy him."

Kylo Ren was Supreme Leader of the First Order. Before that, he'd been the leader of the Knights of Ren. Before *that,* he'd been the presumptive heir to the Skywalker legacy and the son of a princess. So he'd been subjected to false flattery and sycophantic compliments his whole life, and he refused to give them power. Then, and especially now. "Who are *you* to speak of *me*?"

The voice deepened, shaking with barely restrained power. "I am the one who led you here. Who has foreseen your destiny . . ."

The figure moved closer. He was unspeakably frail, his body dangling from an enormous mechanism that disappeared into the darkness above. Kylo had seen this before, while studying the Sith, and again while researching clues about Vader's wayfinder. It was an Ommin harness, a mechanical spine once worn by an ancient Sith king.

Without it, the emperor could not survive.

But the Force itself belied any perception of frailty because a cloud of darkness and need swelled from the creature, along with power like Kylo had never before encountered. It was exhilarating.

"The First Order was just a beginning," the creature said. "I will give you so much more."

"You'll die first," Kylo said.

"I've died before. The dark side of the Force is a pathway to abilities some would consider to be . . . unnatural."

Kylo knew better than to allow himself to feel kinship with the creature, but there was no denying that the Jedi would consider Kylo Ren to be unnatural, too. An abomination. *A monster,* the scavenger had said.

He raised the tip of his lightsaber to the creature's face, which brought clarity to his features. The Emperor's eyes were filmed over with milky blindness, and vials punctured his neck.

All the vials were empty of liquid save one, which was nearly depleted. Kylo peered closer. He'd seen this apparatus before, too, when he'd studied the Clone Wars as a boy. The liquid flowing into the living nightmare before him was fighting a losing battle to sustain the Emperor's putrid flesh.

"What could *you* give *me*?" Kylo asked. Emperor Palpatine lived, after a fashion, and Kylo could feel in his very bones that this clone body sheltered the Emperor's actual spirit. It was an imperfect vessel, though, unable to contain his immense power. It couldn't last much longer.

"Everything," Palpatine said. "A New Empire."

The creature raised his ruined hand; Kylo sensed him drawing on the Force, but before he could react, his surroundings disappeared as if into a fog, and a vision filled their place.

A black void, like space without stars. Then lightning flashed, revealing cracked ground. The barren landscape shook, then shattered. A mountain erupted onto the surface. Dirt and chunks of soil fell away, revealing a metal hull, striped with red. Around it, more mountains broke the surface, resolving into massive Star Destroyers, half again the size of the Destroyers from the days of the Empire. A single, giant obelisk erupted also, a navigation tower that would coordinate their final ascension. It unfurled like a metal flower, exposing its petal-antennae to the violent sky.

More ships rose—and more and more—until tens of thousands hovered in the atmosphere.

"For a generation, my disciples have labored," Emperor Palpatine said, his voice dark and deep.

Kylo's heart was racing. So much power. A star*field* of Destroyers. The largest fleet the galaxy had ever known. The rumors were *all* true. Exegol was a world populated by the Sith Eternal, true believers in the dark side of the Force, devoting their lives to *this*.

"They've built a fleet that will bring an end to the galactic rebellion once and for all."

The vision was whisked away, replaced by hundreds of thousands of stormtroopers, shining in crimson armor. Thunderous marching filled his ears, and with it came the barest hint of a scent he recognized . . . blaster-seared blood.

With tremendous effort, Kylo thrust the vision aside. Everything he'd seen would be his. But he was no fool. Nothing was really that easy.

No Sith willingly gave up a throne.

"The might of the Final Order will soon be ready," the Emperor continued, his voice uncannily compelling. "It will be yours if you do as I ask. Kill the girl." Kylo had no doubt as to whom the Emperor was referring. "End the Jedi. And become what your grandfather Vader could not. You will rule all the galaxy as the new Emperor."

His breath became a mechanical wheeze, then stopped completely. The robed creatures hurried over, adjusted the machinery attached to his body. One quickly replaced a filter at the end of a tube. Another used a syringe to insert an additive into the remaining regeneration fluid. Kylo watched with detached interest, trying to gauge the creature's strengths and vulnerabilities.

At last, speech returned to him. "As you can see, you must act now. Before my final breath."

Kylo sensed deception in his words, but also truth. "If I don't?" he said in challenge.

"Then the girl will become a Jedi. The First Order will fall. And you will die."

No deception this time; only truth.

"You have already sensed this," the creature added.

Kylo had tried to turn her once. His second-greatest failure, that he could not convince Rey to join him.

"But beware. The girl feels a stirring, that she is not who she thinks she is."

Kylo's eyes narrowed. Finally, he lowered his lightsaber.

He'd glimpsed her parents in a vision, a poor, frightened couple eking out a meager existence, surviving on the edge of desperation.

He hadn't been lying when he'd told her they were nothing, nobodies.

But Force visions were filled with tricky truths and potential realities. Maybe he had missed something.

Bringing all the power of the Force to bear, Kylo Ren demanded, "*Who is she?*"

The rotting remnant of Emperor Palpatine smiled.

# CHAPTER 3

Rey told Leia after all—at least part of it—and she was so glad she did. The general thought her vision might be connected to the mysterious transmission coming from the Unknown Regions, which made it important enough to send her out for confirmation once the *Falcon* returned. Leia was considering it, anyway.

Even though they both knew Rey wasn't ready to leave her training.

So Rey knelt on the ground near her workbench to do some aspirational packing. Leia and BB-8 watched as she shoved rations and supplies into her bag. Okay, mostly rations. Her Resistance friends were always complaining about the food, saying it was tasteless and unsatisfying, but Rey had no idea what they were talking about. She'd never eaten so well in her life, or so often. She always kept a few nutrient packs stuffed under her cot, though. Just in case.

She eyed the unfinished lightsaber on her workbench. It wasn't ready yet, and the one she'd painstakingly repaired—Luke's—didn't belong to her. So her quarterstaff would have to suffice as a weapon. Which was just fine. It had served her well on Jakku for years. In fact, someday, once she had mastered this lightsaber-building business, she might design one that felt more like a quarterstaff in her hand. Familiar and hefty. Two business ends. Maybe with a hinge in the middle for portability.

She'd learned a lot about lightsabers by reforging Luke's. His Jedi texts had offered some guidance—like how to repair the kyber crystal—and her experience building daily tools from scavenged parts had provided the rest. Rey was confident she'd eventually finish her own from scratch, even though there was no one to teach her how.

"Do you know where the vision came from?" Leia asked as Rey crammed one more ration bar into her pack.

"I wish I knew . . . but I can't tell what the vision was. It . . ." Words failed her. How to describe something so intense? So strangely personal?

Rey hefted her bag and stepped toward Leia, carefully avoiding a power line snaking across the bare ground. Their base on Ajan Kloss was barely cobbled together. Consoles sat outside, exposed to the elements. A massive cave provided some shelter for sleeping, and an old rebel blockade runner called the *Tantive IV*—currently grounded while awaiting replacement parts—served as command quarters for Leia as well as a communications center. Rey, like many Resistance fighters, had chosen to sleep on a cot tucked against a wall of green jungle near the entrance. A footlocker, a workbench, and a lot of mud completed her personal "quarters." Still, it was better than sand. Besides, she liked sleeping out in the open, her subconscious constantly monitoring the comings and goings around her. It was a reminder that she was part of something. That she wasn't alone anymore.

"I'm listening," Leia prompted.

"I didn't finish the training course. I let the visions distract me. I'm just not feeling myself. I know it looks . . . it looks like I'm making excuses."

Leia's eyes narrowed. "Don't tell me what things look like. Tell me what they *are*."

Maybe trying to tell Leia about her vision had been a mistake after all. "I think I'm just tired. That's all."

Leia gave her an arch look that made her feel like the worst liar who had ever been caught lying.

Rey was relieved to be interrupted by Lieutenant Connix's voice. "General?"

Leia looked over. Kaydel Connix wore her hair in braids now, wrapped around her head like a crown—just like Leia. A lot of the young woman were doing that, but Rey was willing to bet Leia hadn't noticed that her Alderaanian hairstyle had started a trend.

"The *Falcon* still hasn't arrived," Connix said. "Commander's asking for guidance."

The general would have to go deal with that, so Rey grabbed Luke's lightsaber and handed it to her. She always returned the lightsaber to Leia. The General had said she might give it to Rey someday, but Rey knew how hard that would be. The lightsaber was the only thing Leia had left of her brother. "I *will* earn your brother's saber," Rey told her. "One day."

BB-8 beeped a question, which coaxed a smile out of Rey.

"No, you can't do it for me."

"Never underestimate a droid," Leia said with a hint of a smile. Then she headed off after Connix, Luke's lightsaber in hand.

"Yes, Master," Rey murmurred at her back.

BB-8 whirred at Rey, and she knelt before him.

"I tried," she said in a near-whisper. "But . . . I couldn't tell her the whole truth. Who knows what she'd think if I did?" Rey *had* tried. Truly. She'd opened her mouth, but the words had caught in her throat. How do you say something so horrible aloud?

BB-8 beeped again, a little more demanding.

"No, I tell *you* everything. Let's get you fixed."

Rey headed through the base toward the mechanic's station. She'd look for Rose first. If Rose wasn't available, she'd fix BB-8 herself, so long as she could get her hands on the right parts.

BB-8 rolled after her, chirping sadly.

"Oh, don't worry about them. They're just picking up parts. I'm sure our friends are fine."

They were not fine. Poe braced himself for the next hit. They were losing, their soldiers crushed by the onslaught, their enemy gloating in their faces. He loved to see them suffer. He gave them a sly look as he started to make a move . . . then changed his mind.

"Are you ever going to go?" Poe said to Chewbacca, as the Wookiee studied the holochess board. They sat around the table, Chewie on one side, Poe and Finn on the other. It was a long ride in the *Falcon* to Sinta Glacier Colony, and they had to pass the time somehow. This was their third game. On the last mission, they'd played two games. Before that . . . well, Poe had lost track.

"He can't beat us *every* time," Finn said.

"And yet, he seems to," Poe grumbled.

Finn's eyes narrowed. "How does he do it?"

"He does it because he cheats," Poe said.

Chewie roared.

"I'm kidding!" Poe said, hands up in surrender. "You're two hundred fifty years old. Of course you're better than us."

"Just make a move already," Finn said.

The *Falcon* beeped, indicating that they were nearing their destination.

Chewbacca rose from the holochess table, moaning with insistence.

"Of course we're not going to turn it off," Poe said, trying to appear affronted.

"Don't worry," Finn assured the Wookiee.

Chewie left and headed toward the cockpit.

Once he was out of earshot, Poe murmured, "He's cheating."

"Definitely," Finn agreed.

They both reached at the same time and turned the board off.

Poe followed Chewie, passing R2-D2 and Klaud on his way to the cockpit. "Klaud, I hope you got that surged fixed," Poe hollered.

They were trying to fix a pesky short that had been working its way through the *Falcon*'s electronics ever since their last mission. Poe had no idea what species Klaud was or where he came from, and he'd thought General Leia was losing her mind when she'd assigned him to Rose's mechanic team. For one, he had no arms; in fact, Poe thought he looked like a giant slug on flippers. For two, he spoke a language only the droids understood. But it turned out to be a good decision because Klaud could occasionally manipulate objects with his prehensile antennae, and his keen mind made short work of mechanical problems. He and R2-D2 worked well together.

Poe reached the cockpit as the *Millennium Falcon* came out of lightspeed in front of a massive, mountainous asteroid made of ice. With a nod to Chewie, he dropped into the pilot's chair. From the viewport window, he could see its comet origins in its uneven surface, the way gas lifted off it like fog. It seemed small, its chasms merely cracks on a glowing white space lump. Just as he hoped, the *Falcon* detected no sign of pursuit. Poe aimed the freighter toward the rendezvous point and plunged toward the mining colony.

Finn passed the entrance to the cockpit and headed toward the top hatch to get ready for their pick-up.

Based on the sparks flying out of the panel that Klaud was repairing, they'd been lucky on their last assignment. If the *Falcon* had suffered one more hit, they would have been a pile of flaming debris.

Well, maybe it wasn't really luck. He and Poe and Chewie made a good team. A great team, on those rare occasions when Rey accompanied them. But Rey had more important things to worry about now. "Force" things that Finn was doing his best to understand. He'd seen what Rey could do, sensed how important she was to their cause. But he had to admit, when he was out here, and she was back on Ajan Kloss, he missed her.

Poe had taken the *Falcon* into the Sinta ice tunnels, where water vapor and mining processes created a bit of atmosphere. The ship felt wobbly beneath Finn's feet, as though it was fishtailing. Not Poe's fault, he was certain. These asteroids were tricky.

The *Falcon* lurched to a stop.

"I'm opening the portal!" Finn called out to Poe.

Finn hit the release, and the round hatch above him revealed a dim icy corridor, a wash of cold, moist air, and the greenish-yellow face of an Ovissian with a wide, horn-to-horn grin.

"Boolio!" Finn said. Boolio was a mine overseer who'd been siphoning surplus minerals to Resistance-friendly transports for months. Finn himself had picked up shipments twice. "What's so important? You got the regulator?"

Leia needed the regulator desperately to get the *Tantive IV* in top flying shape once again, but these old-model parts were hard to come by, and this was one of the few they'd been able to track down. It was also the cheapest.

Boolio shook his head. "No part." he said. "We have a new ally. A spy in the First Order!"

Finn's mouth dropped open. "Who?"

"No idea, but the news is bad. Transfer the spy's message to your droid!" Boolio said, the regulator already forgotten.

Boolio tossed down a data cable.

Finn grabbed it. "Any idea at all who—"

"They wouldn't say. But someone left a datafile in my office after the last First Order inspection." He looked back over his shoulder nervously.

Finn gestured at R2-D2, who rolled toward him. He inserted the cable into the droid's dataport. All the while, his mind was racing.

This was why Boolio had insisted they come all the way across the galaxy for the regulator. This was why he'd told them the part was critical, that it wouldn't last long. It was a rare piece, sure, practically an antique. But Boolio's urgency had seemed excessive, especially in relation to the rock-bottom price he was offering. Now it all made sense. Somehow he'd gotten a message from a First Order spy. And as a mere mine overseer, he didn't have access to a secure frequency. His only choice was to draw them here in person by promising a part that didn't really exist.

"Please hurry," Boolio said. "If they knew to leave the message with me, then someone in the First Order knows I've been in contact with the Resistance."

Which meant the First Order could return at any moment. Finn found himself tapping the side of his thigh, as if to hurry the transfer along. Old tech, low temps . . . who knew what kind of shape that data cable was in? They could be here for hours . . .

Poe slouched in the pilot's seat. He didn't understand what was taking Finn so long. They had to retrieve a part, pay Boolio, get the hell out of here. That was it.

The *Falcon*'s sensor beeped aggressively, startling Poe from his slouch. He gaped at the console. Was he reading this right? Twenty-something objects approaching from all directions. TIEs, based on the size and speed.

"Finn, we're about to be cooked!" He started flicking switches, getting the *Falcon* ready for a hot exit.

"We're almost there!" Finn called back.

*Get there faster*, Poe thought as he looked for ways out of this trap. Options were limited and growing fewer by the second.

Exactly how hard was it to grab a single replacement part?

R2-D2 beeped that the transfer was complete. Finn yanked the cable from the droid's dataport.

Boolio pulled it up fast, hand over hand, saying, "They found me. Go, now!"

"How can we repay you?" Finn asked. They'd brought untraceable currency, on Leia's insistence. The Resistance had a reputation for paying fair, and she would never jeopardize it. But it wouldn't be nearly enough to trade for First Order intel.

"Win the war!" Boolio said, and then he slammed the hatch shut—

—just as Finn heard the familiar scream of approaching TIE fighters.

He dashed past R2-D2 and Klaud and burst into the cockpit. "I've got bad news!" he told Poe.

"I've got worse," Poe said. "Get to the turret!"

Finn scrambled for the guns.

Poe maneuvered the *Falcon* through the vast chasms of Sinta Glacier Colony. Blue-black ice streamed past in a blur, interrupted occasionally by massive machinery. The chasms were testing his skills to their limits, but they also provided an opportunity. The TIEs chasing them were keeping up so far, but he was the better pilot. He and Chewie just had to hang on long enough for the TIEs to make a mistake and hit a wall, or better yet, for Finn to pick them off with the turret.

If only Rey had come along. Then they'd have two operational turrets, and those TIEs wouldn't stand a chance.

A blast tore at the *Falcon,* nearly throwing him from his seat. Chewbacca moaned.

"Finn!" Poe yelled. "You're supposed to be getting rid of those TIEs!"

A TIE jerked out of its flight path and spun into the wall of ice, where it became an exploding fireball. Chewie roared.

"I got one," Finn retorted.

"What do you mean *both* rear shields?" Poe said.

An alarm in the cockpit began screaming. Poe reached to flick it off. Chewie growled something at him.

"What?" Poe said.

Chewie pointed ahead and slightly to the side, where an enormous mining structure jutted from the ice wall. They were seconds away. This was the opportunity Poe had been hoping for.

"Chewie, good thinking." Poe said, diverting all remaning shield power to the top, because for this to work, they'd have to cut it very close. "Finn, we can boulder these TIEs!" he hollered toward the turret station.

"I was just thinking that," Finn hollered back.

This kind of maneuver was tough to pull off in the light grav of a small celestial body, but he was Poe Dameron, renowned Resistance pilot. He flipped the *Falcon* neatly, lining up the shot. Finn spun the lower turret to shoot straight ahead. *Not quite yet, buddy . . . you have to time it just right . . .*

"Now!" Poe yelled.

Finn fired. Metal groaned against metal as the machinery broke away from the wall. The *Falcon* roared under it just as it tumbled, crashing into the three TIEs. Explosions lit up the chasm on all sides, turning the ice walls to fire.

Finn whooped. "Now get us back to base!"

But their celebration was short-lived. More TIEs appeared in the cockpit viewport. Too many. Ahead was a sheer wall of ice, dirty with machinery and slag. There was nowhere to go. No way to . . .

Poe got a terrible idea.

"How thick do you think that ice wall is?" Poe said.

Chewie roared, leaving no doubt what he thought of Poe's plan.

Finn braced himself as best he could in the turret seat as Poe engaged the throttle. The TIEs were nearly on them. The ice wall loomed straight ahead; where did Poe think they could go? They were definitely going to die.

The *Falcon*'s engines roared, and Finn squeezed his eyes shut. His last thought before they hit the wall of ice was that at least he wouldn't die a stormtrooper.

The impact wrenched his neck. Metal screeched, Klaud screeched, and the freighter shook like a leaf in a hurricane. Suddenly they burst into open space. Finn didn't even have time to take a breath of relief before Poe engaged the hyperdrive. Sinta Glacier Colony disappeared into a stream of light.

The TIEs would follow; they had the technological capability now. There was no getting away.

Chewie roared so fast it was hard for Finn to understand.

"Poe's about to *what*?" Finn yelled toward the cockpit.

Chewie moaned that the pilot was about to do nothing good.

"Don't worry, buddy," Poe said, and Finn wasn't sure if he was talking to him or the Wookiee. "We have the fuel for it. Besides, Rose installed gravimetric compensators to make these quick jumps safe."

"Saf*er,*" Finn clarified. "The compensators make jumping *slightly safer.*"

"That's what I said. Hold on!"

The *Falcon* jumped to lightspeed. Finn climbed out of the turret and entered the cockpit.

Moments later, the ship popped out of lightspeed into a massive cavern-like structure dripping with sparkling, ship-killing stalagmites. A bright star reflected daggers of light from the crystal columns into Finn's eyes, but Poe maneuvered through them neatly. The TIEs that popped into view around them weren't so lucky. Several exploded before Poe jumped right back to lightspeed.

Finn felt a little sick to his stomach.

The *Falcon* entered a bright space filled with shining white towers—the readout screen identified the Mirror Spires of Ivexia—and their reflective surfaces made it hard for Finn to tell which ones were real or how many TIEs were still in pursuit. Poe barely avoided collision as more TIEs crashed around them.

Another jump, this time landing them in the middle of the Typhonic Nebula.

The giant, tooth-rimmed maw of a massive space creature loomed before them. "How do you know how to do this?" Finn asked.

Chewie roared disapproval.

"Yeah, well Rey's not here, is she?" Poe shot back. "Okay, last jump, maybe forever!"

Klaud screamed. The *Falcon* lurched into hyperspace, as the last of the TIEs rammed itself down the creature's gullet.

Finn was definitely going to be sick.

"I have your word?" Kylo Ren said to Albrekh.

"It will be stronger than it was before," he hissed back.

Albrekh was the first Symeong whom Kylo had ever encountered. He was small and thin, with a jutting jaw and long, pointed, wide-spaced ears that twitched with every sound or breath of air. Most important, he was a Sith alchemist trained in classic metallurgy, capable of smithing feats unheard of in the modern galaxy. He stood before a heavy stone table, awaiting the shards Ren had promised.

Kylo considered a moment more. He'd been working alone, pursuing the wayfinder without the Knights, without the mask. But he needed them now to help him find the scavenger quickly.

The Knights were arrayed behind him; he sensed Trudgen and Kuruk close at his shoulders. Calling them together again had been unexpectedly and perhaps uncannily easy. They'd accepted him without question, saying the results of his trial years ago still stood. He remained their rightful leader.

Now to reforge the symbol of his leadership.

Then to find Rey.

He dumped the shards—all painstakingly scavenged from the wreckage of the *Supremacy*—onto the stone table. He wasn't sure how the alchemist would pull it off. There were too many pieces, some of them warped beyond recognition.

Albrekh rubbed his gloved hands together in anticipation and got to work. It would take a long time. That was fine. Kylo wasn't known for his patience, but even he found some things worth waiting for.

The alchemist spread all the pieces across the table. With uncanny perception and speed, he solved the puzzle of their fitting, placing them in proximity to one another in such a way that Kylo could begin to see how the pieces would again become a mask.

The alchemist used heat pliers and a special mallet to hammer the warped fragments back into shape. The whole room glowed red from the molten metal stewing in a cauldron off to the side. Sarrassian iron, Albrekh had told him. The toughest ore in the galaxy.

With steady hands, the alchemist placed adjoining pieces side by side, then propped them together with magnetic forceps. He grabbed a long application tool that looked like a metal snake and used it to pour bloody iron into the crack between pieces. It cooled instantly, forming a red adhesive stronger than steel.

Kylo Ren was fascinated by power. Extreme competence was a type of power, and he watched spellbound as Albrekh repeated the process of fitting the shards together, molding them with molten red ore, over and over with severe patience, focus, and precision. Kylo flexed his own hands, wondering how the alchemist's palms weren't cramping, how his flesh wasn't burning to ash. His gloves protected him, no doubt, their fabric yet another Sith secret lost to the rest of the galaxy.

Finally, the alchemist balanced the mask on a stand and reached for a large ladle. He poured water over the reforged helmet. The water hissed, turning to steam that fogged Kylo's view. Albrekh repeated the process, again and again, until the mask was fully cooled.

The alchemist removed his gloves. With his bare, hairy hands, he grabbed the mask and offered it up to Kylo Ren. "It's safe to wear," he said.

He took it, admired it. The mask was a thing of jagged beauty. Shaped just as before, but now full of red fractures like crimson lightning.

Broken and re-formed. Like the Knights. Like his grandfather.

The Knights of Ren raised their weapons in honor as Kylo placed the mask over his head. It was heavier than ever. It reeked of molten metal. It was perfect.

---

Kylo Ren and his Knights charged down a corridor of the *Steadfast,* a phalanx of sweeping black robes and black masks. Stormtroopers and officers flinched away as they passed. He barely paid them any mind. He'd gotten word that a spy had been captured. He knew exactly how to deal with spies.

They came to a halt before Admiral Griss, a dark-skinned man who always kept his uniform in perfect condition. His eyes flicked to the mud Kylo and his Knights were tracking through the ship, but he wisely said nothing.

Behind Admiral Griss, stormtroopers approached, dragging something between them: an alien with yellow-green skin and four horns—two large horns wide against his skull, and two smaller ones hooking under his mandible. He wore an orange mining thermal suit and a defiant expression.

"Supreme Leader," Admiral Griss acknowledged. "Captured at the glacier colony, sir. A traitor."

Kylo did not hesitate. He ignited his lightsaber and brought it down in a single fluid motion. The traitor's head fell. One of its horns smacked the corridor floor with a resounding *thunk.*

All his officers were already seated around the table of the High Command conference room—Quinn, Pryde, Hux, Parnadee, Engell, and a handful of others—when Supreme Leader Kylo Ren strode inside.

He slammed the traitor's head down onto the table. They all flinched, he noted with satisfaction, even Pryde. Kylo turned his back to them and walked toward the viewport. "He should find it more difficult now," he said, gazing out at the stars, "to deliver messages to the Resistance."

Kylo waited for all his officers to take a good, long look at the severed head before he added, "General Pryde has reported to you the details of my journey to Exegol." Well, not *all* the details, of course. Little about the scavenger. But they'd been briefed about the fleet they'd discovered there, that Kylo Ren had made a deal with the remnant of Palpatine and his Sith Eternal movement to commandeer everything for the First Order. "The First Order is about to become a true Empire."

Silence around the table. Green liquid oozed from the alien's head and pooled on the surface. Hux refused to look at it, instead staring fixedly at Kylo and his mask.

To Hux, he added, "I sense unease about my appearance, General Hux."

Hux blinked. "About the mask? No, sir. Well done."

"I like it," General Parnadee agreed.

"These allies on Exegol," came General Quinn's voice. "They sound like a cult. Awaiting the return of the Sith. Conjurers and soothsayers . . ." His voice dripped with contempt. Quinn was old enough to have been a junior officer in the Empire, and he had little patience for anything that even hinted at religion or mysticism. He'd have to get over that if he wanted to keep his position.

Kylo studied his officers. Quinn's words seemed to have made the rest uncomfortable, especially Hux, whose expression had gone completely taut.

"They conjured legions of Star Destroyers," General Pryde pointed out. "The Sith fleet will increase our resources ten thousand fold." He turned to General Hux. "Such range and power will correct the error of Starkiller Base," he said to Hux, leaving no doubt as to whom he thought responsible for that debacle.

Pryde was one of the few officers who never seemed afraid of Kylo Ren, which didn't sit well. Kylo would have gotten rid of him if he weren't so competent. Also, it fed General Hux's insecurity to keep the vastly smarter, wiser, and higher-ranking general around. Petty of Kylo, perhaps, but keeping his officers at odds kept them from uniting against him.

"We'll need to increase recruitments," General Parnadee pointed out to General Engell with more than a hint of glee. "Harvest *more* of the galaxy's young—"

Engell nodded. She'd doubled recruitment already after the death of Phasma had left a void in that area of responsibility. Kylo appreciated her enthusiasm.

"This fleet," General Quinn said. "What is it . . . a gift?"

This was the exact question Kylo did not want to answer.

"What is he asking for in return?" Quinn pressed. "Does he—"

Kylo thrust out his arm, calling on all his anger, all his impatience. General Quinn flew high, slammed into the ceiling. Something in his body fractured loudly, but it didn't matter if the internal wound was mortal or not because Kylo kept him stuffed against the ceiling, gasping like a fish out of water, gradually choking to death.

Kylo stared his officers down. Hux was visibly shaken. Good. "Prepare to crush any worlds that defy us," he spat out. "In the meantime, my Knights and I are going hunting for the scavenger."

The Emperor wanted the scavenger dead. But Kylo had other plans. He wanted to kill the past, yes. Rule supreme over the galaxy, certainly. And the massive fleet on Exegol would help him do it.

But the ambition that cut into his being was the thought of reigning side by side with *her.*

They were connected. They had defeated Snoke. Together they would be invincible.

# CHAPTER 4

The Jedi texts were strewn across her workbench, and Rey was poring over them for the hundredth time. Luke's added notes on training had been invaluable to her and Leia. C-3PO had translated much of the rest, which had helped Rey learn about the history of the Jedi and the Sith. But some of the writings remained a mystery, their language too old or too secret to be in even C-3PO's databanks.

The odd thing was that some of the mysterious notations were in Luke's handwriting, which meant they had been carefully ciphered on purpose. Rey's friend Beaumont—a former historian and current Resistance intelligence officer—had been working to unlock these portions, and Rey hoped to have answers soon.

In the meantime, she was looking for a clue in the translated texts, anything that might help her interpret her vision. Or better yet, something that would help her find peace. Now that the Force was awake inside her, she had more questions than ever before, about Luke, her connection to Kylo, the Jedi of the past, the nightmarish visions that haunted her. If she could embrace Leia's calm, she was certain the visions would stop altogether. She'd sleep better, train better, become a Jedi to make Leia—and Luke, wherever he was—proud of her.

Leia heard her brother's voice once in a while; she'd said as much. But he never revealed himself to her. She didn't want to consider too hard why that might be. She wasn't even sure she knew what it meant for a Jedi Master to die. A remnant of Luke remained; she could feel it. But she didn't understand it. Sometimes the gaping void of what she didn't know overwhelmed her.

She itched to be in the fight, but the girl from Jakku was still inside her, and that girl yearned to *survive*. Leia was right; she had to prepare herself. How could she possibly learn all she needed in time? One thing about her visions was absolutely clear: The fight would soon come to her, whether she was ready or not.

"Rey!" Nimi Chireen called, startling her from her thoughts. "*Falcon*'s back."

Well, that was a relief. Rey had started to legitimately worry about her friends.

"Thanks, Nimi." Nimi was a new pilot who'd just been given charge of her own fighter. Poe thought she had great potential.

Rey hurried over to the landing area, which was no more than a cleared space in the middle of the jungle. Good thing the *Falcon* could land on a credit chip.

She stopped short when she saw her ship, and her heart clenched. Black smoke curled up from the engines. Scorch marks streaked the hull. The sub-alternators were a writhing mass of charred wires and warped housing. What had Poe done?

The pilot himself was striding down the ramp, and she briefly forgot to be angry. She was just glad to see him back safe. "It's on fire!" Poe was yelling, as droids and mechanics started hosing down the smoking bits. "Whole thing's on fire. All of it. On fire!" He spotted her approaching. "Hey!"

"Hey!" she said. "I heard there's a *spy*?"

Poe seemed a bit haggard, sweat sheening his brow, his shirt blotched with oil stains. He'd apparently done his best to conduct some emergency repairs on the trip back. He said, "Really could have used your help out there."

"How'd it go?"

"Really bad."

Something sparked under the *Falcon*'s belly. "Han's ship . . ."

Poe's face fell even farther when he spotted BB-8 and his dislodged tool-bay rim. "What did you do to the droid?

"What did you do to the *Falcon*?" she retorted.

"*Falcon*'s in a lot better shape than he is."

"Beebee-Ate's not on fire."

"What left of him isn't on fire," he threw back.

What was Poe talking about? It was just a tool-bay cover! "Tell me what happened," she said, trying to change the subject.

"You tell me first!"

She gave him a humorless smile. "You know what you are?"

"What?" He raised an eyebrow in challenge.

"You're difficult. You're a really difficult man."

"We'll, you're . . ." Poe made a noise of exasperation.

"Rey!" came Finn's voice.

"Finn! You made it back!"

Finn was descending the ramp, and his face lit up as she approached. "Barely," he said. Finn had grown his hair out a bit in defiance of First Order regulation, giving him a more relaxed air. In general, Finn had become easier in his own skin in the months after Crait.

BB-8 warbled at Poe, telling him about the training mishap, while Rey wrapped her arms around her friend in a tight hug. Letting Finn fly off and put himself in danger without her was one of the hardest things about Jedi training. She was always so relieved when he returned in one piece.

"Buddy, look at you," Poe said, inspecting BB-8's damaged casing.

"Bad mood?" Rey asked Finn.

"Me?"

"No, him," she said, with a nod toward Poe.

"*Always,*" Finn said, drawing the word out with a flourish.

"Do we have a spy?" she asked.

Chewie interjected with an outraged, multisyllabic moan.

Rey's eyes widened. "Lightspeed skipped?"

Finn winced. "Oh, boy . . ."

"I got us back, didn't I?" said Poe.

"The compressor's down," Rey said, and her tone came out more accusing than she intended.

"I know," Poe said. "*I* was there."

"You can't lightspeed skip the *Falcon,*" Rey said, unable to stop herself. How could Poe take that kind of risk with the Resistance's most precious asset? Besides, she *loved* that ship . . .

"Actually, it turns out you can," Poe said, unblinking.

"Guys," Finn said, trying to sound reasonable. "We just landed."

"What happened?" Rey asked.

"Bad news is what happened," Poe said.

Rey felt her frustration build. She understood that Poe had just been through something, but she needed information. She turned to Finn. "Did we make contact with a spy or not?"

"Yeah. We got a mole in the First Order." Finn confirmed. "They sent us a message."

Poe started to head off, but he couldn't resist throwing some final words at Rey over his shoulder: "You dropped a *tree* on him."

"You blew *both* sub-alternators," she slung back.

"Guys," Finn said.

"Maybe you should be out there with us," Poe said, rounding on her. He was good and angry now, but Rey could sense it had little to do with BB-8.

"You know I want to be!"

"Rey . . ." Finn said.

"But you're not," Poe said. "You're here training for what?" He took a deep breath, as if considering. Rey could see the exact moment he decided to give it to her straight. "You're the best fighter we have. We need you out there, not here."

Rey had nothing to say to that. Poe was right. But Leia was right, too. Rey needed all the training she could get to face what was to come. She wished there was a way to make both of them happy.

Poe caught sight of someone, and Rey was relieved to no longer be the subject of his merciless glare. "Junior!" he called out.

Aftab Ackbar, son of the late admiral, approached quickly. The young Mon Calamari was a decent pilot, and he had also displayed some of his father's flair for tactics. Leia had gotten him up to speed as fast as possible and was delighted with his progress.

"Get Artoo's data transferred and into reconditioning," Poe ordered.

"Yes, Commander," Ackbar said. He left with the droid, while Poe and BB-8 headed toward Rose's repair station.

Rey and Finn walked together toward the *Tantive IV* and passed the blockade runner's giant skids.

"What's the message?" she asked Finn.

Everyone had gathered beneath Leia's ship for the debriefing: All Rey's friends, Leia's advisors Maz Kanata and Commander D'Acy, even the droids.

Poe addressed the group. "Thanks to See-Threepio and Beaumont, we've decoded the intel from the First Order spy, and it confirms the worst." He waited a moment, as though reluctant to continue. After a deep breath, he added, "Somehow, Palpatine has returned."

Rey gasped along with everyone else.

Rose frowned. "Wait . . . do we believe this?"

Rey thought of the transmission that had flooded the galaxy, remembered her own dark visions. "We believe it," she said.

Aftab Ackbar was shaking his head. "It cannot be. The Emperor is dead," he insisted. "Killed aboard the second Death Star."

Beaumont murmured, "Dark science . . . cloning. Secrets only the Sith knew." He stared off into the distance as if lost in thought. His mental catalogue of Sith lore was vast, and if he thought it was possible for the Emperor to cheat death, then Rey did, too.

Besides, Luke's notes had mentioned that Sheev Palpatine had been obsessed with the idea of living forever. He'd claimed to Anakin that he'd discovered the secret of eternal life from his own master, Darth Plagueis, right before betraying and killing him. Luke had assumed it was a lie, meant to tempt Anakin to the dark side. But what if there was truth to it?

"He's been planning his revenge," Poe continued. "His followers have been building something for years. The largest fleet the galaxy's ever known. He calls it the Final Order. In sixteen hours, attacks on all free worlds will begin."

Chewie warbled something.

"In the Unknown Regions," Poe answered. "The Emperor and his fleet have been hiding there, on a planet called Exegol."

Rey's eyes flew wide. *Exegol.*

R2-D2 danced in place, demanding that C-3PO tell everyone about Exegol.

"The planet does not appear on any star chart," the protocol droid began, but Rey was hardly paying attention. She'd heard that name in her vision. She'd *seen* it before. She was sure of it. "But legend describes it as the hidden world of the Sith."

Rey had to get back to the Jedi texts. She slipped away while the others continued to talk and sprinted up a rise to the rocky bit of ground that made up her "quarters."

As she reached her workbench, she heard Commander D'Acy say, "He must have been behind the First Order. It was Palpatine."

"Palpatine's been out there all this time," Poe agreed. "Pulling the strings."

"Always," came General Leia's voice. "In the shadows from the very beginning."

"If we want to stop him," Maz said, her gentle voice penetrating the din with quiet authority, "we must find him. We must find Exegol."

Rey rummaged around in the crate where she kept the Jedi texts. Where was it? She tossed one aside. Then another.

"Is that all?" Rose asked.

"I wish it were," C-3PO said. "But I'm afraid that the Emperor has been discovered by Kylo Ren. Now the two are on the verge of . . ."

"What?" Connix prompted.

Rey glanced toward the others as Threepio flicked the switch on a holo disc, saying, "If my decryption is correct, they are on the verge of launching an unstoppable new Empire."

Ships in miniature manifested above the holo disc. They were tiny and blueish, giving little clue to their actual scale. But there were so many. They were like stars in the night sky.

"They'll crush us!" Aftab said. "My father warned this day would come."

Rey dug deeper into the crate. The text she was looking for had a large round seal on the front . . . There! She grabbed it and rushed back down to the group.

They hardly noticed when she returned. Everyone's faces had fallen. They were all thinking the same thing.

"We're not ready," Beaumont said. "Only half our ships are working. We have no large-scale weapons."

Rose raised her chin. "So we fix them. Fast."

"Friends," Leia said, her voice commanding attention. "This is the only moment that counts. Everything we've fought for is at stake."

"If this fleet launches," Beaumont said, "freedom dies in the galaxy."

Softly, Rey interjected: "General. May I speak with you?"

Leia wouldn't have minded if Rey had chosen to show this to everyone at once, but the Jedi texts had last belonged to Luke, and the girl was always respectful of his memory and legacy. So they were alone in Leia's quarters, one of the texts open before them.

"I know how to get to Exegol," Rey said, her finger tracing as she searched, "because your brother wrote about it in the Jedi texts."

Leia perked up. "Tell me!"

"Luke searched for it. He nearly found it." Rey spotted what she was looking for and brought the book closer. "There are ciphers here I can't read, but he said, 'to get there you need one of these.' A

Sith wayfinder." She pointed to a drawing of a pyramidal object. Rey looked up at Leia, eyes wide. "They lead the way to Exegol."

Leia's breath came fast. If Luke had already been searching, then they simply had to find his trail and pick up where he'd left off. This gave them somewhere to start. It gave them hope.

"If we're to find this fleet," Rey continued, "to stop what we both feel is coming, I need to finish what Luke started. Find Exegol. Find the Emperor."

Now Leia's breath came fast for a different reason. "No," she choked out. Rey wasn't ready. There was so much left for the girl to learn! If Rey left too soon, she could be drawn to the dark side. Leia had sensed her pull to the dark, the same way she had sensed it in Ben years ago.

But as Rey's eyes continued to plead with her, Leia had to face the truth: Rey needed more training, it was true. But the real reason she couldn't bear to see the girl go was that she'd grown deeply fond of her. Luke had told her that the Master-Padawan bond was strong. But he hadn't warned her that she might come to see her apprentice as the daughter she'd never had.

"What have I been training for if not for this?" Rey said. "I don't want to go without your blessing. But I will."

Leia was still shaking her head.

"I *will*," Rey insisted. "It's what you would do."

Leia had no answer for that.

After Rey left, Leia sat heavily on a couch inside her cavern quarters. Ramifications were hitting from all sides. The massive fleet Ben—he would always be Ben to her—had discovered could mean an end to the Resistance, the end of hope for the galaxy. Worse, it would be at the hands of Palpatine himself.

Unless the Resistance stopped him, the Sith would rise again.

The Sith had undoubtedly been planning this for years. Maybe generations. The Emperor and her father, Darth Vader, should have been the last of them. But when one fell, another rose. Always. First Snoke, and now her own son seemed poised to take the mantle.

She should have known Palpatine would have a contingency plan in place. After all, Palpatine had been a fixture in her life, from the time she was a toddler princess on Alderaan. Over and over again, she'd watched him encounter setbacks, only to rise more powerful than before. He was smart, determined, and aggravatingly prepared. Always two steps ahead of everyone else.

Leia didn't know what this contingency plan entailed exactly, but she'd bet Han's medal there was so much more to it than merely a colossal fleet of Star Destroyers.

She flashed back to Rey, to the girl's bleak face as she'd attempted to explain her dark vision. Rey was holding something back, but Leia wasn't the kind to push that sort of thing. It wouldn't be good leadership. People were ready when they were ready.

But if Rey's vision had anything to do with the rising Sith fleet, maybe she should make an exception and push a little more.

In any case, they had to do something. Now. Before Ben could claim Darth Vader's legacy once and for all.

It's just that she was so tired. She'd hoped to have a little more time . . . to train Rey in the ways of the Jedi, to train Poe in the ways of command, to see Finn and Connix and Rose all grow into the great leaders she knew they could be.

But she did not have the luxury of time, or rest, or even regret.

Leia sensed Commander D'Acy at her back. "We have to do something," she said to her friend.

D'Acy was a middle-aged blond woman who was far too high-ranking and qualified for the grunt work she'd taken on to get their base operational. But she'd also become a friend and adviser to Leia. Between D'Acy and Maz Kanata, there was the occasional day when Leia could almost forget her grief over losing Amilyn Holdo. Almost.

"We'll think of something," D'Acy said, her voice full of understanding.

"Last time we sent for help, no one came," said Leia. "No one answered the call."

Even as she said the words, she had to concede to herself that it wasn't that simple. Thanks to some risky assignments led by Poe, Rey, Finn, and Snap, they'd learned that the First Order had been doggedly pursuing their sympathizers, restricting communications, cutting off supply lines, capturing or even assassinating allies. In short, no one had answered the call because very few had even heard it.

That day on Crait had been Leia's darkest moment. She'd thought the spark of hope had died. She remembered sitting down in the old rebel outpost, exhausted, out of options, while the First Order deployed a siege cannon that would make short work of the armored hangar doors. They were all going to die, and the Resistance with them.

And then her brother had appeared. Luke had distracted the First Order long enough for them all to escape, and their small remnant had survived to carry on the fight. Since then, they'd been reestablishing contact with old allies, calling in favors, recruiting everyone sympathetic to their cause. Maz Kanata joining up had been a huge win, for instance—she had more connections in more places than the rest of them combined. They were growing. They were almost a force to be reckoned with.

She'd been wrong to lose hope that day. She wouldn't make that mistake again.

Leia stood to go. There was work to be done.

Rey had barely finished packing when Maz found her at her workbench. Maz was tiny and unassuming, but her warm wide eyes and compelling voice made Rey want to do anything Maz asked of her. She braced herself.

"Leia and Rose will stay behind to plan the attack on the fleet," Maz told her. "But there can be no attack until you've completed Luke's mission. To find Exegol."

Rey's heart raced. She knew she had to do this. She *wanted* to do this. But she wasn't ready.

"Maz, I might be a danger to the mission—to everyone. I'm afraid that I—"

"There is no one else," Maz said, somehow managing to sound gentle and firm at the same time. "The search for Exegol is a task for a Jedi."

Rey glanced at the pieces of her unfinished lightsaber. Maz had urged her to take Luke's lightsaber long ago, when Rey found it beneath her castle on Takodana. Maz had seen what Rey would become before anyone else. "I'm not a Jedi. Not yet. I'm not as strong as Leia thinks."

Maz leaned forward. "You won't know how strong you are until you know how strong you have to be."

Rey shook her head. "The dark side has plans for me. If I go, Kylo Ren will find me."

Maz was not impressed by that in the least. "You have faced him before," she reminded her with a shrug.

Rey's voice dropped to a near-whisper. "It's not him I'm afraid of."

Maz studied her a moment. Finally, she said, "To find the darkest place in the galaxy you will need to face the darkest part of yourself."

Somehow she knew what Rey was up against. Somehow, Maz always knew.

"You must go," Maz urged. "The Force has led you here. You must trust in it. Always."

Rey disconnected a fuel hose from the *Falcon.* Rose had worked miracles, getting the compressor back online, repairing the subalternators. Rey herself had buffed out some of the scorch marks and fine-tuned the rear shields. Her ship was nearly prepped and ready, and anticipation buzzed in her limbs. She was moments away from being behind those controls again.

She'd run a few assignments with Finn and Poe when they'd first established the base on Ajan Kloss, but for months now she'd been stuck here, training, training, training. Poring over Jedi texts with Beaumont's and C-3PO's help. Working on first Luke's and later her own lightsaber. But she yearned to see space again. To get back in the fight. To feel truly useful.

Wiping her hands, she cut around the *Falcon* toward the on-ramp, and nearly ran into Rose.

"Thank you," she said to the mechanic. "I can't believe how fast you got this ship ready."

Rose smiled. "You know I'd do anything for you and the *Falcon*."

There were so many things Rey ought to say to her. She settled for "You've been so kind to me. You and Beaumont, Connix and Snap . . ."

Rose's smile faltered. Became a straight-up glare. "Why does it feel like you're saying goodbye forever?"

"I'm not! I just . . ." Rey didn't know what she was trying to say.

Before she could figure it out, Rose enveloped her in a hug. "Me too," she said to Rey. "Now go do your Jedi stuff." After a final squeeze, Rose headed toward the *Falcon* for a last-minute inspection of the ship's landing gear.

Rey was about to grab a crate and load it onto the ship when Poe nearly collided with her.

"So you got her up and running," Poe said.

"You were right before," she blurted. "I can't stay. I'm gonna pick up Luke's search for Exegol."

"Yeah, I know," Poe said, giving her shoulder a friendly smack. "We're going with you. Chewie, did you get that compressor fixed?"

Chewie moaned that Rose had helped him.

Rey stood, mouth agape, as Poe grabbed a crate of supplies and started helping Chewie load the ship. Before she could formulate a response, she caught sight of Finn approaching. Him too?

She grabbed Finn's shoulder and yanked him close. "I need to go alone!" she said.

He nodded. "Alone with your friends."

"No. It's too dangerous, Finn."

Poe and Chewie drew near, BB-8 rolling after them.

Finn lifted a chin at them in acknowledgment. To Rey he said, "We go together."

Chewie loudly agreed with Finn.

BB-8 beeped his own insistence on going.

"I wholeheartedly agree," C-3PO said.

Rey looked around at them. Poe was giving her an arch look, as if daring her to contradict them. Finn was as earnest and determined as always. Chewie just seemed impatient to be off.

Her friends. She was terrified for them all. But she couldn't keep herself from smiling.

Knowing something in her head was different from knowing it in her heart. Rey had understood on some level that she wasn't alone anymore, but now she *knew* it, and it was so wonderful it hurt. Tears filled her eyes. Loneliness was a kind of agony. But belonging was another.

While they'd packed their things, Beaumont had been doing some final research. Now Rey and her friends gathered with him beneath the jungle canopy to go over what he'd learned.

Beaumont Kin was a slight, sandy-haired man who appeared younger than his years. He wore a mud-speckled field jacket and always carried a holstered blaster—on strict orders from Rose and Connix, who insisted that even an academic had to have a good blaster at his side.

He bent over a console table, Jedi texts arrayed before him. The pages of one had started to curl up at the edges, thanks to the moisture in the air. Once they learned all they could, Rey was determined to have them scanned and preserved properly. Some kind of hermetically sealed container, maybe. Surely Leia could spare the resources for that?

"I've analyzed Luke's ciphers," Beaumont said. "Learned a little more about the wayfinders."

He pointed to a familiar page from one of the texts, the one with the drawing of a pyramidal object.

"Ancient things," Beaumont said. "Only two were made; one for the Sith Master, one for the apprentice."

Rey peered closer. She'd always found the markings on the way-finder odd. Circles with lines leading away from them, like crude navigation charts.

Beaumont pointed to some ciphered text. "Luke was on the hunt for the *Emperor's* wayfinder, but his trail went cold on a desert world called Pasaana."

"In the Middian system?" Finn said. Rey had heard the name. She'd once met a junk dealer at Niima Outpost who made regular stops in the Middian system.

"You been?" Beaumont said. "Can't get a decent meal there. At least Pasaana's unoccupied."

Finn frowned, and Rey knew exactly what that frown meant. For now. Unoccupied *for now.*

"So we start on Pasaana," Poe said.

"Yes," Beaumont agreed. "Luke left coordinates. They point to the Forbidden Valley."

Well, that didn't sound foreboding at all.

*Leia,* came Luke's voice.

"No, Luke," Leia whispered back.

*It's time,* Luke said. He'd been pleading with her for a while now, and his voice was relentless. As if it came from within her very own soul.

"Not just yet."

She stood in her quarters, holding Han's Medal of Bravery. She'd had it with her since the day their son had killed him. She wouldn't be surprised if someday her thumb wore a path through the engraved medal, so often did she find herself rubbing it back and forth, lost in memory.

"When you gave that medal to Han, how could you know?" came another voice at her back, just as relentless, almost as dear. Maz Kanata.

Leia turned. Maz was holding Luke's lightsaber. Once again Leia was struck by how someone so tiny could have such a formidable presence. Maz filled every room she was in.

"How could you know where your life would take you?" Maz said. When Leia didn't answer right away, Maz waved the question away with a flick of her fingers and changed the subject. "I know you fear Rey's pull to the dark side. That you've had visions of her death."

Leia frowned. Maybe she'd shared too much with Maz.

"But as you have often reminded me," Maz went on, "the future is uncertain. The girl must find her true path."

Something about that hit home. "True path . . ." Leia murmured. Had Ben's turn set him on his true path? Leia was resigned to what had happened, but she couldn't believe it was his *true path.* And she couldn't believe it was Rey's, either.

Yet something about Maz's words pestered her. She knew this feeling. The Force was trying to tell her something. About Rey and her journey.

"Your spirit is strong my friend," Maz said. "But you are not well. Your body grows weaker and weaker. Give her your blessing. Give her Luke's lightsaber."

Leia sighed. Being blown off the bridge of the *Raddus* into the vacuum of space had taken a toll. She had saved herself that day through the power of the Force, but her body had paid a steep price.

Maz offered the lightsaber to Leia, who took it reverently.

"While you still can," Maz added. "While there is still hope."

Everyone was saying their goodbyes. Rey looked around, the finality of it all like a weight in her gut. It was possible they wouldn't come back from this. How could the skeleton crew of a single ship discover a way to defeat the greatest fleet the galaxy had ever seen? It seemed ludicrous. But it was their only play.

C-3PO bent over R2-D2, speaking with uncharacteristic softness.

"In the event I do not return," he said, "I want you to know: You have been a superb friend, Artoo. My best one, in fact."

R2-D2 responded with a sorrowful whir.

"Rose, last chance!" Finn was saying.

"The General asked me to study the specs of the old destroyers," Rose said. "So we can stop the fleet if you find them."

"If?" Finn prodded.

Rose smiled. "When."

He nodded. "When."

They hugged, and Rose said, "We'll be on long-range. Take care of Rey." After a moment, she added, "Take care of yourself." She glanced over at Rey, who lifted her chin in acknowledgment. Rey would have loved to have her company on this mission, but Leia was right: Rose was needed on base. In addition to studying Star Destroyer specs, Rose would be doing everything she could to get what ships they had in top fighting shape.

Rey watched them hug again, feeling a little left out. Because there was someone she despearately wanted to say goodbye to, but she wasn't sure how to go about it. Rey had been alone for so much of her life. Having relationships with people was a new skill, far more difficult to learn than floating rocks with your mind or fighting remotes with your lightsaber.

Uncertain, Rey turned and looked around the base. This mess of jungle and wires and exposed terminals had become home, and it would be harder to leave than she thought.

She loved the foliage, the way rain collected on broad waxy leaves, the scent of loamy soil. Green, she had decided—the color of jungles and forests and grass and *life*—was her favorite.

"We should get going," came Poe's voice. When he noticed her staring off into space, he added, "What is it?"

"Nothing," Rey said, a soft and gentle lie.

"Rey?" came another voice, and relief filled her. Leia.

She hurried toward the general, blurting, "There's so much I want to tell you!" Rey should have told the truth about her vision. She should say how much Leia's training had meant to her. Thank her for giving her a place with the Resistance and letting her make the *Falcon* her own. Tell her how much she admired—

"Tell me when you get back," Leia said.

The general's hands came up, and Rey gasped at what they held. Leia was offering her Luke's lightsaber.

Gingerly, reverently, Rey took it. She wasn't sure she'd earned the right to carry it. But Luke's lightsaber always fit so perfectly in her hand. Like two pieces of a puzzle clicking together.

She couldn't help herself; she reached to embrace Leia. Which turned out to be fine because Leia reached for her at the same time and hugged her tight, like she never wanted to let go. Rey closed her eyes, absorbing Leia's strength and calm. They stood together a long moment.

Finally, Leia said, "Never be afraid of who you are."

Rey's eyes flew open. Leia's voice was filled with power. With finality. Maybe the Force had shown her something. Or maybe it was just damn good advice.

Overwhelmed, Rey could only nod in grateful acknowledgment.

Rey settled into the pilot seat. Beside her, Chewie huffed a warm greeting. They locked eyes, and she smiled.

"It is," she responded. "Let's take her up."

Poe and Finn entered the cockpit, followed by C-3PO and BB-8. Her skeleton crew. The best crew.

As they lifted off, Maz and Leia stood together on the jungle floor, watching them go. Leia's heart ached. It was just like watching Ben leave to go train with Luke. Like watching Han go off on a mission without her. It was like saying goodbye to part of her own self.

"If she finds Exegol," Maz said, "she may just survive." Like Leia, Maz occasionally caught glimpses of people and places, presents and futures, through the power of the Force. Like Leia, she rarely understood what they meant. "But if she doesn't," Maz added, "the galaxy will surely not."

Leia had done her best to hide her worry from Rey, if not her affection. That girl might be their last hope.

# CHAPTER 5

General Hux strode down the corridor of the command ship, barely keeping pace with Ren and Pryde. Behind him came the bass-drum boot steps of the Knights. They were always around now, stuck like adhesive to their master, Kylo Ren. Hux hated the fact that he couldn't see their faces behind their masks. Maybe they had something to hide. They were probably hideous, scarred beyond recognition. It was cold comfort.

Allegiant General Pryde was updating Ren on their progress, or rather lack thereof. Hux wasn't sure how Pryde was able to deliver bad news without getting his head lopped off with a lightsaber or getting choked to death with the Force. Ren had no soft spots for anyone—except maybe the scavenger—so there had to be something else about Pryde. Something that kept him immune. Safe. Unafraid. Hux currently had resources devoted to finding out exactly what that was.

"Sir," Pryde was saying. "No leads yet, but the search for the girl continues."

"There's no time," said Ren. His voice was distant and mechanical now that he'd re-donned the mask. Hux distrusted masks on principle, but he was glad for Ren's because it spared him the indignant assault of the Supreme Leader's hair. A good leader led by example, and Ren's hair was the furthest thing from regulation. A small detail, to be sure, but details mattered, and this one represented everything Hux hated about Ren. He was the exception to everything. Outside the rules. Disordered.

When Hux finally took his rightful place as Supreme Leader, the first thing he'd do was make Ren cut off his hair.

With uncharacteristic acceptance, Ren said to Pryde, "Then I'll need to locate her myself."

"Yes, Supreme Leader," said Pryde.

"When she's found," Hux interjected, "I'll personally take the kill squads to—"

"Scan all systems for a Corellian YT-1300," Ren said to Pryde, ignoring Hux. "The *Millennium Falcon* is the ship she'll be in."

He turned to Hux and added, "The Knights of Ren will lead this hunt, General Hux. There is no room for error."

There was no smear of contempt in his voice, no impatience or irritation. Just dismissal.

Hux stood alone in the corridor and watched Ren stride away from him, Pryde and the Knights close at his heels. It was fine that they all thought him a useless imbecile, he assured himself. Advantageous, even. In a way, Hux had his own mask.

After all, the fact that they underestimated him had allowed him to put certain things in motion. This was all part of his plan.

Rey peered through the quadnocs at the endless ocher desert. Pasaana reminded her so much of Jakku that it gave her an unexpected pang. The sand was redder in color, and the air smelled tangier, as though life thrived here in a way it didn't on Jakku. But the sun was just as relentless, the sand just as insidious, the wind just as dusty and dry.

How had she ever survived in a place like this? With no green anywhere to be found? Without the protective embrace of humidity? Without good Resistance-requisitioned boots and a freighter full of water stores parked nearby?

"You sure this is it?" Poe asked at her back.

"Oh, yes," C-3PO answered. "These are the exact coordinates that Master Luke left behind."

Poe opened his mouth to speak, but a colossal drumbeat pierced the sky, so deep it thrummed in Rey's chest. It was followed by a single syllabic thunderclap, as though a giant crowd shouted a word in unison.

"What was that?" Poe said.

They all crept forward, following their ears. Rey knew how tricky things could be in the desert. The wind and sand and snaking buttes made it nearly impossible to tell which direction a noise was coming from.

C-3PO waddled forward faster than all of them. "It sounds like the end of a local Aki-Aki prayer—" he began.

"Shhh! Threeps!" Finn warned.

The drum sounded again, rolling into a series of beats like a coming storm. Then a mass of voices rose in joyful chorus, and the desert was suddenly filled with alien music that was as beautiful as it was startling.

"Why it *is*!" C-3PO exclaimed. "We happen to have arrived the very day of their Festival of the Ancestors!"

Rey's heart was already sinking by the time they rounded a rocky outcropping to reveal a wide valley stretching below them—and the unspeakably huge crowd of Aki-Aki gathered there. Tens of thousands, whirling about in their cloaks, waving colorful flags. No, hundreds of thousands.

Kites and banners floated in the air, tents and canopies provided spots of shade, and everywhere were cloaked figures, their movements marking them as not-quite-human. They danced and mingled, sang and ate, bought wares and sold them, from the near edge of the valley, all the way to the world's rocky horizon.

For a "forbidden" valley there sure were a lot of beings down there.

"This only happens once every forty-two years!" C-3PO informed his companions.

Poe grabbed the quadnocs from Finn, peered through them.

Even without the 'nocs, a few figures at the valley's near edge clarified in Rey's view. They were indeed humanoid, with double, prehensile trunks and thick skin well suited to sun and sand.

All at once the Aki-Aki flowed together like a wave and broke into a celebratory dance centered on a circle of bonfires. Brightly colored smoke rose from the fires, yellow, red, and teal dominating. Building-sized treadable vehicles circled the entire camp, their massive treads kicking up sprays of sand.

Rey would have found it all inspiring and beautiful, if it were not so disappointing. Picking up Luke's trail would be nearly impossible in this giant crowd.

"Well, *that's* lucky," Finn said glumly.

"Indeed!" C-3PO said. "The festival is known for its colorful kites and delectable sweets!"

They glared at him.

Few paid them any mind as they wandered through the festival. Though the vast majority of attendees were Aki-Aki, it appeared species from all over the galaxy had come to the celebration. Poe and Finn scanned the crowd, unsmiling, focused, all business. A clue had to be here somewhere. If they looked hard enough—*stay alert, stay smart,* Poe had said—they'd figure out their next move.

But Rey found it hard to pay attention to the task at hand. The dancing was beautiful, so full of life and color, flowing like water, joyful. She saw a tiny Aki-Aki girl stumble in the crowd. Her parents shot forward to rescue her, yanked her up and cuddled her close before she could come to harm. The little girl went right back to dancing as though nothing had happened, without a care in the world because she had others to care for her.

"I've never seen anything like it," Rey said, half to herself.

"I've never seen so few wayfinders," Finn replied drily.

"There are always random First Order patrols in crowds like

these," Poe reminded them. "Keep your heads down. Especially you, Chewie."

Chewie obliged by hunching over, but Rey wasn't sure it made him any less noticeable.

"Let's split up, see what the locals know," Poe said.

He and Finn headed off, but Rey's legs were rooted in place. A group of Aki-Aki were performing a puppet show. The children stared wide-eyed, sometimes laughing. A mother dressed in bright pink sat with them, holding her infant in her arms. Unlike the adults, the little ones didn't possess long, bifurcated trunks but rather stubby little noses and plump cheeks. Rey thought they were adorable.

Something tugged on her tunic, and she looked down to find a young Aki-Aki girl in a green robe trying to get her attention. Rey knelt before her.

The girl held a trinket in her hands, made from woven jute strands and beaded with colorful grain—some kind of corn, maybe. Rey allowed her to place it around her neck. The Aki girl chattered the whole time, in a language Rey had never heard in all her years on Jakku.

BB-8 warbled at the girl, and Rey translated: "My friend's asking what the fires are for?"

C-3PO repeated the question in the Aki language, and the girl answered without hesitation.

"Their ancestors live in the fire," C-3PO said. "This is how they show their gratitude. She says her name is Nambi Ghima."

Rey said, "Oh, that's an *excellent* name. I'm Rey."

Nambi asked a question, and C-3PO said, "She would be honored to know your family name."

Rey's smile froze. "I . . . don't have one. I'm just Rey."

The words echoed in her head. *Just Rey.*

Her gut twinged with a sudden warning. She'd learned to trust this kind of warning, ever since connecting with the Force. She stood, seeking its source.

All at once the sky darkened, as though day changed to night in the space of a moment. The bonfires were suddenly bright, casting the Forbidden Valley in ethereal light. The sounds of the festival faded. Something rumbled deep in her chest, something angry and desperate and . . . familiar.

Then the festival was gone, whisked away and replaced by endless sand, whipped into flurries by the wind.

She sensed him before she saw him, the familiar thing, as close as her own breath. It was Kylo Ren, black clad as always, his cape sweeping the ground. He stared at her in foreboding silence through his mask. The mask was different now, a patchwork of wicked black pieced together with angry red lines. Her skin dimpled with sudden cold.

This wasn't a vision. It was a Force connection, their first since Crait. And with the connection came a certainty that turned the blood in her veins to ice: He'd been looking for her.

"Palpatine wants you dead," he said, simply and without preamble.

"Serving another master?" she asked, feeling strangely disappointed.

"No. I have other plans."

Of course he did.

"I offered you my hand once," he said in that maddeningly calm voice. "You wanted to take it."

She didn't deny it.

"Why didn't you?" he asked.

"You could have killed me," she said. "Why didn't you?"

"You can't hide, Rey. Not from me."

It did something strange to her, to hear her name on his lips. Had he ever spoken it aloud before? She couldn't remember . . .

Now that the shock of seeing him again was wearing off, Rey began to notice other things. Like the fact that his voice carried an undercurrent of tension, or maybe even regret. That his boots were muddy. That his cloaked form cast a shadow on the desert floor, as though he were really, truly there with her.

"I see through the cracks in your mask," she said. "You're haunted. You can't stop seeing what you did to your father." She imagined that moment as clearly as she could, Han's hand on Kylo's cheek, gazing at his son with love even as his dying body slumped over the chaotic red lightsaber that had skewered him.

Rey wrapped her mind around the image. Threw it at Kylo.

He flinched.

Then he threw an image right back at her. Tally marks, scratched into the wall of her downed, sand-filled AT-AT. "Do you still count the days since your parents left? Such pain in you. Such anger." He began walking toward her.

She steeled herself.

"Where are you?" he asked, reaching for her mind, grabbing something before she could barricade her thoughts. "Somewhere that reminds you of home on Jakku. Of waiting for your parents. The ache of being alone."

She would not show weakness. She would not let tears fill her eyes. She would *not.*

"My mother doesn't see the darkness in you," he went on relentlessly. "Your friends don't, either. But I do."

And that was Kylo's mistake. Because he was deeply wrong about all of it. Leia knew about her dark visions, about the rage and impatience that always threatened their training sessions. Maz knew it, too.

She opened her mouth to tell him to go kiss a rathtar, but he moved too fast, into her space so that he loomed over her. He smelled of molten iron.

"I don't want to have to kill you," he said. "I'm going to find you, and I'm going to turn you to the dark side. When I offer you my hand again, you'll take it."

Not a chance. "We'll see," she snapped.

Before Rey could blink, he ripped the necklace from her neck, leaving her nape stinging.

The ground tilted. The empty desert disappeared, and Rey was back at the festival, Aki-Aki whirling around her. A tall male approached, a yoke around his neck that branched out into a magnificent display of wares—grain jewelry, colorful fans, candies. Her fingers drifted to her neck, to the empty space where the necklace should have been. Her nape still smarted.

It had been their most powerful Force connection yet. Even when she'd been in the hut on Ahch-To and their hands had met, it had been nothing like this—so vivid, so dangerously palpable. This time, they'd been in each other's spaces.

While she'd been occupied with Kylo, the crowd had pushed in around her, separating her from her friends. She dodged the merchant, searching for the droids—there! She waved at them to follow as she hurried off in the direction she'd last seen Poe and Finn and Chewie. She had to reach them *now.* She had to get her friends to safety.

She spotted Chewie first; even slouching he was at least a head taller than anyone else in the crowd. He stood with Poe and Finn just outside a tent, talking to one of the locals. She wasted no time.

"We have to go," Rey said, interrupting their conversation. "Back to the *Falcon,* now."

"Where were you?" Poe asked.

But Finn read her face and said, "What's wrong? What happened?"

"Ren," she replied. "He knows we're here." Or at least he would soon enough.

Poe and Finn did not question or hesitate. They took off around the tent, heading in the general direction of the parked *Falcon.* BB-8 rolled along with them as C-3PO struggled to catch up. They'd find another way to investigate the Forbidden Valley. After dark, maybe she could send C-3PO to—

They almost collided with a stormtrooper, who whipped up his blaster.

"Hold it right there!" he said.

They froze. Rey began reaching for the Force.

Over his comlink, he added, "I've located the Resistance fugitives. All units report to—"

Suddenly there was a resounding *crack.* The stormtrooper's head jerked backward, an arrow shaft sticking out of his left eye lens. He toppled into the sand, where he twitched once, then went completely still.

They whirled, seeking the source of the arrow. A tall helmeted figure stood just inside the tent, holding back the flap with a walking stick. In the other hand was a scoped dart shooter that looked like a smaller, lighter version of Chewie's bowcaster.

"Follow me," came a distinctly male voice. "Hurry."

Rey exchanged quick glances with her friends, who all nodded, and they set off after the helmeted figure. He hurried in the opposite direction, away from the *Falcon,* but he'd just saved them a lot of trouble so no one protested.

That had been an amazing shot, which meant they were in dangerous company. It had happened fast enough that the stormtrooper had been unable to relay their exact location. So Rey hoped they were doing the right thing by trusting the stranger.

They passed C-3PO, who was still hurrying to catch up to them. "Oh, slow *down*!" the droid protested to their backs. "What sort of friends *are* you?"

The helmeted figure weaved through the crowd, leading them to one of the giant treadable vehicles. The entirety of the vehicle sheltered within its massive treads—the huge drum wheels, the cabin, the entrance portal. It sparked with familiarity; the propulsion system, the drive shaft, even the hanging cargo nets all reminded her of the speeder she'd cobbled together on Jakku, even though this vehicle was ten times the size and lacked any repulsorlift.

What had happened to it? A Teedo had likely grabbed it. No, Unkar Plutt had undoubtedly scavenged it for parts. He probably hadn't even waited a day after Rey was gone.

The helmeted figure hurried them through the entrance into the hot, claustrophobic cabin. Supplies and trinkets dangled from the ceiling, and the drive shaft ran right through the center, barely allowing enough headroom. C-3PO was the last to board.

"To the east passage, Kalo'ne!" the helmeted figure called to the driver.

The treadable jerked, then lumbered forward. This was no getaway vehicle; it was much too slow. But it did get them out of sight and away from the last location where they'd been spotted. The First Order would inevitably find them again, but Rey dared to hope they'd bought themselves some time.

Their mysterious rescuer was putting himself at great risk to help them.

"Leia sent me a transmission," the stranger said.

Finn perked up. "How'd you find us?"

The figure reached for his helmet and lifted it from his head, revealing dark skin, close-cropped hair, and a handsome, mustached grin. "Wookiees stand out in a crowd," he said.

Chewie roared a name and practically leapt over Finn to reach the man.

*Lando?* Rey thought. Well, no wonder. She'd heard so much about him from Leia and Chewie. The *Falcon* had once belonged to him!

Chewie grabbed Lando in a hug, lifting him from the ground, nearly crushing the poor fellow.

Lando just laughed. "Good to see you, too, old buddy."

"This is General Lando Calrissian!" C-3PO announced. "Allow me to give you a complete history of—"

"We know who he is, Threepio," said Rey.

"It's an honor to meet you, General," Finn said.

Chewie talked fast, and Finn frowned. Finn had been working hard to learn Shyriiwook and Binary—Rey was impressed with how fast he'd picked them up—but he still struggled to understand when things got intense.

"Yes, Leia told me to keep an eye out for you," Lando said.

"General Calrissian, we're looking for Exegol," Poe said.

Lando froze for a split second, but then he softened with resignation. "Of course you are."

---

"You're certain?" General Pryde asked.

"It was her," Kylo insisted. Strange how anyone could doubt the power of the Force, after everything that had happened. Or maybe it was *him* they doubted.

"In that case, once the necklace is analyzed, we'll know exactly where she is," Pryde said.

Tishra Kandia hurried toward them, Rey's necklace dangling from her hand. Kandia was a top intelligence officer, and one of the few who never balked at his orders to expend First Order resources to find the girl.

"Sir," said Officer Kandia. "Microanalysis says this comes from the Middian system, Pasaana, Forbidden Valley."

Kylo felt a surge of hope. He'd have to move fast. Their Force connection had alerted Rey to his intentions, and she'd flee Pasaana as soon as she'd gotten what she'd come for—whatever that was.

"Prepare my ship and alert the local troops," he ordered General Pryde. "Send a division."

Kylo Ren turned and strode toward the TIE hangar.

"Yes, Supreme Leader," Pryde said to his back.

Lando Calrissian leaned forward so they could all hear him over the rumble of the treadable. "Luke and I were chasing down a real scoundrel," he said. "His name was Ochi of Bestoon."

The name gave Rey a start, though she wasn't sure why. *Ochi of Bestoon.*

"A Jedi killer since the Clone Wars. He was searching for Sith relics," Lando continued. "Evil, old things."

He activated his wristlink, showing a holo of the Jedi assassin. Ochi of Bestoon seemed not-quite human, with large black eyes, soft features, and some kind of cybernetic headgear. He didn't look dangerous at all.

"Like the Emperor's wayfinder," Poe said.

"That's it," Lando confirmed, switching the holo display to a pyramidal object. "Ochi bragged at a cantina that he had a clue to the wayfinder's location. That he had its coordinates inscribed."

"Inscribed *where*?" Rey asked.

"That's the question, kiddo," Lando said. "We chased Ochi halfway across the galaxy."

"Here to Pasaana," Finn said.

Lando nodded. "Where the trail went cold. Ochi disappeared into the desert. Luke sensed he was still here. We found his ship—abandoned—but no Ochi. No clue. No wayfinder."

Something about the way he said it . . . "So you stayed here?" she asked.

"Here and there. The desert helps you forget," Lando said, and sadness tinged his voice. The cabin jerked as the treadable lurched over a boulder. C-3PO grabbed a hanging net to steady himself. Lando went on: "First Order went after us—the leaders from the old wars. They took our kids." His gaze grew distant. "My girl wasn't even old enough to walk. Far as I know, she's a stormtrooper now."

Finn's face turned grim. Rey resisted the urge to put a hand on his shoulder; sometimes, sympathy was hard to bear.

"They turned our kids into our enemies," Lando said in a defeated voice. "My girl. Han and Leia's son, Ben. To kill the spirit of the Rebellion for good."

Rey and Finn locked eyes, and she knew he was thinking along the same lines she was. Ripping children away from their homes and pressing them into service wasn't only about filling ranks. It was about crushing the opposition's spirit. Because wars weren't fought with just ships and weapons, but with grit and resolve. That's why Leia was always talking about hope. It was as essential to victory as good supply lines or reliable intel.

"We need to get to that ship," Rey said. "Search it again."

The treadable lurched to a halt. A familiar screaming sound pierced the air. TIE fighters. They peeked out from the entrance portal and spotted them gliding along the horizon.

The First Order's reach now extended throughout the galaxy, which was why they'd run into a stormtrooper even here. That meant Ren could have backup troops on the ground in the space of an hour. Maybe less. Those TIEs could be an advance unit, scouting on the Supreme Leader's behalf. Come to think of it, Ren had certainly deployed scouts and probe droids everywhere already. She'd sensed how desperate he was to find her.

They would have to be very fast, and very careful.

"I've got a bad feeling about this," Lando said. "Ochi's ship is growing rust out past Lurch Canyon. It's the only clue I've got. Go."

They tumbled out of the treadable, all except Chewie who moaned mournfully at Lando. Lando reached for Chewie's arm and squeezed, as though saying goodbye.

Rey said, "Leia needs pilots, General."

"My flying days are long gone," Lando said. "But give Leia my love."

Rey thought of how she'd almost missed an opportunity to say goodbye to Leia, and she tried one last time: "You should give it to her yourself. Thank you."

Though Lando was practically a stranger to her, she could read the yearning in his face plain as a desert day. Maybe she'd gotten through.

Lando's treadable had taken them across the valley to the other end of the festival grounds, far away from the tent where they'd encountered the stormtrooper. Now they just had to find transportation to the canyon Lando had mentioned.

"There!" Poe said, pointing. "Those speeders!" They all sprinted toward a group of parked skimmers. C-3PO struggled to keep up.

Some of the skimmers were empty—probably for rent to festivalgoers—and several others were loaded with goods. Rey had no idea how they'd pay; they knew better than to walk these crowds carrying hard, untraceable currency, and had left most of it on the *Falcon*.

Poe rolled beneath one of the skimmers, ripped open a panel, and quickly set about rewiring.

“How do you know how to do that?” Finn asked.

“No need to worry,” C-3PO said, finally catching up. “I made it.”

An older Aki-Aki with a missing trunk began running toward them, yelling and waving his huge calloused hands. Undaunted, Poe did the same thing to a second speeder.

“We gotta go!” he said, hopping into it. Finn gaped at Poe, and Rey shared his astonishment. The pilot had somehow overridden the ident locks in the space of mere moments. They’d have to get Poe to teach them that one.

But as Rey grabbed the tiller of the first skimmer, a weight settled in her stomach. She hated stealing, even when it was absolutely necessary. Chewie and BB-8 climbed in behind her, and she gunned the engine. The old Aki-Aki screamed insults at their backs as they raced away.

The desert flew by around them, a sea of wind-rippled sand interspersed with islands of layered buttes that scraped the sky. It was beautiful, in its way.

BB-8 warbled at her.

“It doesn’t go any faster, Beebee-Ate!”

Back on Jakku, Rey had loved climbing onto her speeder after a hard day’s work and whipping across the dunes. It cooled the sweat from her skin, made her feel a little bit free.

As the speeder skimmed the sand, peppering her face with grit, she decided that she’d try to enjoy the ride. She just hoped they were going in the right direction.

# CHAPTER 6

Wind and sand stung Finn's cheeks, and without protective goggles he could hardly keep his eyes open. He had no idea how Poe was piloting this thing—it was like no speeder he'd encountered before. Come to think of it, he had no idea how Poe did a lot of things.

"Ripping speeders, lightspeed skipping," he yelled to Poe. "How do you know how to do shifty stuff like that?"

"Just stuff I picked up," Poe said.

"Where?" Finn pressed. Not in the Resistance, surely. Leia and Poe tried to keep their operations above board as much as possible. Poe had been Finn's very first friend outside the First Order. But it turned out there was plenty he still didn't know about the pilot.

Before Poe could respond, the skimmer jerked sideways with an impact. Finn smelled blaster scorching as more laser bolts missed, sailing past them.

The First Order had found them. Stealing the speeders had probably triggered alarms and informant networks all across the valley—which was still better than getting caught and arrested at the festival. But now two treadspeeders pursued them, each one carrying two troopers. Their treads kicked up sand in their wakes as they closed fast.

Finn and C-3PO clung to the steering vane as Poe began evasive maneuvers, swerving back and forth to make them as difficult a target as possible. Off to their right, running parallel, Rey was doing the same. Netted bundles of goods swung around in the cargo basket, threatening to spill. Finn yanked out his blaster and started firing, but Poe's veering made his shots go wide.

Behind Rey, Chewie's luck with his bowcaster was just as terrible. Still, their shots were making it dangerous for the First Order speeders to close the distance, so Finn kept at it. Gradually, he sensed a rhythm to Poe's maneuvering, and he timed his shots accordingly, getting closer and closer to his target.

Almost there . . . just a little to the left. He lined up the shot, anticipated Poe's swerve . . .

Right before he pulled the trigger, the rear passengers of each treadspeeder, launched into the air with jetpacks.

"They *fly now*!" C-3PO said.

"They fly now?!" Finn yelled.

Poe gripped the tiller. "They fly now," he echoed, because of course they did.

Finn got off a few experimental shots with his blaster, but hitting a flying object from the back of a swerving skimmer was harder than impossible.

"Rey!" Poe yelled. "We should split—"

"Split up," she yelled back.

"Yeah!"

They peeled off, Rey angling right with Chewie and BB-8 toward a dust grain farm. Poe steered Finn and C-3PO leftward into a narrow rocky canyon.

Their pursuing treadspeeders split up just as Finn had hoped. But his breath caught when he realized *both* of the flying jet troopers had disappeared, as though Rey were their true quarry.

The canyon closed in around them. Poe's driving took them so close to the walls that Finn could have reached out and scraped them with the tip of his blaster.

The treadspeeder was gaining on them. "Hold on!" Poe yelled, aiming directly for the canyon's wall.

"Oh, my!" said C-3PO as Poe lifted the skimmer's nose, and suddenly they were racing up the cliff's edge. Goods shifted to the back of the speeder. C-3PO's golden grip on the steering vane slipped, filling the air with a horrible metal-on-metal screeching.

Finn had completed minimum stormtrooper training with speeders, but even he knew that repulsorlift technology wasn't robust enough for them to continue skimming a cliff wall for long. And in an outdated junker like this, things were probably even worse than he knew.

"Did we lose them?" Poe hollered, bumping the speeder back down to the canyon floor.

Finn searched their surroundings. Just sand and outcroppings and walls as far as the eye could see. "Looks like it."

"Excellent job, sir!" C-3PO shouted. But he spoke too soon because the prow of a treadspeeder cornered a butte and came screaming toward them. "Nope, still there!" Finn said.

"Terrible job, sir," said the droid.

Poe laid into the throttle, but the skimmer didn't have any more to give. Finn resumed firing with his blaster—calmer now, letting his instincts guide him—a shot landed! The treadspeeder jerked sideways but resumed the chase in the blink of an eye. Finn hadn't damaged it at all.

The treadspeeder had shields.

Emboldened, the trooper lifted his blaster and fired. Finn hit the deck just in time as the trooper's shot impacted a bundle of dried goods, which blackened to smoke.

He was about to jump to his feet and fire back, but right at his nose was a long coiled rope with large metal hooks on each end. They stuck to the magnetized floor—a nice feature for holding down cargo, but not exactly helpful now. He muscled one away from the floor, lifted it, threw it toward the speeder.

The hook landed on the ground. Just as he'd hoped, the speeder drove right over it. The hook punctured the rubberized tread, caught, and held. The rope at Finn's feet uncoiled at an alarming rate as it wound around the trooper's tread.

Maybe he should have thought this through better . . . Their skimmer was slower than the treadspeeder, but it was also heavier. That gave him an idea.

The vane C-3PO clung to was solid metal, sturdy enough to provide additional steering and stability, just like a mast. Finn grabbed the second hook and secured it to the pole, making sure it held tight.

"Poe," he warned.

The pilot turned, saw the hook wrapped around the vane. "I gotcha!"

The treadspeeder was eating up their rope. It went taut; the skimmer jerked, and Finn nearly lost his footing. Poe angled the rudder sharply left, pushing them into an impossible right turn. They cornered so hard it felt as though Finn's cheeks were struggling to stay on his face.

The rope remained taut between them. The treadspeeder skidded in an arc around the fulcrum of Poe's hairpin turn, skidded, skidded, sand flying everywhere . . . and finally slammed into the side of the canyon, where it exploded into a ball of fire and dust.

"Wooo!" Finn yelled. He couldn't believe that had worked.

Even though they'd split up, Rey was left to deal with three pursuers. At least Poe and Finn would have a chance.

Chewbacca fired doggedly at the treadspeeder with his bowcaster, but he paused when the jet troopers suddenly hit the throttle and pulled even with them—and then confusingly moved ahead. Their strategy quickly became clear when they started firing charges to the ground in front of their skimmer.

Rey yanked the tiller, turning the skimmer at the last moment, barely dodging an explosion. She ducked away from the ensuing debris cloud even as she dodged again, turning away from the treadspeeder. Good thing the controls on this skimmer were sensitive, but she still found it necessary to anticipate, reacting a split second sooner than should be humanly possible. It was taking all her concentration.

The speeder and jet troopers were still in pursuit. Rey knew she couldn't keep this up forever. She'd eventually make a mistake.

"Get them!" she yelled to Chewie. "I'll go for the speeder."

It was possible to dodge obstacles ahead of them while shooting at something behind them, right? Well, she was about to find out.

Chewie kept the jet troopers busy with his bowcaster, but Rey found herself slaloming through grain-processing pipes that jutted from the ground, like an orchard of metal. She yanked up the blaster Han had given her, let the Force fill her, fired several times in quick succession at the treadspeeder.

Her shots hit, but they did no damage.

"The front shields are up," Rey said.

BB-8 began to beep excitedly about something he'd found.

"Not now, Beebee-Ate!" Rey hollered.

Chewie yelled, pointing.

Rey saw a lump in the distance. No, a ship. Ochi's freighter?! It hunkered atop a sandstone bluff, overlooking a vast, windswept valley interspersed with dark sand like blots of spilled ink. The ship's hull was blasted by sand and wind, its landing struts drowning in small dunes. "I see it!"

She ducked instinctively as a laser blast heated the air by her ear. One of Chewie's shots landed square on a jet trooper, who bulleted to the ground. The Wookiee roared.

Two to go.

The treadspeeder continued to fire at them, and the remaining jet trooper seemed inspired by the death of his comrade to double his efforts, lobbing charge after charge. Between evasions, Rey managed to get a few shots off with her blaster. Many of them hit the treadspeeder. None did any damage.

"Their shields are too strong," she yelled, ducking another cloud of stinging grit.

BB-8 had lodged himself behind Rey's tiller, taking advantage of the mag plates to keep himself from rolling off the skiff. One of his compartments opened, and his welding arm shot out toward one of the many containers in the cargo area. Rey didn't bother to ask or admonish; she focused on dodging charges and grain pipes, letting the little droid do whatever he was going to do.

BB-8 reached toward a metal canister with his welding arm and pecked at it, opening up a dark hole. Before anything could escape the now-compromised canister, BB-8 body-bumped it, hard enough to disengage the maglocks and send it flying into the air behind them.

It released a cloud of smoke as it fell—bright, sunshiny yellow, just like the colored smoke at the festival. Opaque as a wall.

The stormtrooper driving the speeder couldn't react fast enough to avoid it. The cloud blinded him, and he panicked, swerving left and launching up the slope of a rock. The speeder shot high, exposing a fuel tank that was unprotected by its forward shields. Rey aimed her blaster and pulled the trigger. The treadspeeder exploded.

BB-8 beeped smugly.

"Never underestimate a droid!" Rey said.

One to go. But neither Rey nor Chewie could spot him anywhere. The remaining jet trooper had disappeared.

Rey's senses were on high alert as she steered the skiff toward the abandoned freighter. As they approached, the lines of the hull manifested into something recognizable. Familiar. Her palms grew damp, and her breath became shallow and fast. "Ochi's ship . . ." she murmured. "I've seen that ship before."

Poe's skimmer appeared over the rise. Everyone seemed haggard and windblown, but were otherwise fine.

"You get them all?" Finn called.

"There's one left," she called back, searching the wide blue sky. Nothing in sight.

No help for it but to continue on. Together, the skimmers raced for the ship.

The closer they got to the freighter, the more its familiarity troubled Rey. Where had she seen it? Maybe one like it had stopped on Jakku. Small freighters landed at Niima Outpost all the time. It was the place to go to trade junk no one else in the galaxy wanted.

Rey steered toward the on-ramp. A ship like this would never survive long on Jakku. It would be stripped for parts within days. Maybe the Forbidden Valley really was forbidden, only used once every forty-two years during the Festival of Ancestors. There had to be an explanation for why this ship remained untouched.

As she and her friends were about to jump out of their skimmers, something roared overhead. Charges exploded all around them, throwing them to the sand and blowing their speeders to smithereens.

Everyone whipped up their weapons and fired; Rey wasn't sure which of them hit, but the jet trooper spiraled out of the sky and slammed into a cliff. His jetpack detonated, shooting him into yet another bluff and out of sight.

Rey had just enough time to register that the sand around her was a different color—more black than ocher—and that she'd seen this kind of sand before . . .

She sank up to her hips.

Her friends were descending around her, especially Poe. ". . . the hell is this?" he said, trying to extricate himself, but his movement only made him sink farther and faster.

"Sinking fields!" Rey said. The Sinking Fields of Jakku had taken many an unwary soul. She should have recognized the sand right away. "Grab onto something!"

But there was nothing to grab onto. Chewie called out, panicked.

C-3PO dropped all the way to his recharge coupling. "Oh, what an ignoble end!" he exclaimed.

BB-8's round body spun wildly in the mire, to no avail. Within the space of a breath, the little droid disappeared beneath the surface.

"Beebee-Ate!" Rey yelled.

Tears filled her eyes as she panic-thrashed against the sand. Rey was going to lose them all. Not to a dark and powerful enemy, but to a natural phenomenon she should have recognized. Jakku was going to have its last word after all.

She locked eyes with Finn. Her friend's face was stricken. "Rey!" he said. "I never told you—" He dropped, the sand reaching his shoulders.

"What?" she cried.

Finn slid down to his chin. "Rey!"

*No!* "Finn!"

Finn disappeared beneath the surface. C-3PO and Poe followed. She reached for Chewie as if in apology, and he reached back. She held her breath as sand covered her mouth, her nose, her eyes. Grit filled her ears, scraped her skin. The world went dark.

General Leia was in the command center, getting briefed by Rose Tico on the status of their tiny-but-growing fleet. "Everyone who can hold a wrench or pilex driver is repairing and upgrading ships," Rose said. "We're working as fast as we can."

Leia nodded. Just outside, sparks were flying everywhere, and she was about to ask for status updates on a few specific ships, but Snap Wexley hurried toward her, interrupting them.

"General, we're getting reports of a raid at the Festival of Ancestors."

Of course they were. Of course the First Order had found her people. "This mission is everything," Leia said. "It cannot fail." Then, her voice a little plaintive, she asked, "Any word from Rey?"

He shook his head. "The *Falcon*'s not responding."

At the look on Leia's face, Rose said to Snap, "Do you have to say it like that?"

"Like . . . what?" he said.

"Do me a personal favor," Leia said to him. "Be optimistic."

"Yes, ma'am," said Snap, forcing his features into bland pleasantness. "This is . . . this is *terrific*. You're not gonna believe how well . . . This is gonna turn out great."

Leia resisted rolling her eyes. But she said, "Major Wexley, requiring optimism doesn't mean hiding the truth."

"Yeah, what aren't you telling us?" Rose demanded.

Snap shuffled his feet. "The raid at the Festival . . . General Leia . . . Our eyes on the ground say it's the Knights of Ren."

Sand was scraping Poe's eyelids, shoving into his ears, up his nostrils. Any moment now, he'd lose control and inhale a mouthful of grit. The sand would scrape away at his lungs in the painful seconds it would take to choke to death.

Just when he thought he couldn't hold his breath a moment more, his feet met air. His torso broke through a layer of packed sand, and he dropped, hitting the ground hard.

BB-8 dropped after him, plunking down just a few meters away. Poe gasped to replenish his lungs, shaking sand out of his hair, blinking rapidly to clear the grit from his eyes. He looked around; BB-8 was right beside him. It was too dark to see well, but they had fallen into some kind of tunnel made of hard-packed sand. A gaping dark maw marked what might be an adjoining tunnel. Hopefully, he'd find the rest of his friends there. He got to his feet, dusted himself off, and stepped toward the maw. "Rey? Finn?" he called out.

"You didn't say my name, sir, but I'm all right," C-3PO responded from a few meters away.

A squelching noise made Poe turn; it was Rey, her legs dangling from the ceiling. He hurried over to keep her from dropping as hard as he had. After he lowered her to the ground, she bent over, coughing.

"I should have used the Force," she muttered between coughs. "I panicked . . . I didn't even think to . . ."

"Rey? You all right?"

She nodded. Her face was covered in sand. "Where's Finn?"

"And where's Chewie?" Poe said.

Chewbacca dropped through the ceiling and *thunk*ed to the ground. Poe winced at the impact, but Chewie shook himself off, seemingly unscathed.

"Finn?" Rey repeated.

He appeared in the entrance to the adjoining tunnel. Sand peppered his black hair. "Yeah, I'm good," he said. "What is this place?"

C-3PO doddered toward them. "This isn't the afterlife, is it?" he asked. "Are droids allowed here?"

Poe felt like he could *truly* breathe again, now that everyone was accounted for. He'd had it with people dying on his watch. "Thought we were goners," he said.

"We might still be, sir," C-3PO reminded him helpfully.

"Which way out?" Finn asked, looking around.

Rey unhooked her lightsaber and turned it on. Its blade lit the walls around them in soft blue, and Poe could feel its hum in the back of his throat as she waved it around, studying the walls.

Poe reached for his glow rod and turned it on. Its glow compared with the lightsaber's was like that of a moon to a sun. He shrugged and aimed it forward anyway, seeking an exit.

"This way," Rey said, and headed off.

He thought of protesting, of asking how Rey could possibly know which equally unremarkable direction was the right one. But Poe had learned that when Rey said things that way, her face determined, her voice unwavering, a fellow ought to just follow.

Lando Calrissian crouched on a rock outcropping, making himself as small as possible. Directly below and within spitting distance was the *Millennium Falcon,* surrounded by stormtroopers. Behind them was a high rock cliff, and Lando could make out several dark figures. His helmet zoomed in on the image until he could identify them: the Knights of Ren. They eyed his ship like vultures.

*His* ship. He hadn't been prepared for the sting of nostalgia that overcame him when he laid eyes on the *Falcon* again.

Lando had re-donned his mask and crept to this viewing perch, hoping he could grab the *Falcon* and return it to Chewie before the First Order found it. But he hadn't been fast enough.

A desert trooper wearing a colored pauldron strode forward. "Confiscate, scan, and destroy that ship," the stormtrooper commander ordered. "By order of the Supreme Leader."

Lando's breath grew tight with rage, and his helmet hummed to keep up with the task of filtration. The First Order always destroyed what you loved.

He'd been spending a lot of time on Pasaana to get away from all that. The Aki-Aki were joyful and nonviolent, and they'd welcomed him without question or reservation. He'd had to don the helmet, sure, because an old Rebellion general was nothing if not recognizable. A small price to pay for a little peace and quiet.

But maybe scoundrels like him didn't get to have peace. Maybe trouble always came looking, no matter what.

He watched, his determination growing, as the desert troopers broke the locks and forced the *Falcon* open. Then the best ship in the whole galaxy lifted off and screamed out of the atmosphere, its fusion engines glowing blue, no doubt heading for an incineration hangar.

Lando knew what he had to do.

# CHAPTER 7

The sand burrow made for easy traveling with its flat, hard-packed ground and cooler air—which was good because Rey had no idea how long it would take to find an exit. She only knew that a strange instinct drew her forward. *Let it guide you,* she imagined Leia saying. She'd been doing that a lot lately, imagining what Leia would counsel her to do.

She should have let the Force guide her when she and her friends were sinking into the sand. Rey wasn't sure what she would have done, but . . . something. Calling on the Force was easy. But she needed to make it her first instinct. Leia had observed that her formative years on Jakku had taught her to look for tactile solutions to impossible problems. Leia thought that could be why it took so long for the Force to awaken inside her, and why it might take even longer to shake that kind of conditioning.

But Rey didn't have that kind of time, and she wouldn't let herself make that mistake again.

BB-8 beeped a question.

"I don't *want* to know what made these tunnels," Poe answered.

"Judging by the bore circumference," C-3PO said, "any number of deadly species could—"

"Do *not* want to know," Poe repeated. "*Not.*"

The tunnel curved around, and Rey followed. "So what was it?" she asked Finn, mostly to keep her mind off C-3PO's words.

"What?" Finn said.

"What were you going to tell me?"

"When?"

"When you were sinking in the sand, you said, 'I never told you . . .' "

Finn avoided her gaze. "I'll tell you later," he mumbled.

"When you're not 'with Poe'?" Poe said.

"Yeah!" said Finn, with a mock glare.

"Great," said Poe. "We're gonna die in a sand burrow, and we're all keeping secrets . . ."

"I'll tell you," Finn said, "when you tell us how you know how to do all that shifty stuff!"

BB-8 warbled at something ahead, which brought them up short. Something metallic flashed in the glow of Rey's lightsaber as they peered closer.

"What's that?" Poe said, aiming his glow rod.

"A speeder?" Finn asked.

"An old one," Rey said. Its steering vane was bent at an impossible angle, and it was outdated by at least a decade, but the dry, windless tunnel had largely preserved the acceleration module and repulsorlift. If she stripped this thing for parts, she could get at least three portions for her trouble.

"Perhaps we'll find the driver," C-3PO said.

BB-8 told C-3PO what he thought of that.

"Yeah, I think dead, too," Poe said.

Chewie complained that he was getting thirsty.

C-3PO waddled over to the speeder's hood ornament and bent over, peering close. "It's a hex charm," he said.

"A what?" Poe said.

"A common emblem of Sith loyalists!" C-3PO said, delighted.

"The Sith . . ." Rey murmured. This was the place her instincts had been leading her to, no doubt about it. But it was not the hex charm that had drawn her. Something else . . .

"Luke sensed it," Rey said. "Ochi never left this place." *Disappeared into the desert,* Lando had told them.

"He was headed away from his ship," Poe said. "Same thing happened to us happened to him."

That explained why the freighter had remained untouched for all these years. Anyone familiar with Pasaana knew better than to go near this place, the same way the residents of Jakku knew to stay clear of the Sinking Fields.

"So how did Ochi get out?" Finn asked, looking around for an exit.

Rey stepped toward the speeder, her limbs tingling. "He didn't," she said.

At her feet was a pile of old bones.

"No, he didn't," Finn agreed.

"Bones," said Poe, looking away in disgust. "I don't like bones."

Ochi's speeder had fallen into the tunnel, and either he'd died on impact, or he'd injured himself so badly that he'd died slowly, trapped and alone.

BB-8 warbled that he'd found something.

Rey moved next to him and peered closer at the pile of bones. Tattered clothes clung to the remains. A leather belt with a knife sheath circled his pelvis. The sheath was empty.

BB-8 extended a tube from his tool compartment and began blowing away some nearby sand. Gradually, an object appeared—long and metallic, with a still-sharp blade.

Rey's heart began to race as she picked it up, gripped its cold handle. This dagger. Those runes . . .

*Screams rending the air, the metallic scent of blood, the feel of blade against bone and sinew . . .*

Rey blinked the vision away, feeling sick. "Horrible things have happened with this," she murmured.

Poe took it from her, and a weight lifted from her shoulders when the dagger left her hand.

"It has writing on it," Poe said, studying the blade's etchings.

"Of course it does, sir!" C-3PO said cheerfully. "Perhaps I can translate."

It was an archaic text Rey had never encountered in all her years at Niima Outpost. The blade itself was silvery but untarnished, with a scalloped edge designed to do as much damage coming out of a body as sliding into it. A hefty, curved crossguard protected a leather-wrapped handle. She'd never seen anything like it.

C-3PO took it from Poe, and a weight was lifted from her shoulders when the dagger left her hand.

"What does it say?" Poe asked.

"Sith assassins often inscribed their secrets on . . ." the droid observed. "Oh! Look! The location of the wayfinder!"

They all practically knocked heads trying to get a closer look.

"What's it say?" Poe demanded again.

"Where's the wayfinder?" Finn said.

"I'm afraid I cannot tell you," C-3PO said.

Poe gaped at him. "Twenty-point-three-fazillion languages, and you can't read that?"

"Oh, I have read it, sir!" C-3PO enthused. "I know exactly where the wayfinder is. Unfortunately, it's written in the runic language of the Sith."

"So what?" Rey said.

"My programming forbids me from translating it. I am physically incapable!"

"Wait," said Poe. "*Wait.* The one time we want you to talk you *can't*?"

"Irony, sir."

Rey was surprised to learn that C-3PO knew what irony was.

"My vocal processors cannot phonate words translated from Sith," the droid said. A hulking shadow moved behind him. Something huge, and—Rey sensed—in great pain. Rey lifted her lightsaber in readiness. Oblivious, C-3PO added, "I believe the rule was passed by the Senate of the Old Repub—"

The thing in the shadows hissed, manifested into a serpent more massive than a happabore with a segmented body and wicked red eyes. C-3PO turned. The droid dropped the dagger into the dirt and screamed, "Serpent!" as the snake opened its massive jaw to reveal sharp fangs dripping venom. It drew back into a striking position.

"Rey," Finn whispered.

BB-8 rolled behind Rey as Chewie whipped up his bowcaster, preparing to fire.

The Force should always be her first instinct. So Rey reached out to the bowcaster to lower it, her eyes glued to the snake's huge fangs. She'd once heard about this creature—a vexis—from a trader. He'd been complaining about Jakku, and how it was hard to get a decent drink anywhere on the planet, but at least Jakku had never been home to a vexis, like some of the other desert planets.

Poe said, "I'm gonna blast it."

"Don't blast it," Finn said, his gaze fixed on the snake.

The vexis rose even higher. It hiss-roared, blowing Chewie's fur back.

It was terrifying. Rey could sense its rage, its hunger. But she also sensed great pain. Unsure exactly what she was doing, she handed her lightsaber to Finn and stepped forward.

"Rey—" Finn protested.

"It might be injured," she said.

"Might just be a giant killer sand snake," Poe said.

Rey narrowed her eyes as she approached the serpent's body. "More light," she ordered.

Poe aimed his glow rod where she pointed, illuminating the creature.

Yes, the serpent was definitely wounded. A giant gash ran across several segments. She just had to reach it. Carefully, slowly, she climbed over the vexis's curved body until she stood within its coils. If it decided to kill her, all it had to do was squeeze . . .

She spoke gently, to comfort herself as much as the snake. "Leia says when something's trying to hurt you, it was usually hurt by something bigger." Like farm equipment. A grain farmer had probably rolled a tilling blade right across this creature's lair, flaying it open.

Rey reached for the wound. The vexis hissed, and she hesitated. But it didn't attack. Heart in her throat, she stretched her hand forward, touched the serpent's cool segments.

She was acting on pure instinct now. Rey closed her eyes. Reached for the Force.

Whenever she fought, or leapt through the jungles of Ajan Kloss, or even mind-tricked a stormtrooper into releasing her shackles, she *channeled* the Force, using it for her own advantage in some way. But this would call for a different technique, something she'd learned from the Jedi texts when she was mending Luke's kyber crystal. This time, she would *give.*

A hum resonated in her chest as she gathered something inside her, offered it up to the serpent. Her own energy. Her own life. It was part of the Force, too, and she didn't have to keep it all to herself.

She felt the vexis calming. Its pain was receding.

After a moment, she dared to open her eyes. What she saw made her gasp. The wound had closed.

The vexis lowered its head to hers. It was so huge. It could devour her in a single gulp. Its tongue flicked out, and it hissed, blowing her hair back—a kiss of sorts.

The snake uncoiled around her, leaving her free. It slithered away into the dark, forging a new path in the hard-packed sand as easily as if it were an eel swimming through water. When it disappeared, they could see a clear circle of sky.

Poe and Finn exchanged a look.

BB-8 rolled up to Rey, beeping softly.

"I just transferred a bit of life. Force energy, from me to him."

BB-8 whirred.

"You would have done the same."

"Well," Finn said. "We've got our way out." He started after the vexis. Chewie bent down to retrieve the dagger, stuffed it into his pack, then he followed Finn toward the light of day.

Rey wasn't in a hurry to get to the surface, though. Her breath came fast, her very bones ached with weariness, and unaccountably, her hand stung. Healing the vexis had felt so normal and natural and right. But it had cost her.

The tunnel dumped them even closer to Ochi's rusty freighter. It perched atop a huge rock platform, an island of stability in a sea of shifting mires. Rey and her friends climbed toward it.

"We cannot possibly fly in that old wreck!" C-3PO protested. He struggled to keep up over the jutting rocks. If they survived this, Rey would make sure he got an oil bath.

"We gotta keep moving," Poe urged from just ahead. "Find someone who can translate that dagger . . . like, a *helpful* droid."

"I suggest we return to the *Millennium Falcon* at once." C-3PO said.

"They'll be waiting at the *Falcon,*" Poe said.

"They'll send *us* to the pits of Griq," Finn said.

"And use *you* as a target droid," Poe added.

"You both make excellent points at times," C-3PO said.

Rey frowned. Finn and Poe were having a bit of fun with the droid, but it was true that the *Falcon* was probably in First Order hands by now. Chewie had locked it down tight, but the First Order would get past all their security precautions eventually. It was possible she'd never see her ship again.

A familiar presence hit her like a thunderclap, and she froze in place.

"Rey?" Finn turned to see what had made her pause.

His face was still dusty from their tour of the tunnels, and as usual his inherent kindness and concern were smeared all over his features. She would *not* allow him to be hurt by what was coming. She would protect her friend, even if it meant doing something she was pretty sure Leia wouldn't approve of.

"I'll be right behind you," she said gently.

He frowned.

She gave a little push with the Force and added, "It's okay."

He was wordless as she handed over her haversack and

quarterstaff—everything save the lightsaber hooked to her belt. She felt his eyes on her back as she descended the rocks and—avoiding the shifting mires this time—sprinted out onto a wide, flat stretch of desert.

*Go, Finn,* she thought, pushing a little harder with the Force.

She didn't dare to look and see if he obeyed, because all her attention was drawn to a black mote on the horizon, flying fast and low, approaching her.

She squared her shoulders as the mote became a TIE fighter. *His* TIE fighter. She wasn't sure how yet, but she would not give ground. She would protect her friends. At any cost.

Finn's head was fuzzy. Maybe it was the heat. Maybe it was the fact that Rey had told him to go, and he'd just left her in the desert without question. Something about that didn't make sense.

Poe hit the freighter's hatch release, and the access ramp descended. Finn followed Poe, Chewie, and the droids into a dark central hold choking in sand. Ochi hadn't sealed this place up before being swallowed by the mires. He must have thought he'd be returning before long.

The hold was filled with junk, and the walls remained mostly open to the ship's inner workings—Finn recognized emergency atmo tanks, a particle shield booster, along with endless wires and ducts and latches whose uses remained a mystery, though he'd bet Poe or Rey would know what they were. The interior was so messy it made the *Falcon* look almost tidy.

On a wall near the entrance to the sleeping quarters, a metal plaque identified the ship: BESTOON LEGACY.

"Let's try waking up the converters," Poe said, heading toward the cockpit, pushing cobwebs and junk out of the way.

"This ship is filthy!" C-3PO said, and Finn had to agree. Phasma would have made his entire unit scrub latrines with their toothbrushes if she'd ever caught them failing to lash down cargo or mop up dirt.

While Poe started hitting switches, Finn peered inside a cargo box. It was filled with blaster pistols. He looked around, noting several other boxes. Were they *all* filled with weapons?

Lights flickered on around him. The floor began to vibrate as the power plant cranked to life.

"Look at that," Poe said.

Finally, some luck. But they couldn't leave without Rey, who still hadn't entered the ship.

"Where is she?" Finn asked no one in particular. He hurried to the cockpit viewport and searched the vast desert. There. A tiny, wind-whipped figure. She'd managed to travel quite a distance.

"Chewie," Finn said, thinking of the Wookiee's long stride and superior speed. "Tell Rey we gotta go."

Chewie moaned assent, then headed out to fetch her. A moment later the Wookiee appeared in view of the viewport, but he promptly disappeared behind a rock formation on his way toward the desert floor and Rey.

Kylo Ren sensed her before he saw her. As he flew his TIE whisper along the flat desert, she was a bright presence in his mind, practically glowing with determination and ferocity. Something odd pulled at his chest. It was the same feeling he'd had when he'd faced his father for the last time, when he'd made the decision to kill Han Solo. You had to kill the past, yes, but you had to kill the light, too, to fully claim the darkness.

He finally understood. Han Solo was his past. But Rey was his light.

That's why Kylo was still in agony. That's why he couldn't shake the memory of his father's hand against his cheek, of those eyes full of love and understanding. Kylo hadn't yet destroyed his light.

Maybe the Emperor was right. She needed to die. That, or he needed to kill the light in her.

And there she stood, barely a dot against the ocher sand, her shoulders squared, facing him down. The girl was terrified; he could sense it like he could sense the sweat dampening his gloves. Yet despite her terror, she was unwavering, ready and waiting.

She should be *mindless* with fear. She should be cowering. She should have turned to the dark when he gave her the chance. How could she resist? How *dared* she?

Rage turned his vision red. He didn't care about the Emperor. He didn't care about the Star Destroyer fleet. He just wanted his pain to end.

If Rey wanted to survive what came next, she would have to manifest more power than she ever had before. Show him who she was.

He watched as Rey unhooked her lightsaber and lit it.

Kylo Ren hit the throttle.

Rey saw the TIE approach, felt his intentions. Kylo Ren's pain and killing rage were breathtaking.

But she knew just what to do now. Healing the vexis had exhausted her, but it had also opened up new avenues of the Force to her—something about both giving and taking, about a more perfect oneness than she'd understood before. She yearned to talk it over with Leia.

For now, though, she had no choice but to let the Force thrum in her blood, fill her limbs with readiness. She was terrified, yes, but she was also strangely calm. Luke had told her that fear leads to the dark side. But it turned out that terror and calm could coexist. Maybe this is what Leia had been trying to teach her.

She allowed the TIE to approach. Sensing it was the right time, she turned away, lowered herself into a fighting lunge.

Rey glanced back. He was close enough that she could see the shape of his helmet through the cockpit viewport.

Finn hated feeling useless as Poe flicked the controls, made adjustments. The rumbling floor beneath his feet steadied, and the clanking of the turbines smoothed into a steady hum. They had achieved flight readiness.

But Chewie had not returned with Rey.

"What the hell's she doing?" Poe demanded. "Where is Chewie?"

Finn peered out the cockpit viewport. It was hard to make out details from here, but it seemed she was crouched, her lightsaber lit. He should be out there, helping her . . .

The strangest thing happened. In yearning to help her, in reaching for her, he sensed something. A danger. A presence. "It's Ren," he whispered.

Probably just a bad feeling . . . right?

Just in case, he put a hand to his holster to check his blaster and jogged down the ramp into the desert.

He headed for the outcropping Chewbacca had disappeared behind, but he stopped short and hunkered down when he heard footsteps. Slowly, carefully, he peered around the rock—and nearly gasped.

Chewie had been captured. Manacles circled his furry wrists. Tall figures with dark armor and strange weapons shoved him forward, toward a handful of stormtroopers and their transports. Malevolence radiated from the dark figures in waves; Finn felt like he was choking on it.

The Knights of Ren. They could be no one else. He should flee.

But within moments Chewie would be loaded onto a transport and taken away. Finn had no choice but to act now.

He drew his blaster, intending to charge forward, but he froze when a dozen more stormtroopers poured down the ramp in formation. Attacking them all at once would be suicide.

Finn would have to creep back to the *Bestoon Legacy* and come up with another plan. No, that wouldn't work. The fact that an entire transport was here, along with the Knights of Ren and—if his feeling was correct—Kylo Ren himself, could only mean one thing. They were after Rey and her power.

Finn had to warn her.

---

The *Bestoon Legacy* was ready to take off, but now Poe was sitting alone in the cockpit without a crew. First Rey and Chewie, and now Finn was gone, too. Where the hell were—

He gasped. Rey had started to run, her lightsaber whipping beside her with each stride. A TIE was bearing down on her, flying so low that it kicked up clouds of sand. It would be on her in moments.

Rey sucked air as she sprinted. She would only pull this off with good speed and a lot of help from the Force, but her training with Leia was paying off. She was fit and her limbs were strong. Her lungs were capable. More important, her mind was ready.

She pressed forward, picking up more speed. The TIE was close now; its scream was bright in her ears.

Still not close enough. She reached out for the connection she shared with Kylo and felt his determination. She threw a wave of ferocity right back at him.

Her shoulder blades prickled as the ship bore down on her. Not just yet . . . a few strides more . . . now!

She leapt up and flipped backward, sweeping her legs in an aerial arc.

Below her, Kylo Ren craned his neck to track her flight.

She whipped her lightsaber down at the support pylon.

The TIE screamed past in a cloud of choking dust.

She landed neatly in the sand. Eyes narrowed, ready for anything, she watched the TIE start to wobble. She sensed Kylo's frustration as he compensated at the controls. The support pylon buckled, and the left wing clipped the ground.

Out of control, the TIE tumbled, wings ripping off their struts. The remaining ball holding Kylo Ren rolled at an impossible speed, leaving a ditch in the sand. Finally it slammed into an embankment, where it lay still.

Rey turned off her lightsaber. She hoped he was dead. No, she didn't. She hoped . . . she didn't know what she hoped.

She hooked her lightsaber to her belt and headed toward Ochi's freighter.

A figure appeared ahead, familiar in his blue pants and flight jacket. "Rey!" Finn screamed at her across the desert plain. "They got Chewie!"

A transport lifted into view, its drive thrusters already glowing blue.

Finn punched the air with his finger. "Chewie's in there!"

No. *No, no, no, no.*

She'd been here before, standing helplessly as sand blasted her skin, watching a ship carry away someone she loved.

Where there had been calm, now there was only terror. It filled her mind, overflowed into pure, hot power. She reached out with the Force, imagined herself grabbing the transport, wrenching it back planetside.

It actually slowed. Wobbled in the air. Its engines began to whine.

Rey gritted her teeth. Sweat poured from her forehead. She would not let them take Chewie from her.

Kylo Ren yanked off his mask to get some fresh air. He was an idiot. His stomach roiled with this inevitable certainty as he gingerly stepped around the burning wreckage of his TIE. She had run like a frightened womp rat, and in his blind rage he had succumbed to the temptation, not pausing to consider that maybe she had a plan.

With this realization came another certainty, even more gut wrenching: He was relieved he hadn't killed her.

Snoke had always encouraged him to pursue his impulses. They were a shortcut to the dark side—and unimaginable power. But his impulse to kill Rey had almost ruined everything he'd been planning.

Kylo didn't know how to reconcile that. The path to the dark side lay in succumbing to one's desires. But his deepest desire, the thing he wanted most, would require planning and patience. The

Emperor had figured out how to embrace a plan so long suffering and painstakingly careful it boggled the mind—and he did it without being tempted by the light even a little.

There was a way. He just had to learn it.

Kylo sensed a tug in the Force as he stepped from billowing smoke into clear air. Far away, Rey stood in the sand, straining, her arm reaching toward—

A flying transport? And she was succeeding in slowing it down!

It didn't matter what—or who—was inside that transport that made Rey desperate to prevent its escape. He was not going to let her have it.

He reached out, felt the massive machinery in his mind, yanked it toward himself.

The transport almost jerked out of her grip, and she gasped at the familiar presence. Kylo, alive and well. Rey would not let him have Chewie. Chewie was *hers*.

She strained to regain control, and she felt the ship lurch in her direction, but then it whipped right back.

Rey tried to remember her training. *Let the Force guide your actions,* Leia would say. But thinking of Leia, her training, even for the briefest moment made her lose concentration, and the ship listed again in Kylo's direction.

So Rey bore down with all the strength of her being. Blood screamed in her ears, and her heart was a massive drum in her chest. She drew on her rage at Kylo, at the First Order, even at Unkar Plutt. She drew on her terror for Chewie's life, remembered what it felt like to watch Han Solo drop into the abyss at Starkiller base. She drew on pain too: the aching hollowness of an empty stomach, the bruised knuckles with no bacta to soothe them, the feel of grit in her molars after a windy day, the dagger-sharp silence of loneliness. Rey opened her mouth in a silent scream.

Raw power burst from her fingertips, arced toward the freighter. It was blue lightning, pure Force energy, brighter than a lightsaber, hotter than a sun. It wrapped its deadly, crooked fingers around the transport, which jerked sideways for the briefest instant and then exploded into a sickening fireball.

Rey stumbled back, gasping for air, as bits of wreckage rained down onto the desert plain. The transport—and everyone inside—reduced to nothingness.

She stared down at her hand in horror. Then at the bits of wreckage. Her stomach heaved, and finally she screamed, "Chewiiieeeeeeee!" as tears poured down her cheeks. What had she done?

A voice penetrated her haze of guilt-madness: "Rey!" It was Poe, calling to her. "They're coming!"

He pointed toward the horizon, and she turned. Half a dozen First Order TIEs were quickly approaching.

"But Chewie . . . He . . ."

"I'm sorry!" Poe yelled. "But we have to go. Now!"

His voice, along with Finn's rapid approach, convinced her feet to move. She would not lose any more friends. She hurried toward Finn, and together they ran for the ship.

From a distance Kylo Ren watched the freighter rise into the sky, Rey inside it. She had beaten him *again,* and yet he was filled with triumph.

He'd been right to push her.

She had just demonstrated unbelievable, mind-blowing power. Dark power. *Sith* power.

The scavenger was almost ready to turn. And when she did, they would *both* kill their light, embrace their darkness. Then the Star Destroyer fleet—and the Sith throne—would be theirs.

# CHAPTER 8

Ochi's freighter may have been flightworthy, but that didn't mean it was in good shape. The *Legacy* had been grounded on Pasaana for years, which meant they didn't dare take it far until Rey and her friends could hide out for a bit, do a thorough check of the ship's systems, and regain their bearings.

Poe told everyone he knew exactly where to go, and Rey was happy to cede that decision to him. She sat in the copilot's seat and provided support as he guided the *Legacy* into the rings of a large, glowing planet. The rings were made mostly of ice drifts. They reflected plenty of light from the system's cool sun, and constantly shed vapor. It was a good hiding spot, one that would confuse most ships' sensor sweeps—perfect for smugglers. One of these days, she might ask Poe how he knew about this place.

"Rey," Poe began, as he set the ship to drift alongside an ice floe, but when he saw her face, he changed his mind about whatever he was going to say. Instead, he went with: "I'll start some diagnostics. Why don't you . . . take a moment?"

It was the gentlest he'd been with her for a long time. She nodded wordlessly and headed into the central hold, found a cushioned bench near the back, and plunked down.

*What have I done?*

Fear led to the dark side after all. She'd been fine so long as her fear was tempered by peace and resolve. But the moment she gave in to rage and terror . . . Chewbacca was gone. The *Falcon* was probably gone. Ochi's dagger was gone. She had ruined everything.

Leia would be so disappointed in her when she found out.

As if reading her thoughts, BB-8 gave her a long, mournful beep.

C-3PO said, "Poor, poor Chewbacca."

Tears were pouring down her cheeks. She couldn't stop them. Chewie had done so much for her. The *Falcon* was arguably his by right, but after Han died, Chewie had offered the pilot's seat to *her*. And she had repaid this act of enormous generosity and respect by killing him.

Finn stepped forward. His face was stricken. He said, "It wasn't your fault."

"It was," Rey said, unable to look at him. "I lost control."

"No, it was *Ren*. He made you do it."

Rey shook her head. "You saw what happened. That power came from me. Finn, there are things you don't know."

"Then tell me." He gazed at her, waiting patiently, no trace of judgment on his face.

Rey hadn't been able to bring herself to tell Leia. But maybe she could tell Finn. She had to tell someone or the secret would devour her from within.

She whispered, "I had a vision. Of the throne of the Sith. I saw who was on it."

Finn's eyes narrowed. "Ren?"

Rey nodded. "And . . . *me*."

Finn's mouth parted.

She looked away, unable to face him. Rey wished she could run, from Finn's inevitable disappointment, the shock in his voice when he finally spoke next. But on this tiny freighter, there was nowhere to go.

Poe stepped into the hold from the cockpit. His face was haggard, but he seemed as determined as ever. He'd been so serious lately, often on the verge of anger ever since Crait. He felt responsible for the decimation of the Resistance, Rey knew. She understood what that was like, and she braced herself. She wasn't going to blame him one bit for laying into her; she was just going to take it.

He didn't lay into her. Poe said, "We've only got eight hours left. So what are we gonna do?"

"What *can* we do?" Finn said. "We gotta go back to base."

Poe was shaking his head. "We don't have time to go back. We are not giving up. If we do that, Chewie died for nothing."

Poe was right. Rey was selfish to wallow in misery. She still had the Resistance to think about, their plan to find the Sith fleet. Chewie would want her to press on.

"What is there to do?" Finn asked, his voice as despairing as she felt. "Chewie had the dagger. That was the only clue to the wayfinder. It's gone."

"So true," C-3PO said sadly. "The inscription lives only in my memory now."

Finn's and Poe's heads whipped toward C-3PO, and they pinned him with a collective glare.

"Hold on," Poe said. "You got the dagger inscription in your memory?"

"Oh, yes, Master Poe. But a translation from a forbidden language cannot be retrieved. That is, short of a complete redactive memory bypass."

"A complete what?" said Finn.

C-3PO flailed his arms. "Oh, it's a terribly dangerous act, performed on unwitting droids by degenerates and criminals!"

Finn brightened. "So we do that!"

Poe's eyes were narrowed in thought. "I know a black-market droidsmith."

"Black-market droidsmith!" C-3PO exclaimed.

Poe seemed almost apologetic when he added, "But he's on Kijimi."

"What's wrong with Kijimi?" Finn asked.

Poe seemed hesitant to answer. At Finn's look of insistence, he said, "I had a little bad luck on Kijimi . . ." Poe sighed, then added, "But if this mission fails, it was all for nothing. All we've done. All this time."

Finn was nodding. "We're in this to the end."

Rey had been looking back and forth between them as they talked, offering nothing, still expecting them to blame her, maybe even start yelling. But they hadn't. Not once. Instead, they both looked to her for input. They both still trusted her, even Finn, who knew her darkest secret.

She couldn't bring herself to speak as she reached out and took Finn's hand. In turn, Finn looked to Poe and extended his own hand. Poe shrugged once and then took it.

"For Chewie," Rey choked out.

C-3PO teetered over to them and valiantly attempted to join hands, too, despite the fact that he didn't have full articulation of his elbows or adequate spatial awareness.

Oblivious that he'd accidentally knocked Finn's feet with his own hard, metal ones, C-3PO solemnly said, "For the Wookiee."

*Never underestimate a droid,* Rey thought.

They held hands for a long moment.

Poe was the first to let go. "To Kijimi." he said, and left for the cockpit to finish his diagnostics. Finn followed. Rey was about to go after them and make herself useful, but BB-8 caught her eye as he rolled away toward the corner, where an old, lumpy cloth sat discarded. He opened a port and reached out with his grip arm, yanked back the cloth.

Beneath it was a rusty green droid, as lifeless and cold as a piece of scrap. It was tiny, with a conical head and a unicycle mechanism. The only droids Rey had ever encountered that were so small were used strictly for maintenance and janitorial work. This one seemed different. It had a motivator compartment and a higher-end transmitter array.

BB-8 opened a side panel on the tiny, rusty droid, plugged in, and began to charge him. Rey wasn't sure how well that would work out, but she couldn't blame BB-8 for trying to give a little of his own life force to help another.

Suddenly, the little droid was stirring to life. "B-b-battery charged!" he announced. He tried to roll forward, but his uni-wheel squealed in protest. He stared up at BB-8 in awe and wonder, whirring at the larger droid in a worshipful tone.

"He-hello!" the little droid said.

BB-8 warbled back, telling him to follow. Together, they rolled toward Rey, the tiny droid's wheel squeaking with each rotation.

"Hello-hello!" the droid said to Rey. "I'm D-O."

"Hello," Rey said, reaching out to touch him, but D-O recoiled, cowering in the corner.

"No-no-no thank you," he said.

She respected his wishes, withdrawing her hand. He needed lubricant badly, but Rey didn't see droid maintenance supplies anywhere in the hold. What kind of horrible person kept a droid but never maintained them?

BB-8 beeped a question.

"Looks like someone treated him badly," Rey answered.

Little D-O cocked his head at her.

"It's okay," she told him. "You're with *us* now."

General Hux took a deep breath before stepping onto the bridge of the *Steadfast*. The *Millennium Falcon* had been commandeered. He himself had supervised as three TIEs towed it into the incineration hangar.

But it would not be enough.

Ren was not currently aboard, but Allegiant General Pryde was, and he had the ear and favor of Ren. Whatever Hux reported to him, and *how* it was said, would be relayed in exact detail. Hux had one card to play. He had to play it carefully.

He squared his shoulders and strode in as though he had every confidence in the galaxy. Bridge officers ignored him as he headed toward General Pryde and joined him on the upper walkway. A janitor droid scurried out of his way.

"We recovered the scavenger's ship," Hux began. "But she got away."

General Pryde said nothing.

"Under command *of the Knights of Ren,*" Hux said pointedly, "we suffered losses. Troops, TIEs, a transport was destroyed—"

"I've seen the report," Pryde snapped. "Is that all?"

"No, Allegiant General," Hux said.

He often left little things out of his reports. Hux justified these redactions to his superiors by citing security concerns. But really, it was for moments like this. Hux needed to *see* Pryde's reaction, understand the older man's response in real time. If Pryde were allowed to read it while behind a desk, in the privacy of his office, Hux would never know how the news landed.

"There was another transport in the desert," Hux said. "It brought back a valuable prisoner."

Pryde's stride hitched. The Resistance forces had been greatly depleted at Crait. Anyone left was immensely valuable. "Prisoner?" Pryde asked.

Hux smiled. "Come with me."

Hux led Pryde to the door of a holding cell just outside the incineration hangar. The shiny black floor around it was peppered with sand and dust from the planet Pasaana. Hux was about to point it out to the stormtrooper guarding the door, but an MSE-6 series droid scurried over to take care of the mess, and Hux decided to let it go. For now.

Instead, he signaled to the stormtrooper that they were ready.

The door *swick*ed away, revealing an impossibly tall and hairy creature in manacles, surrounded by more troopers. When it saw Hux and Pryde, it moaned loudly, revealing long teeth. Its breath smelled like something had crawled up into its throat and died. Sweet stars, but Wookiees were disgusting creatures.

"The beast used to fly with Han Solo," Hux said to Pryde.

The Wookiee roared, blowing Hux's hair back. The general managed to keep from recoiling, but he felt his cheeks quiver with the effort.

"Have it sent to Interrogation Six," Pryde said dismissively.

Pryde headed away and Hux followed, secretly relieved to get out of range of those teeth.

Kijimi City was an ancient, once-grand city that had been slowly carved into a snowy mountainside over the course of centuries. Its cobblestone streets twisted at steep, narrow angles, and slippery steps limned in ice and snow had caused more than one unwary person to regret their visit.

Poe hurried down an alleyway, the hood of his coat tight against his face, his breath frosting the air. Snow flurried down, making every step slick and dangerous. He was lightheaded, his heart pattered fast, and he felt a tight headache coming on. He knew from experience that a body adjusted to the altitude eventually, but he hoped they wouldn't be around long enough. In the meantime, he couldn't afford to get altitude sickness. As he traveled, he took lots of slow deep breaths to give his body as much oxygen to work with as possible.

It was nighttime, but like all large cities, Kijimi never quite slept. Oil lamps, sodium sconces, and the occasional cantina window pooled light onto the flagstone streets. He tried to avoid them all, sticking to darkness.

Because First Order troopers were everywhere.

Poe watched from the shadows as a group of troopers pounded on a door, demanding entry. Down the street a way, he found a small family huddled beneath an overhang, trying to disappear into the stone. Another turn, another set of steps, and Poe watched a snowtrooper drag a tiny, wailing girl away from her mother. He wished there was something he could do to help.

There was. Finding that droidsmith, translating the dagger, and obliterating the Star Destroyer fleet could put a stop to all of this for good. He just had to figure out how.

Poe entered the Thieves' Quarter, and the alleys narrowed. A noxious stink made him wince. The sewer was backed up. Which meant one of the criminal syndicates had taken over this territory. Probably the Intracluster Gatherers, who were notorious for deferring maintenance, letting basic amenities like plumbing and power fall into disrepair just to save a few credits.

It broke his heart a little. His memories of Kijimi were a mixed bag at best, but he hated to see the place even more run down, strangled by First Order occupation. It was happening in the Yavin system, on Corellia, and now even distant worlds like Pasaana weren't safe. The First Order burned away everything that made the galaxy light and beautiful. Kijimi, like so many others, was now a shadow of what it used to be.

Poe finally reached his friends, who had been waiting for him in a dark alcove. Rey, Finn, and even C-3PO wore long, hooded coats, which Poe had liberated from the Opranko Guildhouse. The protocol droid had informed Poe that his internal thermostat made a coat unnecessary, but thanked him nonetheless. Poe had ordered C-3PO to keep his hood up over his bright, stupid, golden head no matter what.

Only BB-8 and his tiny new friend went undisguised.

"Snowtroopers are everywhere," Poe told them all. "We gotta find another way around."

"Then I suggest we leave," C-3PO said, too loudly. "Who votes we leave?"

"Threepio, clam it," Poe ordered. Did the droid *ever* modulate the volume of his voice? "Follow me."

They'd only gone two steps before Poe stopped them again. The cone-headed droid was squealing like a dying rodent. "Is there anything we can do about that?" he asked.

"Master Poe," C-3PO said. "I will carry him."

He leaned down, scooped up the tiny droid, and cradled him under his arm. Rey reached over and pulled C-3PO's coat closed, shrouding them both.

"Thank you, thank you," came a muffled voice.

They set off again. His nose and cheeks were going numb in the icy air. They would tingle and itch like mad when they finally warmed up. Back in the day, plenty of his buddies had suffered frostbite in this place. One of the many reasons he'd been glad to leave it behind.

Poe led them through the twisted streets, up a flight of stairs, all the while doing his best to avoid trooper squads and lookouts. He half expected Finn or Rey to needle him about how he knew so much about this place; they'd been relentless on the flight over, asking him about hot-wiring speeders, finding smugglers' hideouts, all of it. But they were as silent as a grave as they crept through the narrow passageways, tense with alertness.

They were nearly to their destination. "All right," Poe whispered. "Let's head down this—"

The tip of a blaster barrel was suddenly boring into his skull. Poe closed his eyes. He'd been afraid of this. No matter how sneaky you were, on Kijimi someone else was sneakier.

"Heard you were spotted at Monk's Gate," came a female voice, filtered through a helmet vocoder. He knew that voice, even through a vocoder. "I thought," she continued, *"He's not stupid enough to come back here."*

"Oh, you'd be surprised," he said.

He dared to look at her.

Zorii Bliss. She was tall and lithe, in a maroon flight suit trimmed in coppery bronzium. Just like he remembered. Except her twin blasters were newer, and her helmet and visor—which shrouded her entire face—had a few more dings in it.

"What's going on?" Finn demanded.

"Who's this?" said Rey.

"Uh, Zorii, this is Rey, Finn, and—"

The pressure of the blaster against his skull deepened. "I could pull this trigger right now," she said.

"I've seen you do worse."

"For a lot less."

"Can we try talking this out?" he asked.

"Nope. I wanna see your brains in the snow."

"So . . . you're still mad?"

"What *is* this?" Rey said. Poe knew that look. His friend was drawing on the Force. He had to defuse this situation quick.

Zorii said, "Really hoped I'd never see you again, Poe Dameron of the Resistance." She said the word *Resistance* like it tasted rotten in her mouth.

"Oh, we're *all* in the Resistance!" C-3PO said.

"Threepio!" Finn snapped. "Shut. *Up.*"

Once in a while, it was actually best to lead with the truth. *Here goes nothing,* Poe thought. "We need *help,* Zorii," he said. "We gotta crack this droid's head open."

"Pardon me?" C-3PO said.

"We're on our way to Babu Frik," Poe added.

"You're outta luck," Zorii said. "Babu only works for crew nowadays. That's not you anymore." With the word *you,* the pressure on his skull became unbearable.

Rey looked back and forth between them. "What 'crew'?" she asked.

"Funny he never mentioned it," Zorii said, in a tone that meant it wasn't funny at all. "Your friend's old job was running spice."

Poe's shoulders deflated. There it was. Now there'd be no end to it.

"Waitwaitwaitwait," said Finn on cue. "You were a *spice runner*?"

"You were a stormtrooper!" Poe retorted.

"*Were* you a spice runner?" Rey prodded.

"Were you a scavenger? We could do this all night . . ."

Two figures materialized out of the darkness, tall, armed beings, one from each direction, blocking their exits. Zorii shifted her blaster to Poe's neck.

"You don't have all night," Zorii spat at him. "You don't even have *now.* You know, I'm still digging out of the hole you put me in when you left to join the cause." Her gaze shifted to Rey. "You? You're the one they're looking for. Bounty for her just might cover us." To the oncoming thugs, she ordered, "Djak'kankah! All of them!"

"No Djak'kankah!" Poe protested, but Rey was already moving like lightning, swinging up her staff to knock Zorii's blaster out of her hand. In the same, single fluid movement, she whipped her staff around, slammed the end into the face of one of Zorii's thugs, then hefted it and threw it like a spear into the face of the other.

Before anyone could react, Rey had ignited her lightsaber and brought the tip to Zorii's neck. Zorii had to hear the crackle near her ear, had to realize she'd been pinned with an ancient Jedi weapon.

But Zorii's reactions were always hidden by that helmet.

Poe didn't mind admitting that he was feeling a little bit smug as Rey said, in a preternaturally kind voice, "We really could use your help. *Please.*"

Zorii studied Rey through her mask. Poe could hear her breathing, hear her *thinking.*

"Not that you care," Zorii said at last, her voice as cool and steady as ever, her mask still closed, "but I think you're okay."

Rey blinked. "I . . . care." Rey retracted her lightsaber, clipped it to her belt.

Zorii looked at Poe. A bit of tension left her shoulders as she came to a decision. "We can get to Babu's through the Thieves' Quarter."

She headed off, and Poe indicated for his friends to follow. Behind them came the unmistakable *tat-tat* of stormtroopers marching in formation. They slipped out of the alley before they could be spotted.

As they traveled a snowy passageway, Finn leaned over to him and whispered, "Poe Dameron: Spice Runner."

"Don't."

"Runner of Spice."

"All *right.*"

He glanced over at Rey, who was silent and frowning, lost in her own thoughts. Or maybe she was focused. Sensing something.

# CHAPTER 9

Rey couldn't help trying to calculate the portion value of everything she saw.

Babu Frik's workshop was a cramped maze of tools and droid parts. The walls were wholly obscured by shelves, piled with wires and electronics. Every table surface was covered, every nook and cranny filled to overflowing. Parts even draped from the ceiling overhead; Rey noted a pair of dismembered legs hanging, possibly from an old battle droid.

It was a fortune in parts. That astromech head dome, for instance, was in great condition. It was made of plastex, which meant it would be easy to buff out the scorch marks and sell it for—

Something bumped her foot. A janitor droid mopped up a bit of melted snow they'd tracked in, then scurried away.

"I haven't the faintest idea why I agreed to this," C-3PO said, drawing Rey's attention back to the droid, "I must be malfunctioning."

He was reclined on a workbench, with so many wires sticking out of his head it almost looked like he'd grown fur.

"You're going to be okay," Rey assured him.

Babu Frik himself was nearly invisible, hidden behind C-3PO's rear head plate. He was one of the tiniest beings Rey had ever seen, his height barely stretching as long as her forearm. He poked around in C-3PO's head with an electroprobe, muttering in Anzellan, occasionally interspersed with words in Basic. He had a grizzled face highlighted by bright, intelligent eyes, and gray brows as long and stiff as whisk brooms. The welding goggles he wore on the top of his head were armored against scorching. What kind of dangerous work was this fellow involved in to require weapons-grade work armor?

Rey crouched beside him. "Babu Frik?" she said. "Can you help us with this?

Babu responded, but Rey had no idea what he was saying.

She looked toward the spice runner. "Zorii?" Rey said. "Is this going to work?"

Zorii said something in Anzellan, and Babu responded as though annoyed at being interrupted. The words were delightful, clanging against one another fast and curt, like metal parts tumbling into a melting vat. Rey wished she had time to learn the language.

"Babu says he's found something in your droid's forbidden memory bank," Zorii said. "Words translated from . . . Sith?"

"Yes!" Rey said.

"That's what we need," Poe affirmed.

The spice runner turned on Poe. "Who are you hanging around with that speaks *Sith*?" Zorii asked, and Rey could have sworn that Zorii glanced toward the lightsaber at her belt.

"Can we make him translate it?" Finn said.

Zorii and Babu spoke back and forth. Then Zorii said, "Yes. But doing so will trigger a complete memory wipe."

". . . Complete memory wipe?" C-3PO said in a tremulous voice.

"Waitwait," Poe said to Babu. "You're saying we make him translate . . . and he won't remember anything?"

"Droid remember go blank!" Babu said.

"No!" said C-3PO.

"Blankblank," said Babu.

"There must be some other way," C-3PO pleaded.

"Doesn't Artoo back up your memory?" Finn said.

"Please sir," C-3PO said. "Artoo's storage units are famously unreliable."

Rey hated this. C-3PO was right, of course—in a way. Leia had told her a little about the droid's history. Along with R2-D2, he'd survived the Clone Wars, the Galactic Civil War, and now the Resistance against the First Order. Leia's father, Anakin, had built C-3PO when he was a little boy. But the golden droid remembered little of it. His memory had been wiped at least once that Leia knew of. Rey wasn't sure she could stomach doing that to him again.

"*You* know the odds better than any of us," Rey said gently. "Is there any other choice?"

C-3PO was silent a long moment, considering. He muttered, "If this mission fails, it was all for nothing. All we've done . . . all this time . . ."

Poe's exact words from earlier, before they'd all held hands and vowed to press on. Droids continued to amaze her.

C-3PO looked up. His gaze moved to each of them in turn, lingering on one face then another.

"What, uh . . . what're you doing there, Threepio?" Poe asked.

"Taking one last look, sir. At my friends."

They all stood in silence, watching C-3PO quietly say goodbye. Rey could hardly believe this was happening. She'd lost Chewie, and now she might lose C-3PO. How much loss could a person take?

"Sad," said D-O.

The sound of a large vehicle filtered in through the walls. Babu cocked his head and said, "Uh-oh."

Zorii cleared her throat. "Night raids are starting. I'll keep a lookout." She moved as if to leave.

"I'm coming with you," said Poe.

"You never did trust me," Zorii said, laughing a little.

"Do you trust me?" he asked.

"Nope."

Together Zorii and Poe exited the workshop. Rey watched them go, wondering how far she could push Poe to talk about his history with the spice runner.

After they were gone, C-3PO addressed Babu Frik in a brave and steady voice: "You may proceed."

Poe and Zorii sat on the rooftop of Babu's workshop. The city spread out before them, dark and icy. Kijimi used to quiet down during this deep hour of the night, but no longer. Laser flashes glowed briefly between buildings. Distant shouts echoed strangely over the rooftops. Several blocks away, a First Order UA-TT walker thudded through the streets. Poe watched a small figure dart away from its heavy steps, fleeing for their life.

He was glad Zorii had brought a flask, because he really needed a drink.

Poe lifted the flask and sipped. The liquid burned his throat, warmed his insides. He sighed. It had been years since any skordu had passed his lips. It was a popular drink on Kijimi, distilled from a high-altitude fungus that grew in icy caves and crevices. Local legend was that the Dai Bendu monks had first invented it, back when Kijimi City had been a religious stronghold—almost a holy site—before the city was overtaken by thieves and squatters and refugees. Poe wasn't sure he believed that Kijimi City had ever been a place of peace and contemplation. But with a little skordu in his belly, he could almost pretend.

"Is every night this bad?" Poe asked. He stared off over the rooftops. Kijimi City was a drinking town, because drinking kept a body warm. Cantinas selling skordu or Ultra-Ox made a killing. If he could do it all over again, he might consider running booze instead of spice. He offered Zorii the flask.

"Most nights, worse," she said. "First Order's taken most of the children. I can't stand the cries anymore. I've saved up enough to get out. I'm going to the Colonies."

Poe whipped his head to look at her.

She took the flask, turned her face away. Out of sight, her mask *swick*ed open. She tilted her head back to take a swig. The mask thumped closed. Zorii handed the flask back to him, her face shrouded once again.

"How?" he asked. "They blocked those hyperlanes." No one was getting to the Colonies these days without special authorization. The First Order wanted everyone to stay right here in well-mapped sectors, where they could be controlled.

Zorii fished into a belt compartment, drawing out a small object that flashed in the pale glow of a nearby oil lamp. It was round like a coin and latticed, with a port for connectivity.

Poe whistled in appreciation. "First Order captain's medallion. I've never even *seen* a real one," he said.

"Free passage through any blockade. Landing privileges at any garrison."

"Who'd you bribe? What'd you pay?" Poe asked, his voice incredulous.

Zorii touched the side of her mask. Her visor shield retracted, finally revealing depthless wide-spaced green eyes that seemed almost yellow in the lamp light. Poe swallowed hard. Her eyes had always affected him strangely.

"Wanna come with me?" she said, sounding suddenly vulnerable.

It was a quick shuttle trip back to the command ship, and it hadn't given Kylo Ren nearly enough time to prepare. He stopped before the door of Interrogation Six, rallying his thoughts.

He had all the power now, he reminded himself. The Wookiee was his past. He meant nothing to him.

Kylo opened the door.

Chewbacca was shackled to the wall. He looked up at Ren, fury in his eyes.

"I have not forgotten that you shot me," Kylo said. That wound had resulted in a defeat at Rey's hands. Had he been in top fighting form, the scavenger never would have gotten the best of him.

With a wave of Kylo's hand, Chewbacca's shackles opened and clanked to the floor. He removed the lightsaber from his belt. Dropped it to the ground.

"Kill me," Kylo taunted. "I'm unarmed. Now's your chance. Have your revenge for Han Solo."

Chewbacca had never been stupid, and so he made no move. But he growled, dark and low.

"Feel that?" Kylo continued, merciless. "It makes you feel alive, doesn't it? That burning. The dark side. It makes you *powerful*. You understand that. The scavenger will understand it, too."

He sensed a stab of fear from the Wookiee, on Rey's behalf. Kylo smiled, for he'd just been given his way in. Chewbacca *loved* the girl. In time, he would love her as much as he'd loved Han Solo.

The way he'd never really loved Ben. Snoke had been the one to show him that.

Kylo's voice crackled with rage. "What was her mission? Where is she going? Give me the answer . . . or I'll take it myself."

It should have been satisfying to watch Chewbacca wince in fear. Kylo should have felt pleasure in reaching out with the Force, inserting himself into the Wookiee's mind, ripping away his memories and thoughts.

Instead, it was exhausting. He saw flashes of the Wookiee laughing with a much younger Han Solo than he himself remembered. Felt Chewbacca's joy when his best friend married the woman he'd come to love like a sister. Saw the Wookiee cuddling a human toddler, teaching an older boy to fly a speeder, target practice with a young man, their blasters set on stun against a haphazard dummy made of rocks.

*Uncle Chewie,* he'd called him back then.

Nausea rolled around in the pit of Kylo's stomach when he finally walked away from Interrogation Six. He'd gotten what he needed. Surely the sense of triumph would follow soon.

---

Inside the workshop, Rey watched Babu operate on C-3PO. The protocol droid's head plate had been removed, and Babu was elbow-deep inside C-3PO's head. Distantly, through the building's stone walls, came the muted sound of screaming. Occasional blasterfire. Rey wasn't sure if the First Order was tearing the city apart looking for them, or if it was like this all the time.

She looked toward Finn, who winced at every sound of battle. Not in fear, she noted, but in empathy. He was one of the kindest people she'd ever met. No, the kindest.

Rey had waited so long on Jakku for her parents to come back for her, scratching out the days against the metal wall of her AT-AT scavenged home. No one ever did. She had vague memories of Unkar Plutt raising her for a few years in a halfhearted, ham-fisted way, before booting her out into the desert to fend for herself as a little girl. Even he had never bothered to check on her. To care.

But then she'd met Finn, and after a short time together, she'd been captured by Kylo Ren and taken to Starkiller Base.

That's when Finn had done something no one in her life had done before, the thing she'd yearned for her parents to do: He'd come to get her. At tremendous peril to himself. Before anyone knew she could wield a lightsaber or use the Force or any of it. She was nothing, just another scavenger from another godforsaken planet, when he'd risked his life to save hers. And she'd never forget it.

Sparks flew from C-3PO's head, startling her. She couldn't stand to watch anymore.

Rey stepped away, out of view, and hunkered down on the floor. BB-8 rolled over and whirred at her softly. Behind him came D-O, trailing BB-8 eagerly, his uni-wheel squeaking with every revolution.

Rey grabbed an oil can and moved toward the tiny droid, who recoiled at the sight of Rey looming over him, an unfamiliar object in her hand.

"It's just oil," she said gently. "Won't hurt. I promise."

---

Hux joined Pryde and Admiral Griss in following Supreme Leader Kylo Ren as he strode away from the hangar bay and interrogation rooms.

Ren said, "I want all the Wookiee's belongings brought to my quarters."

Hux hid his smile. Ren was practically frothing at the mouth. He had a history with his father's copilot, and seeing the Wookiee had done something to him. The Supreme Leader was likely not thinking with a clear head. Good.

"Sir," Allegiant General Pryde said. "The Knights of Ren have tracked the scavenger."

Ren's stride hitched.

"To a settlement called Kijimi," Admiral Griss added.

"They're searching there now," Pryde said.

Hux needed to insert himself before his peers brought any more good news. He asked, "Shall we destroy the city, Supreme—"

Ren stuck a long finger in Hux's face, effectively shushing him. "Set a course for Kijimi," he said. "I want her taken alive."

His words dismissed them all, and Kylo Ren hurried off alone. Hux stood with his hands clasped behind his back and watched him go, wondering how he always managed to say the wrong thing.

Snow was drifting down, melting against Zorii's helmet. Poe stared at her. How do you say no to eyes like that?

He sighed. You think of everyone else you care about, that's how. "I can't walk out on this war," Poe told Zorii. "Not until it's over."

As the Kijimi night grew even colder, Poe remembered something Leia was constantly reminding him: *Always be recruiting.*

"The Resistance could use a pilot like you," he said to Zorii. Truly, she was one heck of a pilot, thanks in no small part to *his* teaching and encouragement. "We're down to almost no one."

Then he slammed his mouth shut. Admitting how dire things had become was likely *not* the best recruitment strategy. It was the damn skordu making him so flippant.

"Why?" she said. "You hear about pockets of rebellion all over the galaxy."

"Just stories," he murmured, looking down at his hands. "We put out a call for help at the Battle of Crait. Nobody came. First Order's made everyone so afraid . . . that *I'm* afraid maybe everyone's given up."

Since then, it had become clear that the First Order controlled so many lines of communication, had so many jammers operating at strategic locations throughout the galaxy, that they couldn't be sure their call for help had even been heard. Leia and Poe had spent the ensuing months trying to reconnect with old allies and friends, re-establish communications, bolster their network of sympathizers and spies. They'd even made contact with former Imperials and rescued some high-profile First Order targets from imprisonment. But their progress had been painfully incremental, and Poe couldn't shake his greatest fear, that the real reason no one came was because they'd all lost hope.

"I don't believe you believe that," she said. She stared up at the jagged mountain peaks; this time of night they looked like massive razors of shadow. "They win by making you think you're alone. Remember? There're more of us than there are of them."

Along the dark horizon, a handful of ships appeared, small at first but growing ever larger as they approached. When they breached the city boundaries, they spread out and flashed on huge searchlights. The lights swept back and forth, lighting up sections of the city brighter than day.

"The hell are those?" Poe asked.

Zorii stood. "Your cue to leave."

The first few drops of lubricant Rey applied to D-O did absolutely nothing. He was drier than the Rakith Plateau in high summer. But he made soft whirring sounds of happiness, so she kept at it—applying it to his head joint, his wheel rotor, even the base of his communications array.

"Squeaky wheel," he informed her solemnly. "I-I-I-I have a squeeeeeaky wheel."

"Now try," Rey said.

He rolled back and forth experimentally. Not a sound. "Squeak eliminated," he said. Then he shrieked in delight and took off on a freewheeling rampage, running circles around the workshop, whipping about BB-8 as if enticing him to play. "Thank you. Very kind."

Finn stepped over to see what the fuss was about and smiled. He gave Rey a light elbow to the side as if to say: *Good job.*

"Finn," Rey said, her gaze on the tiny droid. "I know where I've seen it . . . the ship he was on . . . Ochi's ship."

Finn flinched a little. "What?"

Rey took a deep breath. Saying it aloud was going to make it real. "The day my parents left. They were on that ship."

Finn leaned toward her, concern all over his features. He understood how important this was. "Are you *sure*?"

Zorii dashed inside, Poe at her heels. "The scanners are coming," she said.

"Did we get it?" Poe said. "Babu?"

Rey and Finn exchanged a startled glance. They couldn't leave; Babu wasn't done yet!

But another spark popped over C-3PO's head, and Babu climbed down to give the droid some space. "Ay-yep," Babu said. "Droid is ready!"

Something inside C-3PO seemed to purr, as if he was powering up after a long nap. His eyes flashed on—bright, eerie red. He cocked his head to look at them all—a sharp, jerky, almost hostile motion.

"Is okay," Babu said. "Is unlock! Droid unlock!"

But Rey's heart sank. No matter what happened next, no matter if they were successful, she had lost another friend.

The droid who used to be C-3PO sat up and spoke, his vocal intonators using a strange new modulation that was dark and low. "The Emperor's wayfinder," he said, "is sealed inside the Imperial Vaults. At delta-three-six transient nine-three-six bearing three-two on a moon in the Endor system. From the southern shore. Only this blade tells, only this blade tells . . ."

The droid jerked once, then slumped as if powering down. His eyes went dark, his body stilled.

*Oh, Threepio, I'm so sorry,* Rey thought.

"The Endor system?" Finn said. "Where the last war ended?"

"Endor!" Babu enthused. "I know this. Babu will help."

The little droidsmith started to reach for something, but the entire workshop began rattling. Bolts and screws spilled from shelves. The battle droid legs hanging from the ceiling swung violently.

Poe ran to the nearest window, and Rey followed. Together they peered up into the night.

A massive Star Destroyer cruised low over the mountains, blocking out the sky. The blowback from its thrusters shook the city, tossing trash and loose snow about, creating chaos.

"Ren's Destroyer," said Poe.

He had found them again. Rey tensed to flee. If they ran for Ochi's freighter right this second, they might have a chance. She was about to say as much, but she gasped instead.

Kylo Ren was near. And his conflicted mind was dwelling on torture. He'd ripped away someone's thoughts, the same way he'd tried to rip away hers when they'd first met, except with far greater results . . .

Her stomach turned over.

"Rey?" Finn said.

"Chewie . . ." Ren had done something to him. Recently. Maybe only moments ago.

"What about him?"

"He's on Ren's ship." She hadn't killed Chewie after all. She could still save him. "He's alive, I feel it! Finn, he must've been on a different transport!"

"We have to go get him!" Finn said.

Zorii's voice came out almost like a squeak. "Your friend's on that sky trash?"

"I guess he is," Poe said, in a voice as glad as Rey felt

Something inside the workshop clattered, and they all whirled. Poe's hand flew to his blaster.

It was C-3PO, rebooting. His eyes flashed a familiar gold. "Allow me to introduce myself! I am See-Threepio, human–cyborg relations! And you are?"

"Okay, that's gonna be a problem," Poe said, but Rey's relief was like a punch to the gut. The droid was back, in some semblance of his former self.

"Helloooo," said Babu. "I, Babu Frik."

"You've got bigger problems," Zorii reminded them. "To the alleys. Let's go!"

The sounds of pursuit were all around them as Poe and his friends hurried through the crooked streets of Kijimi City, keeping low to avoid troopers. But their group was only as fast as their slowest member, which was C-3PO. Always C-3PO, shuffling along at half the speed of everyone else. If Leia were here, she'd no doubt make a lesson in leadership out of that.

But she wasn't here. Poe said, "Threepio, move your metal ass!"

"How *dare* you!" the droid said. "We've only just *met*!"

They turned a corner. Ochi's freighter was straight ahead, and Poe's chest was suddenly aching and empty. At least this time he wouldn't leave without saying goodbye.

Zorii and Rey exchanged a nod, and then by silent mutual agreement, Rey ran ahead with Finn and the droids, giving Poe and Zorii a moment alone.

Zorii pulled the captain's medallion from her belt and handed it to him. "Might get you on a capital ship," she said. "Go help your friend."

Poe stared at the medallion, his breath catching in his throat. The fact that Zorii refused to talk about its acquisition meant she'd done unspeakable things to obtain it.

He said, "I don't think I can take this."

"I don't care what you think."

Poe smiled. Still the same Zorii.

"Poe!" came Rey's voice. "It's the Knights. Come *on*!"

Poe took the medallion, but his feet were rooted. How could he leave Zorii *again*? What do you even say in a moment like this? He settled for, "Can I kiss you?"

"Go," she ordered, giving his chest a shove, but he smugly noted the amusement in her voice.

Reluctantly, smiling just a little, he stepped away from Zorii and then dashed after his friends.

# CHAPTER 10

Finn followed Poe and Rey as they raced into the cockpit. Rey took the pilot's seat, and Poe slipped into the seat beside her. Both started flicking a dizzying array of switches. Lights came on, and the engines hummed to life. Finn tried to pay attention. Unlike Rey and Poe, he was not a natural pilot, but he was still supposed to be learning piloty things. Leia expected every member of her core team to be able to fly something in a pinch.

"Hang tight," Poe said. "We're going up hot."

In the *Falcon,* "going up hot" meant Finn had better get himself to the turret station, but there was nothing for a third passenger to do in the *Bestoon Legacy;* the cockpit didn't even have a place to sit. Until there was something for him to shoot at with a blaster, Finn would have to settle for holding on tight and offering encouragement. He was good at encouraging. He could encourage all day.

"Uh, you're both doing great," he muttered.

Rey lifted them away from the planet at such a fast, steep angle that the acceleration compensators couldn't keep Finn's stomach from dropping into his feet and pressing like lead against the floor. Within moments they had cleared the atmosphere and were quickly approaching the massive Star Destroyer that was most certainly Kylo Ren's command ship.

How was it that he always ended up flying *toward* First Order ships?

Rey slipped Zorii's captain's medallion into the dash slot. BB-8 and D-O rolled into the cockpit, which made the place a bit cramped, but Finn didn't mind. When you were about to try to sneak aboard an enemy ship—*again*—and your heart was racing and your feet twitched to flee, it was helpful to have something blocking your exit.

Everyone in the cockpit was dead silent as they waited to see if they would get blown to bits.

Something beeped, and Poe's shoulders slumped with relief. "Medallion works," he said. "Cleared for cargo hangar twelve."

"Hang on, Chewie," Rey murmured. "We're coming."

"Whoever this Chewie is," said C-3PO, "this is madness."

There'd been a time when Finn would have agreed with the droid, before he'd had friends.

Traffic was heavy, with supply ships, TIEs, and shuttles flying to and from the various hangars. Rey angled them neatly toward one, slowing to regulation speed, slipping through the containment field, touching the freighter down onto the shiny hangar floor with the lightest kiss.

Together they rushed down the ramp. Two patrol troopers approached, stepping in unison. One said, "Credentials and manife—"

Finn blasted him. Poe got the other. Both collapsed to the ground. So much for sneaking.

Rey turned to the droids, who were attempting to follow. "You three stay there," she said.

"Happily," said C-3PO.

"Which way?" Poe asked.

"No idea. Follow me!" Finn said. Because he had a feeling. Besides, there was a pattern to First Order construction and organization that was fleet-universal. If he wandered around a little, he'd be able to figure out where to go.

They jogged down a corridor. Just as in Starkiller Base, the floors were pristine, the light panels, dataports, and even support struts sparkling with newness and state-of-the-art technology. Finn knew exactly how much work it took to keep everything looking like it just came off a Corellian assembly line. He preferred the dirt and fallen leaves and intruding tree roots of the Ajan Kloss base any day.

They turned a corner and came face-to-face with another pair of patrol troopers, who raised their rifles.

"Drop your weapons!" one ordered.

Finn did not want to kill anyone else. Leaving a trail of bodies throughout the ship would just make it all the harder to rescue Chewie and escape. But if he had no choice . . . He moved his finger to the trigger.

Rey said, her voice full of quiet strength: "It's okay that we're here."

Finn held his breath.

"It's okay that you're here," the stormtrooper echoed.

The other trooper nodded. "It's good," he added.

"You're *relieved* that we're here," Rey said.

"Thank goodness you're here!" said the first trooper, his shoulders going slack.

"Welcome, guys!" said the second.

Poe leaned over and whispered in Finn's ear: "Does she do that to us?"

Of course not. She'd never—no, wait . . . she definitely would. To protect them. To keep one of them from following her into the desert and getting run down by Kylo Ren's TIE fighter.

*Oh, hell.*

"We're looking for a prisoner," Rey said.

The stormtroopers cheerfully gave directions to the cellblock where Chewie was being held. After the troopers resumed their patrol, Finn and his friends raced away. Within moments, they came to a split in the corridor, just like the troopers had described.

Rey stopped in her tracks, and Finn's heart thudded in his chest. He knew that look. It meant their plan was about to take a detour.

"Chewie's this way," he reminded her.

Half to herself, Rey said, "The dagger's on this ship. We need it."

"Why?" Poe said.

C-3PO had already translated it, already given them the coordinates of the Emperor's wayfinder.

"A feeling!" Rey said.

"Rey, you can't just—" Poe grabbed Finn's arm to silence him.

"I'll meet you back in the hangar." She dashed off before either of them could protest.

"Chewie," Poe reminded him.

Finn nodded, and together they jogged down the corridor.

Zorii Bliss crouched on the rooftop of the Kozinarg Guildhouse, spying on the squad of snowtroopers who gathered at the steps to Monk's Gate. Her left foot slipped on the steep, icy tiles, dislodging a bit of ice and snow, which slid off the roof and plunked down at a snowtrooper's foot. She froze, hardly daring to breathe.

The trooper gave a small kick to rid his foot of snow, but otherwise did not react.

Slowly, quietly, Zorii reached down to the tread of her boots and flicked a small switch built into the arch. Her cleats popped out—tiny metal gripping stars that were a lot noisier to walk around in, but they would dig into the toughest ice, keeping her from sliding off the roof. They were also pretty great in a fight.

Her perch now secure, Zorii leaned forward to hear better.

A tall, black-clad humanoid with an odd helmet and a long cloak swept toward the stormtroopers. At his back were a band of similarly clad warriors. She could see none of their faces, but their weapons expressed volumes. One carried an ax, with a long weighted handle even taller than he was. Another a giant club. Still another a wicked scythe. The scythe dripped with something dark and viscous.

Not warriors then. More like butchers.

As the black-clad man approached, the squad's officer snapped to attention. "Supreme Leader," he said.

Zorii barely managed to hold her gasp in check. The man standing below with his gang of butchers was Kylo Ren himself. The man responsible for all the horror she'd witnessed these last months.

"Lieutenant Barok," the Supreme Leader said. His voice was tight and calm, though Zorii got the feeling that he was barely containing his rage. He looked around, almost as though he was sniffing the air.

"We have a perimeter around the city—" the lieutenant began, but Kylo Ren cut him off.

"We're too late," he snapped. "The scavenger is gone."

The *scavenger* . . . Why was the Supreme Leader of the First Order specifically here for the girl Zorii had just met? Rey was remarkable, that much was clear. That lightsaber, those fighting skills . . . What had Poe gotten himself into?

Well, she would waste no more time worrying about that nerf herder. The lieutenant had mentioned a "perimeter" around the city, and that was bad for business. As soon as the First Order troopers left Monk's Gate, she'd hurry back to the Spice Runners' den and tell her people to—

Supreme Leader Kylo Ren whipped out a lightsaber that teemed and sparked with chaotic red light. He slashed it back and forth in a rage, toppling a column of stone, slicing a neehwa oil lantern in two. The snowtrooper squad slunk away from his wrath, but his butchers looked on as though amused.

When he was done, boulders and lantern scrap lay scattered on the ground, the melted water pooling beneath them already freezing back up at the edges.

"She had help," said the Supreme Leader, his voice calm once again. "Find them. Destroy them."

Zorii adjusted her plan. Now, somehow, she'd have to sneak back to the spice runners' den, and instead of telling them to cash in a few favors and open their emergency smuggling routes, she'd order them to get the hell out of the city.

Finn and Poe reached the prisoner cellblock and found the cell that supposedly held Chewie. Finn hit the switch, and the door whooshed open to reveal the Wookiee, manacled to the wall. He growled and moaned excitedly, almost too fast for Finn to follow with his rudimentary understanding of Shyriiwook—he only caught the words for "surprised" and "danger" and "much gladness."

"Of course we came for you!" Poe said.

Chewie rattled off a question.

"Rey's here," Finn said. "She's gonna get the dagger."

Chewbacca started to chatter, something about Kylo Ren and information and how very sorry he was, but they didn't have time. It would take moments for the First Order to figure out that Ochi's freighter didn't belong in hangar twelve, if they hadn't already. And once that happened, even off-duty stormtroopers would be called upon to join the search for intruders. Finn had endured that drill a hundred times.

"We've got Ochi's ship," Finn said to the Wookiee, interrupting him. "Follow me."

He hurried down the corridor to a door and hit the release. It whooshed up—revealing a stormtrooper who raised his blaster.

Finn hit the release again, slamming the door down. "Wrong way!"

They sprinted away in the opposite direction—and ran right into another stormtrooper, who began to fire. They'd caught him by surprise, and his first shots were wild.

"Not really a right way, is there?" Poe said, taking out the stormtrooper. He crouched over the fallen trooper, dislodged his blaster rifle from beneath the body and slid it along the floor toward Chewie.

The Wookiee grabbed it, and brought the rifle to bear just in time to blast two stormtroopers who had come up behind them.

They ducked around a corner—

And almost collided with an entire squad. Rifles whipped up, and the corridor became hot with laser blasts. Poe dropped to the ground, and Finn watched in horror as his friend clutched his arm in pain.

"Poe!" he yelled. The pilot's arm was charred and oozing. He needed medical attention right away.

Suddenly they were surrounded by troopers, way too many for the three of them to fight off. "You there, put your weapons down. Hands up! Now!"

Finn raised his hands in surrender. He knew exactly what would happen next: interrogation, execution. He'd been on the verge of execution before, on the *Supremacy,* Phasma looming over him. A fellow couldn't reasonably expect to get out of that kind of situation more than once.

"Hey, fellas," Poe said.

"Shut up, scum," said a stormtrooper, in a voice that reminded Finn so much of Phasma that he had to resist the urge to snap back.

He hoped Rey was faring better. If she found that dagger and got back to the ship, their mission still stood a chance.

Rey entered a bright, white space with soaring ceilings and clean perfection. Kylo Ren's private quarters.

She stepped slowly, carefully, still drawn to the dagger. The room was beautiful and light-filled, but devoid of warmth. As though he didn't care about anything or anyone.

Or maybe that wasn't entirely true, because a few more steps brought her to a pedestal, deep black in contrast with its surroundings, jutting unchallenged from the shiny white floor. A place of honor.

Displayed atop the pedestal was a warped black mask, its eyeholes and vocoder still gaping but melted like heated wax, smeared into a display of perpetual agony. She stared at it a long time—too long—unable to look away. She'd seen this mask in Ren's thoughts, when he'd tried to pull Luke's map from her mind on Starkiller Base. It had belonged to his grandfather.

But that horrible mask was not what she'd come for, and she wanted nothing to do with it. She glanced around . . . there! On a table opposite the pedestal were Chewie's things—his bowcaster, his satchel, and Ochi's dagger.

She reached for the dagger. Wrapped her fingers around the handle—

*Screams. A woman crying out, "Rey!" A ship's engines roaring . . .*

"No," Rey whispered, even as pieces of a lifelong puzzle began to click together in her head. She'd dreamed of finding out about her parents, but as the knowledge began to clarify inside her, Rey finally considered that maybe she'd rather not know.

The floor shifted beneath her feet, and the air went dark. What had begun as a Force vision changed, became a *connection.*

"Where are you?" came Kylo Ren's voice.

Rey whirled. Ren stood alone before her, masked, surrounded by darkness. Snow dusted his cape.

"You're hard to find," he said.

"You're hard to get rid of." She began to turn away. He was worth no more of her time.

"I pushed you in the desert because I needed to see it. I needed *you* to see it. Who you are. I know the rest of your story. Rey . . ."

She spun back around. Whipped up her lightsaber and aimed it at his throat. "You're lying."

"I've never lied to you."

Oh, but he had deceived. Kylo's words always had an element of truth, even when their intent was pure falsehood.

"Your parents were no one," he said. "They chose to be. To keep you safe."

"Don't!" she said through gritted teeth. She hated this. That he had knowledge of her that she didn't, that he was the one to tell her.

"You remember more than you say." As she backed away, he reminded her, "I've been in your head."

"No. I don't want this." And she didn't. Not from him.

"Search your memory," he demanded.

"No!" She swung the lightsaber. He brought his own to bear, and they clashed, blue on red.

"Remember them," he said, relentless. "See them."

*A beautiful woman in a blue hood, tears in her wide brown eyes. She hugged a tiny girl to her chest. "I know," she said. "Rey, be brave."*

*A young man, stubble along his jaw, staring at the tiny girl with such love and hope and desperation. "You'll be safe here. I promise."*

*The* Bestoon Legacy *flying away, disappearing into the clear Jakku sky. "Come back!" the little girl cried, but Unkar was yanking her arm, yanking her away from the last sight of her parents . . .*

Rey pushed the vision away, even as she pushed against Kylo's lightsaber, thrusting him back.

"They sold you to protect you," Kylo said. They circled each other.

"Stop talking."

"I know what happened to them."

His calm was maddening. She rushed him, swiped and stabbed with a series of blows. She was faster now, the lightsaber more like an extension of herself than a separate weapon, but he countered easily.

Rey swung; he dodged. Her lightsaber sliced through a basket. Red berries came from nowhere, spilled out, brighter than blood against the . . . white floor of Ren's quarters?

They were together *and* they were separate, in each other's minds *and* spaces, but Rey didn't care, she just wanted to land a blow, to *hurt* him. Their blades sizzled with impact as they fought, creeping closer to Vader's mask.

"Tell me where you are," Kylo demanded. "You don't know the whole story."

Rey attacked again. He dodged, stepped back to give them some space.

"It was Palpatine who had your parents taken," he said, like a patient teacher, as though they weren't in the fight of their lives. "He was looking for you. But they wouldn't say where you were."

She circled him slowly, looking for an opening. Anything to get him to stop talking.

"So he gave the order."

A vision filled her mind again, and Rey was helpless against it: *Black-eyed Ochi of Bestoon raising his horrible dagger.*

*Rey's mother pleading with the assassin. "She isn't on Jakku! She's gone—No!"*

*Ochi thrusting the dagger into her father's gut. Her mother's cry of anguish becoming sudden silence.*

"No!" Rey screamed, launching at Kylo.

Their blades clashed, hummed with impact, and all at once she glimpsed his location, or maybe she was actually there for a split second—the shadowy stone rooftop, the icy air. Kijimi. He had probably just missed her.

She was having no luck getting past his guard, so she swung blindly, chaotically. He moved to block.

The pedestal shattered. Darth Vader's mask tumbled toward the ground . . . and disappeared.

"So that's where you are," Kylo said, looking down, presumably at the mask. "Do you know why the Emperor's always wanted you dead?"

"No," she said, but the confusion on her face was the only answer he needed.

Immense satisfaction tinged his voice as he said, "I'll come and tell you."

Rey took several steps backward. What had she done? She'd let her anger get the best of her again. Let herself get distracted. Now Ren knew exactly where she and her friends were.

She half expected him to renew the attack, but he didn't. All went silent. Her vision of him winked out. Her own breathing was loud in her ears. The shattered black remains of the pedestal were strewn at her feet.

*What just happened?*

No time. She had to get everyone off this ship now, before Ren returned. She hefted the dagger, grabbed Chewie's things, and sprinted for the freighter.

---

It took Zorii nearly half an hour to reach the Spice Runners' den, even though it was usually a ten-minute walk from Monk's Gate. Snowtroopers were everywhere, kicking down doors, rounding up everyone at blasterpoint to interrogate them about the scavenger. Zorii was forced to travel rooftops, ducking behind venting chimneys and fuel tanks whenever a scanner ship swept by.

She ended up reaching the den through the Monastery, an underground cantina in the Thieves' Quarter. Her spice runners had an agreement with the Monastery's owner—unlimited access to the cantina's cellar in exchange for a heavy discount on spice.

The secret cellar door dumped her into the lounge area, with stained couches surrounding a creaky furnace. She was hugely relieved to see that many of her gang were already there.

"Zorii!" said Lluda. Lluda was a young human girl with close-cropped white hair and a knack for slicing. Her parents had been killed by the Lantillian Spacers' Brotherhood. The spice runners had taken her in when they'd caught her slicing identichips. Useful kid. "I was getting worried. It's bad out there," Lluda said.

"It's bad out there," Zorii agreed.

"What do we do?"

"Zorii," came a lower, gruffer voice, and she turned.

"Jarraban," she said to the tall, mustached spicer. "Just the person I need to see. First Order's got the city in lockdown. He's looking for—"

"Your boyfriend," he said, getting right in her face.

"He's not my boy—"

"You left Vicii and Vibbo unconscious in an alley because of him."

Damn. Word traveled fast.

The two beings—Vicii and Vibbo—stepped forward, their mandibles smeared with anger and blood. Rey had definitely given them a faceful with that quarterstaff.

"I had no choice. Some girl put a lightsaber to my throat. I got back here fast as I could."

Jarraban turned to Vicii and Vibbo. "That true?"

They looked at each other. Shrugged. "It's possible I was unconscious for that part," Vicii admitted.

"I don't even remember getting back to the den," Vibbo added.

Zorii glared at them. "Glad we had this talk. Now everyone, listen up!"

She told them about the Supreme Leader locking down the city and ordering it turned inside out. "He's looking for any Resistance associates, and I'm sorry to say, Poe Dameron used to be one of us, and he brought them all to our door. So we have to get *out.* All of us. Right now."

Jarraban plunked down into a squishy, threadbare sofa and put his face in his hands. "We'll need to scatter, reconvene when things die down. How many ships do we have right now?"

"The Voyam sisters are out on a run," Lluda reminded him. "They've got the freighter and a support fighter."

"That leaves three ships," Jarraban said. "For over twenty people."

"I can go underground for a while," said Vibbo. "I know a place."

"Nineteen people," Jarraban said.

"I can take Lluda in my Y-wing," Zorii said. "It'll be a tight, uncomfortable ride, but we can fit."

"Thanks, Zorii," Lluda said.

"Seventeen people."

"Carib Diss owes me a favor," Vicii said. "I helped him collect a pretty bounty last week. His ship can take three passengers."

"Fourteen—"

Pounding at the door. Blasterfire that made the whole building quake.

"Those weren't hand blasters," Lluda said, her voice low.

"A walker just clawed through our front door," said Zorii. "Grab your go-packs and scatter. Lluda, meet me at my Y-wing; you know where I park it, right?"

The girl's face was frozen with fear, but after a precious wasted moment, she nodded.

"Okay, go!" Zorii yelled, and her people fled. She raced back through the secret entrance to the Monastery, muttering under her breath, "What have you gotten me into, Dameron?"

It didn't take long for First Order officers to appear on the scene. Finn glared as General Hux approached. The other guy was new to Finn, a slender, severe fellow with a perpetual frown and a piercing blue gaze. Rank insignias in the First Order were subtle, but Finn knew them all. This man had extra shoulder pleats and a double rank band on his left forearm. He could be none other than Allegiant General Pryde, outranked only by the Supreme Leader himself.

They were so dead.

"The girl's not with them," blurted one of the stormtroopers holding them prisoner.

Allegiant General Pryde seemed bored. "Take them away. Terminate them."

Finn couldn't believe it. No interrogation? Not even a single question from the allegiant general? What was so important about Rey that they'd ignore the opportunity to get intel about the Resistance from members of its core leadership?

Hux stepped into Finn's space, so close he could feel the general's hot breath on his skin. They locked eyes. "At last," Hux said.

If Finn had a credit for everyone who wanted him dead for deserting the First Order . . . Well, he had no regrets, no matter what happened next.

Pryde left, but Hux tagged along as stormtroopers thrust rifle butts into their backs and shoved them down the corridor toward the execution chamber.

It was a small room, with jets built into the walls. Once they were dead, the jets would release heat and toxins to break down their remains, then vacuum everything up, leaving a perfectly sterile chamber. All physical trace of their existence would be obliterated.

"Turn around," a stormtrooper ordered.

They faced the wall.

"Actually, I'd like to do this one myself," Hux said, and Finn heard the click of a blaster accepting a new identiprint.

Suddenly Finn realized he *did* have one regret: that he couldn't see Rey one last time. Tell her that—

"What were you going to tell Rey?" Poe asked, as if sensing his thoughts. "In the tunnels."

"You still on that?" Finn awaited the inevitable.

"Oh, I'm sorry, is this a bad time?" Poe said.

Finn nodded. "It sort of *is* a bad time, actually, the worst—"

Chewie complained that he was going to die hungry.

"I suppose *later* is better?" Poe said. "I mean if you want to get something off your chest, now is not the *worst* time—"

A blaster shrieked.

Death did not come. Finn opened his eyes and turned.

Hux stood over the stormtroopers' dead bodies, his blaster tip smoking after close-range fire on the highest setting.

"I'm the spy," Hux announced.

"*What?*" Poe said.

"*You?*" said Finn.

"We don't have much time," Hux said.

Finn, Poe, and Chewie all gaped at him.

"*I knew it!*" Poe said, sticking a finger in Hux's face.

"You did *not*," Finn said, rolling his eyes, which he knew was petty, but who cared? They were *alive*.

# CHAPTER 11

Rey peeked around the corner. The droids were being questioned outside the ship by stormtroopers. For once, she was glad of C-3PO's memory wipe. She trusted BB-8 to say nothing. But D-O was an unknown factor.

"What's your operating number?" a stormtrooper was asking C-3PO.

The droid responded with an unintelligible soup of syllables.

"That's not even a language!" the stormtrooper said.

Rey took a moment to focus, line up her shots, fired . . . one, two, three shots: three hits. The stormtroopers crumpled to the ground as Rey sprinted for the freighter.

"Oh, dear!" said C-3PO. "I've never been in a laser battle before!"

Rey was nearly to the on-ramp when she sensed a familiar presence. Kylo.

"Where are the others?" she asked the droid.

"They haven't come back."

A TIE screamed into the hangar bay and landed hard. *He* was on that fighter, and he was looking for her.

She thrust everything she was carrying at C-3PO—her quarterstaff, the dagger, Chewie's satchel—and yelled to the droids, "Find them! Go!" Better for them to take their chances inside the maze of a Star Destroyer than face Kylo Ren.

Rey was vaguely aware of C-3PO scurrying out of the hangar with BB-8 and D-O on his heels as she took a deep breath and advanced on the TIE.

The hatch opened and Kylo emerged. His face was hidden behind his mask, and his cloak whipped at his heels.

Hux had good news for Finn and Poe: The *Millennium Falcon* had been commandeered by the First Order and was right here on the *Steadfast.* Finn could hardly believe their luck.

But he also had bad news: It was scheduled to be incinerated, by order of Supreme Leader Kylo Ren. They could save the ship and get away in it, but they'd have to be quick. And they'd have to leave the droids behind. Finn would come back for them somehow. And Rey.

General Hux led the way. They passed officers and stormtroopers, droids and maintenance crew, and although a giant, hairy Wookiee occasionally made someone do a double take, Hux's presence gave them unhindered passage through the ship's corridors.

"Look!" came a familiar mechanical voice behind them. "There they are!"

Finn spun. C-3PO! Looking ridiculous in Chewie's bandolier, and carrying the Wookiee's satchel and bowcaster. With him were BB-8 and the little cone-head droid.

"Friends!" said Cone-head.

Poe seemed as relieved as Finn felt. "Beebee-Ate, Threepio, come on," the pilot urged.

Hux hustled them toward a door. "I shut down the impeders," he said. "You've got seconds."

The general opened the door revealing the *Falcon,* unscathed except for the entrance lock, which was a conspicuous mess of charred wires. No worries; Rose could have that lock working in no time.

"There she is," said Poe. "She's a survivor."

They headed toward the ship, but Finn felt a hand on his shoulder. "Wait!" said Hux. "Blast me in the arm. Quick."

"What?"

"Or they'll know."

Finn raised his blaster.

"I could kill you," Finn said, testing the thought, letting it roll around inside him. He did not enjoy killing. He hadn't even enjoyed watching Phasma fall into the flaming wreckage of the *Supremacy.*

Maybe he could make an exception for Hux.

"You need me," Hux said.

True. But Finn could still make it *hurt.*

He shot Hux in the leg, doing as much external skin damage as possible. Hux grunted, and sweat broke out on his suddenly red face.

"Why are you helping us?" Finn asked. Hux hated the Resistance. Hated them all. Finn was certain of it.

"I don't care if you win," Hux spat out through his pain. "I need Kylo Ren to lose."

Rey and Kylo circled each other like stalking wolves, slow and intense. An audience formed around them as stormtroopers charged into the hangar to watch.

He was going to tell her something important. She was desperate to hear it. Maybe she should just kill him. Or maybe she should flee.

She remembered what Leia said to her. *Never be afraid of who you are.* Spoken as Rey was wrapped in a loving embrace, with no trace of judgment. Only acceptance.

The memory filled her with resolve. With strength. And she asked: "Why did the Emperor come for me? Why did he want to kill a child? Tell me."

He stepped toward her. "Because he saw what you would become. You don't just have power. You have *his* power."

Dread was a dark miasma, filling her until she was sick with it. She knew what he was going to say. She *knew* it.

"You're his granddaughter. You're a Palpatine." He let the words settle for a moment.

She backed away toward the hangar entrance, away from his words, away from the certainty rising within her. It was true. She sensed it. All the darkness inside her, the rage . . .

Kylo pressed forward mercilessly, backing her closer and closer to the void. "My mother was the daughter of Vader. Your father was the son of the Emperor. What Palpatine doesn't know is that we are a dyad in the Force, Rey. Two that are one."

Her heart stopped. The *dyad.*

His words rang with truth, deep in her very soul. They shattered her, emptied her of everything.

She forced herself to continue edging toward the abyss where the hangar ended and the high atmosphere of Kijimi began. Rey peered over, gauged the distance to the hazy ground. Too high a jump, even with the help of the Force. Maybe she should try it anyway.

"We'll kill him," Kylo said. "Together. Take the throne."

He removed his mask. A gesture of vulnerability. Of trust. It suddenly occurred to her how long it had been since she'd seen his face. The scar on his cheek had faded, but it would still mark him forever. "You know what you need to do," he said. "You know."

He extended his black-gloved hand to her.

She looked at it. Remembered. The last time he'd extended a hand to her had been in the wreakage of Snoke's throne room. Their combined power had defeated him. It was true that together they could do such incredible things.

Suddenly, she sensed a weight at her back and along with it, Finn, his presence a bright beacon of light, piercing the dark.

"I do know," she told Kylo. Rey turned toward the abyss.

The *Falcon* rose before her. Stormtroopers volleyed blasts at the ship, but the *Falcon* swiveled on an invisible axis. Poe hit the thrusters, blowing back everything in the hanger. Stormtroopers slid away helplessly.

Rey braced herself. She sensed Kylo doing the same behind her.

The *Falcon* remained hovering in the air as the access ramp descended, revealing Finn, wearing a breather and wielding a blaster. "Rey!" he called.

Debris flew past her, kicked up by the wash of the *Falcon*'s engines.

She turned back to Kylo one last time. She hated him for telling her. And yet she was glad he had. A *dyad* . . .

"C'mon!" yelled Finn.

She sprinted for the edge, then launched herself toward the *Falcon*. Finn grabbed her arm before she could sail by, and swung her onto the ramp. They sprinted into the *Falcon*'s belly as the ramp rose, closing them in, and the floor shuddered beneath her feet as Poe whipped the ship around and hit the accelerator.

Leia held her breath. Lieutenant Connix had run to fetch her the moment they'd received the signal, but it was coded. *Please be the* Falcon, she thought.

She listened on her headset as Beaumont worked the console controls, decrypting. A red light turned blue, and the console beeped.

Beaumont grinned. "We're picking up their flight signature! General, the *Falcon*'s flying again!"

Leia couldn't even savor her relief because a wave of weakness washed over her, making her stumble. The headset was suddenly too hot and tight. She jerked it off, let it fall to the ground.

*Leia,* came her brother's maddening voice. *It's time.*

*I can't,* she told him. *There's too much to do.*

She felt his understanding, his love, maybe even a touch of amusement. *There is only one thing left,* he said. *And then you can rest.*

Dizziness overtook her. She felt herself falling, the edges of the world caving in on her. She was vaguely aware of Connix's arms wrapping around her, boosting her, the lieutenant's worried voice: "General?"

Connix guided her to her quarters. Leia just needed to lie down for a bit. That's all.

Kylo Ren and Allegiant General Pryde surveyed the hangar bay. They'd lost four stormtroopers, one cargo pilot, and two maintenance workers when the *Falcon's* engine wash had flooded the hanger, pushing them into the high atmosphere of Kijimi. Kylo considered it a small price to pay to encounter Rey again, to provoke her into a rage, to say the word *dyad* and watch the truth of it wash over her lovely face.

The remaining maintenance crew had quickly restored the hanger to working order, but small fires burned throughout the bay. A few troopers lay injured on the floor; one bled badly from a leg wound.

He hardly paid attention. He kept seeing her face, the way her lips had parted with surprise, the way her body had canted toward him. If the *Millennium Falcon* hadn't appeared, she might have come to him, taken his hand.

Kylo *really* hated that ship.

"Are you sure we shouldn't pursue?" Pryde said.

"You scanned the dagger?"

"Of course, sir."

"Then we know where she's going."

He'd been so very close. But now she knew the truth. She would accept it. She would come to understand that darkness was her destiny. Next time he saw her, she would turn.

# CHAPTER 12

Rey found herself engulfed in a giant, hairy hug.

"I missed you, too," she said. She'd gotten Chewie back. She hadn't killed him. But the fact remained that she had lost control. The only reason her friend wasn't dead was pure, dumb luck.

She'd lost control twice since then, with Kylo. Something had been happening to her, and she finally understood what it was. The darkness growing inside her; it all made sense now.

She was a Palpatine. Born of pure evil.

More than anything in the galaxy, she wanted to run back to Leia, beg her teacher for help. But there was no time. Rey was still committed to their mission, now more than ever. The mission was all that mattered.

Finn exited the cockpit and ran past them, saying, "Gear regulator's out." He paused when he saw her face. "You okay?"

Rey nodded, and Finn hurried toward the back to start repairs.

Chewie moaned his thanks for coming after him.

Rey forced a smile and said, "I'm so happy to . . ." Her voice trailed off.

Chewie shrugged and headed into the cockpit to help Poe.

Rey stood there a moment, a little relieved to be alone. She just needed to collect her thoughts. She leaned against the wall outside the cockpit and closed her eyes.

From inside came the sound of alarms beeping, then Chewie asking why they weren't being followed.

"I dunno why they're not following us," Poe said. "But I don't trust it."

Because he already knew where they were going, that's why. She was putting her friends in danger just by being here. Kylo Ren would always find her, no matter what.

Chewie gave Poe a rundown of damage to the *Falcon.*

"What do you mean, landing gear's busted? How busted?"

Chewie told him to look at the readout himself if Poe didn't believe him.

"Well," said Poe. "That's something else we gotta fix. I'm just glad we got you back. I'm not sure General Leia would have survived losing you."

And it would have been her fault.

Rey straightened. Time to stop feeling sorry for herself and get back to work. She headed into the rear of the ship, where she found Finn at a panel, trying to fix the gear regulator.

Wordlessly, he handed her an electroprobe. They worked together in companionable silence for a while. Sparks shot up from the panel as they rewired, welded, and tested.

At last, Finn said, "Whatever Ren said to you, you can't trust it."

"All that matters is the wayfinder," Rey said. "Getting to Exegol."

"That's what we're doing," Finn said, giving the command junction one last solder.

Rey lowered her electroprobe. She felt dazed. Her mind kept replaying the sickening vision in her head, over and over: Ochi's dagger, piercing the people who loved her.

She should have been able to know them.

"He killed my mother, and my father," she whispered.

Finn paused what he was doing to stare at her.

"I'm going to find Palpatine. And destroy him." She lifted the probe and tested Finn's newly wired junction. She could feel his eyes on her as he considered her words.

"Rey," he said. "That doesn't sound like you."

Oh, but it did. Maybe she was revenge made flesh. Maybe she had been all along. She was a Palpatine, after all.

Finn said, "I know you—"

She slammed the panel shut. "People keep telling me they know me. I'm afraid no one does. *I* don't even know."

Rey strode away, knowing she was being a little unfair. Finn knew what it was like to grow up without a family, to finally find belonging and friends in a place you never expected. He understood her better than anyone.

But that didn't mean she'd been wrong. A new Rey was rising inside her, struggling to break free. She'd spent so much time and energy getting to know a new Rey already—one who could use the Force and fight for a cause greater than herself. But maybe *that* Rey was just a skin to be shed. A temporary person.

She felt groundless, adrift. This must be why they identified children so young in the days of the old Jedi Order. They needed a foundation, knowledge, care, because the only way to survive their awakening into power was to be surrounded by those who had done it all before.

Rey had no one. Luke was dead, his voice closed off to her. Leia was half a galaxy away.

She realized that her hand hurt. She'd been gripping the electroprobe so tightly, its ridges were digging into her palm.

Rey took a deep breath. She'd try to fix the landing gear next. It would give her something else to think about.

"The Jedi apprentice still lives," the Emperor said. Kylo was in a corridor of the *Steadfast,* but he was speaking with Emperor Palpatine—whose power was even more vast than Kylo had realized. Only Rey had been powerful enough to communicate over long distances like this—or maybe it was their strange connection that was powerful. Not even Snoke had been able to do it.

But such a demonstration of power was costing the Emperor, because he looked even more frail than before. Kylo didn't know how it was possible for the Emperor's necrotic vessel to appear paler than the last time, but it did. His eyes were nearly closed, and his breathing was labored. "Perhaps you have betrayed me," Palpatine said. "Do not make me turn my fleet against you."

"I know where she's going," Kylo said, shielding his thoughts. "She'll never be a Jedi."

The Emperor's voice was like thunder in his head. "Make sure of it," he said. "Kill her!"

Kylo Ren brought down a mental curtain to cut off their connection. Just in time, for he could hardly contain his sense of triumph.

The Emperor was terrified of Rey. Of her power. Once she accepted her destiny as part of their dyad, they would be unstoppable.

Zorii's plan to flee to the Colonies had been two-pronged. Prong one: Acquire a decent ship. Prong two: Buy safe passage.

The second prong of her plan was defunct, now that she'd given her captain's medallion to Dameron. But she still had her ship, a BTA-NR2 Y-wing with an armored cockpit module, upgraded navicomputer, and customizable tactical interface. It had cost her nearly forty thousand credits. Some people considered it crass to name fighter craft, but she'd named hers anyway: *Comeuppance.*

Zorii had a lot of scores to settle.

The Colonies were no longer an option, but as long as she had the *Comeuppance,* she could go *somewhere.* Her ship carried a week's worth of provisions, so she had time to figure it out. Half a week's worth, she corrected herself, if Lluda was on board.

The only problem was that Zorii was *here,* crouched on the city's outer wall at the edge of the Thieves' Quarter, and the *Comeuppance* was *there,* in a small ravine outside city limits, hidden by a snow tarp. Between them was an entire unit of snowtroopers and one of the butchers.

Zorii tapped her helmet to trigger the sensor array. A holographic overlay appeared, and she focused tight on the butcher—his long cloak, his wicked helmet. The holograph zeroed in, circled around, and beeped slightly, identifying him as Ushar, one of the Knights of Ren.

She needed a distraction.

Zorii glanced around for Lluda but saw no sign of the girl. She was probably hiding in a similar perch, waiting for an opportunity to make her move. Lluda always wore gray-and-white camouflage. With her pale skin and white hair, she blended right in with the snowy, stony surroundings. She could also handle Kijimi's freezing temperatures without a mask. Zorii suspected she was a human hybridized with a cold-weather species, but Lluda had never shared details about her parents, beyond the fact that they'd been brutally murdered.

Someone screamed. Screaming wasn't uncommon these days, but the voice pricked her with familiarity. Zorii crept to the roof's edge and looked down. Her stomach turned over hard.

It was Jarraban, bleeding and broken in the snow, a black-clad Knight standing over him. The Knight's massive ax dripped with her friend's blood.

Zorii scuttled back and ducked behind an exhaust flute. She closed her eyes futilely against the image burned into her brain. She and Jarraban had been running together for years. He was her right-hand man.

She would mourn later. She had to get herself and Lluda off this icy rock before they joined Jarraban in the afterlife. If there was an afterlife.

Zorii looked around, desperate for an idea. Her holographic overlay identified an explosive element.

It lay to her right, inside an observation tower, a holdover from the days of religious tourism, where beings once went to meditate and become one with the mountain scenery. Now they were used by various gangs and guilds as lookout perches, but this one was unoccupied, and it contained a neehwa oil lantern, shining bright against the night.

That would do. In the chaos, she'd make a run for the *Comeuppance.*

Cleats out, she crept along the roof's ridgeline. Slow and careful was the trick. She'd feel a lot better with her twin blasters in hand, but she needed her fingers free in case she slipped.

She reached the tower, gripped the stone wall, and heaved herself over and into the tower well. Thick icicles dripped from the tower roof, for the lantern melted the snow above, which refroze on its way down. They created a tiny, icy cage that would shelter her from prying eyes as she worked.

Now, to rig it to blow.

The easiest method would be to just blast the darn thing from a distance, but trained First Order troopers would look for the source of the shot. Best to rig it and be far away when it exploded.

She fished in her utility belt for a fuse and some putty; it wouldn't take much. Zorii pressed the fuse against the oil tank beneath the glass and tapped her helmet to sync the fuse with her detonator.

Zorii climbed out the way she came and paused to evaluate. Once the explosion triggered, the snowtroopers would be drawn . . . that way. Which meant she should be . . . there, near the wall.

She made her way to her chosen spot, a place far enough away from the tower not to be noticed, but an easy drop to the ground outside the city. From there it was a quick sprint to her ship.

Zorii hoped Lluda was somewhere nearby, watching.

With a quick prayer to the Dai Bendu monks of old, all the gods she'd never believed in, and even the Force, Zorii gave a hand signal in front of her helmet, ordering the detonation.

The tower blew. Icicles flew out, shattered against rooftops. The tower roof itself shot upward like a missile.

The troopers standing between her and her ship looked

up . . . and did absolutely nothing. They just went back to their business, hardly giving it any mind.

"You've got to be kidding me," she muttered aloud.

Something tapped her shoulder, and she whirled so fast she almost lost her balance.

It was Lluda.

Her hair glowed against the night. Her cheeks were not red and chapped the way Zorii's would be. Her breath didn't even fog.

"I'll distract them," Lluda said. "You go."

"Not without you."

Lluda smiled. "You already saved my life, taking me in. I do this and we're even."

No. She couldn't stand to lose anyone else. "Lluda, what will you . . . where will you . . ." Zorii opened her mask. Pleaded with her eyes. "We can do this. We can leave together and—"

"You know me. I'll be fine. I always find a way." The girl gave Zorii one last lightning grin and said, "Watch this!" And then she was off, scampering over the rooftops like she was born to it.

Zorii muttered swear words in every language she knew. Then she *swick*ed her mask shut and prepared to run.

"Hey!" Lluda called, waving her arms in plain sight of the troopers. "Down with the First Order! Long live the Resistance!"

Blasterfire erupted around the girl as she took off, screaming insults. As one, they pursued, even the black-clad Knight.

Zorii jumped from the wall and landed in a puff of powder snow. She sprinted for her ship, which proved no easy task with every step sinking shin-deep.

She breathed in relief when she ducked under the tarp and found her ladder still intact. Zorii triggered the lock with her helmet so that the cockpit canopy was opening as she climbed. She leapt inside, hit the converters, pumped the fuel line, and pedaled the repulsorlift for a quick takeoff. She'd leave hot, no lights, and hope they couldn't follow.

Blasterfire shook her Y-wing as she pivoted toward a safer launch trajectory, but her shields held. She'd lose her pursuers, and make a fast jump to lightspeed. But then she'd double back to Kijimi City and do a quick sweep for her crew. She had to try. With a little luck, maybe she could still rescue Lluda or someone else.

But where to after that?

As her ship broke atmo, she decided where she was going. In the very same moment, she forgave Poe Dameron. He hadn't run *away* from her and the gang; he'd run *to* something. Zorii would do the same.

General Armitage Hux stood before Allegiant General Pryde, several stormtroopers beside them. His leg wound had been smothered in bacta gel and bandaged. Now his leg was uncomfortably warm and a little bit itchy. Small price to pay for getting away with treason and murder.

"It was a coordinated incursion, Allegiant General," Hux reported. "They overpowered the guards and forced me to take them to their ship."

Pryde stared at him a moment, nose high, eyes narrowed. "I see."

Hux kept his face perfectly, determinedly blank. The bandage around his pants was stained with blood. A good showing that would bolster his account, he thought. But beneath his pant leg, a bit of bacta gel had oozed through the bandage and begun to slither, wet and warm, down his leg.

Pryde's perpetual frown deepened. Something flashed in his eyes, something Hux had never seen before.

He suddenly found the act of breathing to be nearly impossible.

Pryde turned to the unit leader. "Get me the Supreme Leader." Then he grabbed the stormtrooper's rifle, pointed it at Hux, and shot him point-blank in the chest.

Hux was not dead before he hit the ground. His mouth opened and closed soundlessly as flashes of pain lit up every fiber of his being.

"Tell him we found our spy," he heard Pryde say.

His last thought was of the scavenger. He hated that girl. She had ruined everything. Yet over and over again, she had faced Ren and survived. It gave him one bright shining spark of hope against the oncoming dark: Ren might still lose.

Then that spark, too, was consumed by darkness, and Hux knew no more.

# CHAPTER 13

Kef Bir was technically a moon of Endor, but to Rey it seemed like a whole world. Flying into the atmosphere had revealed vast seas interrupted by tentative patches of land, covered mostly with grass. Shrubbery was scarce, settlements nonexistent.

C-3PO had connected with the HoloNet and informed them that Kef Bir used to be almost entirely underwater. But recent decades had seen several cataclysmic events, which had vented water into the atmosphere and caused tectonic upheaval, revealing more and more landmasses. Some theorized that the destruction of the second Death Star was to blame. Debris from the moon-sized base not only had rained down for years, but had collided with several nearby asteroids, creating a chain reaction of bolide hits to the moon's surface and atmosphere.

Kef Bir had calmed in the past decade, and life was finding a hold. The moon was rumored to have even attracted a small number of settlers and refugees, though this was unconfirmed, and the moon's official designation remained "uninhabited."

Rey hadn't been able to fix the landing gear and repulsors entirely by the time they arrived—just enough to slow their impact a little. Which was why, when they all exited the *Falcon* bruised and shell-shocked, it was to the sight of a massive scar in the damp ground, running behind them in a straight line as far as the eye could see.

Her ship's fuselage was half buried in mud, and they'd had to exit out of the top hatch, but the *Falcon* remained *almost* flight-worthy, and with a few repairs and a little luck they'd be able to take off.

After Rey had gotten what she'd come for.

The air smelled of salt and sun-kissed grass. Water prickled her skin, as though something was kicking up spray. The sky roiled with angry gray clouds, but everything remained bright, for the gas giant Endor provided reflected light in addition to the system's sun.

Rey led them up a steep, grassy slope, following the coordinates they'd gotten from C-3PO. Even the droids followed; D-O's uni-wheel was surprisingly effective against the grassy terrain.

Her breath came hard and her legs burned by the time their heads crested the top. Then Rey forgot to breathe at all.

They stood on the edge of a cliff at least six hundred meters high. Below them, a violent steel sea stretched into fog. Swells the height of a Star Destroyer rolled back to reveal jagged black shoals, only to crash back down in an explosion of white water and froth.

So much water, all in one place, carving cliffs, spearing the sky, spraying them with wetness, even at this distance. Where she'd come from, water was one of the most valuable substances in the galaxy. Turned out, it was also one of the most powerful.

The fog was clearing, and their view of the ocean pushed farther and farther into the horizon. A shape began to emerge, like a mountain of metal. No, a whole mountain *range* of metal. Beside her, Finn gasped.

It was a ship, or rather the remains of one, except this ship was larger than any ship Rey had ever seen. Its tattered hull arched out of the violent swells like an upside-down bowl, the jagged remains of its superlaser focus lens aimed at the sky. It was just like the starship graveyard on Jakku, except wetter. And about a thousand times bigger.

"What-what is that?" D-O asked.

"It's the Death Star," Rey said, staring at the colossal wreck. "It's a bad place, from an old war."

"I don't think General Leia had any idea this was here," Poe said, his voice filled with wonder. "A huge chunk of the second Death Star, still intact . . ."

"Of *course* not, Master Poe!" C-3PO said. "It was likely submerged for more than a decade after the Battle of Endor. A terrible battle, according to the HoloNet. Oh, I would *hate* to endure something so dreadful."

BB-8 warbled a question.

"From the sky, Beebee-Ate," Rey said.

"The wayfinder's in the Imperial Vaults," Finn said, as if saying the words would help him believe it. "In the Death Star."

"I hate to be practical," Poe said, "but it's gonna take us years to find it."

Poe was right. How do you search something the size of a moon? Where do you even start?

Rey blinked, remembering. *From the southern shore . . .* C-3PO had said. She whispered, "Only this blade tells."

She retrieved the dagger of Ochi of Bestoon. Held up its wicked edge so that it shimmered in the light.

The shape of the blade lined up exactly with the outline of the wreck.

Poe leaned forward.

Rey peered closer. The dagger's crossguard was hinged. Keeping the blade aligned exactly where it was, she used her other hand to gently swing the crossguard down until it clicked into place—

—And pointed out a very specific section of ruin, southwest of the superlaser lens: a star-shaped structure, nestled in a crook of the jutting wreckage.

"The wayfinder's there," Rey said.

C-3PO's coordinates hadn't been the location of the wayfinder; instead they'd indicated exactly where to stand so that the dagger would show them the way.

"Heads up," Poe warned.

Rey whirled. Finn and Poe whipped up their blasters.

A young woman about Rey's age rode toward them atop a creature that looked like a fathier with tusks except large-boned and with a more generous coat of fur. The woman had dark skin like Finn's, and beautiful obsidian hair that framed her face like a halo. The only weapon she carried that Rey could see was a bow, and Rey found herself filled with admiration and kinship when she noted that the bow was made of salvaged blaster parts. This woman would have done fine on Jakku.

Then nearly a dozen others rode up behind her, similarly mounted and armed.

"Rough landing?" said the woman.

"I've seen worse," Poe said.

"I've seen better," the woman said. "Are you Resistance?"

"Depends . . ." Poe said carefully.

"We picked up a transmission from someone named Babu Frik."

Poe lowered his blaster.

"Babu Frik!" C-3PO exclaimed. "Oh, he's one of my oldest friends!"

"He said you'd come. He said you were the last hope," the woman said.

Rey stepped forward, feeling a smidge of optimism. "We need to get out to that wreck," she said, pointing. "There's something inside we need."

"That could end the war for good," Poe added.

The rider considered a moment, then said, "We have fishing skimmers. I can take you there by water."

"Do you *see* that water?" Finn said.

"Not now," she agreed. "Too dangerous. We can get there at low tide. First light tomorrow."

"We can't wait that long," Rey said. She turned to Poe and Finn. "Kylo Ren's right behind us."

"Kylo Ren?" the woman said, exchanging a startled look with some of her fellow riders.

"We don't have *time*," Rey said.

"Do we have a choice?" Poe said. "Let's get fixing the ship." To the woman, he said, "Do you have parts here?"

"Some," she said. "I'm Jannah."

"I'm Poe."

They all headed down the hillside toward the *Falcon*, except Rey, who lingered, gazing out over the ocean at the wreckage of the Death Star. To be so close . . .

After a moment, she forced herself to turn and follow her friends.

The riders had dismounted to let their creatures graze and work out some kinks. Orbaks, Jannah had called them. Finn thought they were great, the way they kicked up dirt when they ran, tossed their long manes, play-fought with their huge tusks. They were a lot like the fathier he and Rose had ridden on Canto Bight, except joyful and free. Also stouter, as though built for endurance and cold weather.

He smiled as an orbak snuffled BB-8. It made a noise—half grunt, half whinny—which BB-8 imitated with limited success.

"Hello!" said the little cone droid.

The orbak tossed its mane and roared in response—not an unfriendly gesture—but the tiny droid recoiled. "No, thank you. No, thank you," he said, as BB-8 tried to assure him that the orbak was friendly. Finn left them to get to know one another, entering the *Falcon*.

"What a dreadful situation," C-3PO was saying, as he and Poe ran a diagnostic on the forward shields. "Is every day like this for you people? Madness!"

"Did we ever find his volume control?" Poe said.

Their crash landing had also damaged the *Falcon*'s reserve atmo tank, though it wasn't yet leaking. Fixing it now would prevent a much larger problem later. Finn got to work, glad to have something to fill the time, to distract himself from worrying about Rey.

A while later, Jannah entered, carrying a small rez cylinder—

exactly what he needed to patch the tank. "It's an oh-six, but it'll work," she said.

Finn took the cylinder, stared at it. "That's a First Order part," he said.

"There's an old cruiser on the west ridge, stripped for parts." She paused, as though coming to a decision, then added cautiously, "The one we were assigned to. The one we escaped in."

Finn's eyes flew wide. "Okay, wait. You were First Order?"

"Not by choice," she clarified quickly. "Conscripted as kids. All of us. I was Tee-Zed One-seven-one-nine. Stormtrooper."

Well, that explained the bow made of blaster parts, and the armband containing a transponder.

Finn came to a decision, too. "Eff-En Two-one-eight-seven," he said.

"You?"

He nodded. Then he grinned. Someone like him! He couldn't wait to tell Rey.

He dropped the cylinder. Sat down and leaned forward. "I never knew there were more!"

"Deserters. All of us here were stormtroopers. We mutinied at the Battle of Ansett Island. They told us to fire on civilians."

Finn winced. He knew exactly how that felt.

"We wouldn't do it," Jannah said. "We laid down our weapons."

"All of you?"

She nodded. "The whole company. I don't even know how it happened. Wasn't even a decision really. More like—"

"An instinct. A feeling," he finished for her.

She looked at him in surprise. "Yeah. A feeling."

Finn was nodding again. "The Force," he said emphatically. "It brought me here. Brought me to Rey and Poe."

"You say that like you're sure it's real."

"Oh, it's very real. I wasn't sure then. But . . ." He smiled. "I am now."

Whatever she was about to say in response was cut off when Poe and BB-8 rushed toward them.

Finn's heart thudded. Somehow he knew exactly what Poe had come to tell them.

"Rey's gone," Poe said.

As one, they all rushed from the *Falcon*. Droids trailing, they clambered up the rise.

"She took the skimmer?" Jannah said in disbelief.

Finn raised his quadnocs and swept his gaze across the sea. "I see her," he said. "Waaaayyy out there." He handed the 'nocs to Poe.

"What the hell's she thinking?" Poe said.

Finn knew exactly what she was thinking; she was going after the Sith alone, in a misguided attempt to keep her friends from harm. Stupid, wonderful, maddening Rey. "We gotta go after her," he said.

"We'll fix the *Falcon* and get out there as fast as we can," Poe said, hurrying down the rise toward the ship.

Finn followed. "We're going to lose her!" he said, his voice rising. *Lose her*—not necessarily to death. Possibly to something worse.

Chewie and Jannah kept back, saying nothing as they argued.

"She left us!" Poe said. "What do you want us to do? Swim?"

"She's not herself. You don't know what she's fighting."

Poe stopped. Whirled. "Oh, but you do?"

"I do. And Leia does."

"I'm not Leia!"

"That's for damn sure."

Poe recoiled as if struck, and guilt pierced Finn. That had been too harsh. Too close to the truth of Poe's worries and fears. He should have known better. Before he could apologize, Poe tossed the 'nocs to him and walked away.

Finn sighed, climbing back up the rise. He lifted the 'nocs, and gazed out across the ocean. Rey's skiff was barely more than a mote against the turbulent water. He had no idea how she was managing to navigate that thing, how she hadn't capsized yet.

He couldn't swim to her—that would be suicide. Maybe Poe was right and the only thing to do was repair the *Falcon* as fast as possible.

"Finn?" came Jannah's voice.

He lowered the quadnocs.

"There's another skimmer," she said.

Hope stabbed through him. He started running.

The fact that the *Millennium Falcon* was transmitting again had probably already traveled base-wide, but Leia sensed it was time for a motivational talk. She ordered everyone to gather so she could officially report. It was the perfect time for good news. A brief tropical storm had dropped the temperature. Birds chattered in the jungle canopy above, celebrating the delightful coolness.

"I'm very pleased to report that the *Millennium Falcon* sent us a transmission on long-range," she said. "Their mission is back on track."

People clapped one another on the back. She saw smiles. Connix and Rose even hugged. This had been the right choice.

"Our hope is with them, but our work is here. Commander Tico reports that the two fighters we liberated from the Corellian scrapyard are now flight ready."

More applause.

"My congratulations and thanks to the entire Engineering Corps for pulling off that miracle. But our work has just begun—"

*Leia.* Of course he chose the end of her speech to interrupt.

*You're becoming a pest,* she told Luke.

She felt his smile. *Time to say goodbye,* he said.

*Not just yet . . .*

But the words she'd been planning got stuck in her mouth, and instead she ended with, "I'm so proud of all of you. As long as we never lose hope, our cause lives on."

She stumbled a little on her way to her quarters, but Connix was there in a flash to support her.

As they headed past the *Tantive IV,* she overheard R2-D2 ask Maz a question.

"Yes, Artoo," Maz said. "She knows what she has to do. To reach her son now will take all she has left."

Leia decided to ignore that, like she was ignoring Luke. She was just so tired. If she could lie down . . . Connix helped her to her cot. After the girl left, Leia grabbed Han's medal and lay back, holding it close to her chest.

Before Rey had touched down on Takodana with Han Solo, the only body of water she'd ever seen was the slimy trough at Niima Outpost. Then, on Ahch-To, she'd always eyed the sea with a bit of distrust. The ways of water were terrifying and alien to her, and she knew she'd be facing her most unpredictable enemy yet.

Still, this ocean was even worse than Rey had anticipated. The skimmer she'd stolen was a marvel of recycling ingenuity, with two pontoons made for cutting through waves, bouncing over rough water, turning with her slightest touch of the rudder. But the waves were higher than buildings, creating eddies and whirlpools and massive explosions of froth. It took all her concentration to keep from capsizing.

The skimmer itself became her enemy when an unexpected wave ripped the rudder from her hand, slamming it sideways and almost knocking her into the water. A few more near-disasters and she figured out that she needed to aim *for* the waves instead of against them, and trust the skimmer to make the climb.

Soaked and shivering, she pushed on toward the Death Star, toward the exact spot identified by the dagger. The star-shaped chamber was so high, so isolated. But maybe she could reach it by climbing up the *inside* of the structure, sheltered somewhat from the waves. The wreckage loomed higher and larger as she approached. Water churned against the massive hull, pulled back to reveal tantalizing access points, only to crash back and drown them in the next moment. Rey had no idea how she would get on board with her life intact.

She crested another wave, and her heart leapt into her throat as the skimmer dropped down the other side. She was too close to the wreck. Her momentum was going to slam her into the hull, shatter the skimmer into a thousand pieces . . .

Instead, her skimmer was sucked into a vast canyon of metal that stretched nearly to the horizon. Here the water was somewhat sheltered by the warped walls scraping the sky to either side. Her journey slowed. Compared with the open ocean, it was almost peaceful. She craned her neck. Flying creatures nested far above at the canyon's zenith. They winged in circles, crying out as they came in to land.

The dagger had told her where to go, but she found she didn't need it. Something drew her forward, the pull of it heavy in her bones. For some reason, she found herself reaching out for Luke. *Be with me?*

Of course, there was no answer.

She aimed the skimmer toward a section of wall that seemed to have good hand- and footholds. She tied the skimmer down as best she could, checked that her lightsaber was still attached to her belt, and began to climb.

It had been a while since she'd spelunked through the ruins of a downed starship. Her grip remained strong, but everything was wet and slippery. Patience was the key. *Slow and deliberate, Rey. Test every hold before putting weight on it.*

She was far above the surface of the water, the skimmer a bobbing speck, when she found entry into the hull. Avoiding sharp metal, she ducked inside and scooted along a canted beam to a wide shaft, where she resumed her climb. It was drier here, but also darker, and she found herself working by feel.

Her path of handholds ended. There was nowhere to go except across the empty shaft, where a fallen strut created a way forward. It would be an impossible leap.

She called on the Force, launched with all her might, sailed through the shaft across a depthless maw, landed on hands and feet.

Rey resumed her climb. Her back and shoulders burned by the time the shaft opened into a vast chamber. The floor was sloped upward, slippery with water, covered in seaweed and metal detritus and even pieces of stormtrooper armor, blackened by fire. Wind whistled through gaping holes in the walls, and she shivered. This place had been something once. Something important.

Ahead, the sloped floor led to a huge viewport, half shattered, bayed out to the sky. Before it was a dais of some sort, containing the ocean-soaked remains of a chair. No, a throne.

This had been the Emperor's throne room. Luke had fought Darth Vader here, and the energy—or maybe memory—of that battle still lingered. She closed her eyes and sensed terror, pain, regret, and . . . a determination to save someone who was deeply loved.

Rey stepped toward the throne. The floor quivered beneath her feet, and she leapt back just in time as a large panel dropped away. It clattered on its way down, the sounds growing ever fainter. She did not hear it land.

Rey crept along the shadowy walls, where she hoped the floor was better supported, and came to a door. It had a complicated access mechanism that marked it as valuable and significant. Maybe a vault. What she sought was assuredly inside.

She could get through this lock eventually. The Death Star had been dormant here for decades. She probably just needed to muscle it—

Rey lifted a hand as if to push, but before she made contact, something clicked and the door whooshed open. As if it still had a power source. Like she'd been recognized.

Darkness enveloped her as she stepped inside.

The door slammed down behind her. Rey moved forward, inexplicably drawn.

Shapes manifested around her, fragments of a person. It was *her*, she realized with dawning dismay. She was walking through a hall of shattered mirrors, seeing her own form reflected back at her over and over, like in the cave beneath Ahch-To.

Except here the shattered glass only gave her jagged pieces of herself—an arm here, a boot there, a lock of soaking hair, a bruised temple. The shards of reflection were a puzzle that she ached to solve, as though doing so might make a whole person finally appear.

No, she would not allow herself to go through this again. The tease, the promise of knowledge and insight, only to come up with nothing. Rey closed her mind to the mirrors and continued forward, toward the thing calling to her.

The wayfinder hovered between black fittings, its pyramidal shape glowing soft red from within. She reached for it, took it.

Triumph filled her. *Finally.*

The triumph shifted, became burgeoning dread. Sweat broke out on her forehead, and her neck prickled. She was being watched.

Slowly, still grasping the wayfinder, she turned.

A hooded figure materialized, glided toward her with inexorable purpose, dark cloak sweeping the ground. The figure practically radiated power, and something else . . . a cold and ravenous hunger.

A red lightsaber appeared in the figure's hand, chaotic like Kylo's, with two parallel blades. Light from the blade finally illuminated a face as pale and gaunt as it was fierce.

Rey gasped, stumbling backward. It was *her.* Her face, her form. Cold and dark, wearing a Sith cloak, whole at last.

Horrified, she watched as the dark mirror Rey swung her blades apart, forming a long, fiery quarterstaff. It was the very saber she'd tentatively begun designing in her mind.

This couldn't be real. It was a vision, nothing more. But the dark Rey's steps echoed when they met the floor, and her lightstaff reeked of ozone. Her power was incredible, *intoxicating.* Almost against her will, Rey began to reach with her hand . . .

The mirrored dark visage of Rey spoke: "Don't be afraid of who you are."

It was a lightning strike, hearing Leia's exact words from this creature's mouth.

The dark Rey whipped her lightsaber forward, seeking a killing blow. Rey had her own lightsaber ignited and raised within a split second. Their blades clashed, blue on red, sparking and angry.

Rey refused to lose her grasp on the wayfinder, which gave the dark Rey the advantage. With two hands on her weapon and a fierce gaze, the dark one pushed, pinning Rey's weapon, forcing her back, one step, then another. Rey slid into the throne room.

Her stomach roiled and tears streamed down her face. She was about to be defeated by her own self, her deepest fear made flesh, everything she'd fought for come to nothing—

The dark Rey hissed, revealing pointed teeth.

Rey barely registered the fact that her dark mirror-self disappeared as she stumbled backward, tripping. She fell, the wayfinder slipping from her hand. It slid across the sloped floor. She scrambled after it, reached for the wayfinder.

Another hand got there first, larger, black-gloved. She looked up. Kylo Ren loomed, his shoulders dimpled with drops of ocean.

Despair nearly choked her. To escape a future dark self, only to collide with Kylo Ren. It felt like her worst nightmares coming true. It felt like destiny.

She launched to her feet. Re-ignited her lightsaber.

"Look at yourself," he said. He was maskless. Somehow, she knew that he would never wear his mask for her again. "You wanted to prove to my mother that you were a Jedi." His voice oozed contempt for that notion. "But you've proven something else. You can't go back to her now. Like I can't."

His words cleared her head. Because he was wrong. Her darkest self had told her not to be afraid of who she was. But so had Leia. Leia *knew*. And she had still chosen to train her.

Kylo Ren did not understand his mother at all.

"Give it to me," she ordered.

He seemed confused for a moment, as though surprised that she could still resist. "The dark side is in our nature," he tried again. "Surrender to it."

"Give it. To me," she said, pushing with the Force.

He lifted the wayfinder, stared at it. His expression turned smug. "The only way you're getting to Exegol is with me."

Rey gasped, began shaking her head. *No, no, no . . .*

His grip tightened. The wayfinder shattered. Something viscous oozed out of the remains, slipped through Kylo's fingers. He opened his palm to reveal nothing but sticky dust. The thing she'd come halfway across the galaxy for, risked the lives of her friends for, had been obliterated.

"No!" she screamed.

Hot, primal rage rose inside her like volcanic magma, and she erupted forward, swinging her lightsaber.

He leapt out of the way of her blow, ducked under the next. He whirled away from her, cape flying.

Vaguely, through her haze of fury, she realized he was not attacking her, and somehow this enraged her further. She reached, drew power from the Force as though she were a bottomless whirlpool—more, more, *more.* Her attacks increased in speed.

Finally, he could dodge no longer. His own lightsaber was suddenly brought to bear, and they clashed, their blades crackling and humming with energy.

Over and over she swiped, slammed, stabbed, and he countered with effort, matching her ferocity. But he gave ground.

Kylo stepped back, dropped into the shaft.

Without a second thought, she leapt after him.

She hardly recalled traveling any distance, but somehow they ended up outside the wreckage, on a bridgelike hunk of metal only meters wide. A massive gun turret loomed over them; beyond it and half drowning in spray was Ren's parked TIE. The ocean raged all around, but she pressed her attack, oblivious to the added danger.

Kylo Ren had no choice but to attack in kind, and it was so satisfying to strike, again and again, only to have their blades clash like cymbals. The impacts shivered into her shoulders, bruised her spine and hips. It was better than thinking about what she'd seen, what he'd done. Who she was.

A presence cut through her awareness, shining and bright. And a voice screaming: "Rey!"

Finn was running toward her, leaving Jannah behind to watch their skimmer. Rey's instinct to protect Finn was overwhelming. With no thought at all, she called on the Force and thrust out with her hand. He flew backward toward Jannah at the edge of the bridge-wreck. A wave crashed down on the stretch of bridge between them, cutting Finn and Jannah off from her sight.

The sea was boiling now with a rising tide. As she raged against Kylo Ren, the Force opened itself to her, flooding her with new power, and she found herself leaping out of the way of massive waves, then landing on her feet only to leap again. Kylo leapt after her, using the Force to propel himself into the sky, then again to control his landings.

She would not leave this place until one of them was dead. But her blade was not breaking through his guard. She gritted her teeth and attacked him with Force energy. He flew backward, caught himself, landed neatly.

Kylo advanced, pushing with his own Force energy. Her temples began to throb with pain, but she stood her ground.

He sent the thought directly into her mind: *I know you.*

*No one does,* she shot back.

*But I do.*

She screamed and launched herself at him again.

He was physically stronger. The longer they fought, the clearer it became. But she was a little faster. Their sabers collided. He pushed. She slid backward on the slick metal surface, his chaotic blade gradually getting closer and closer to her face. She felt its vibration near her cheeks.

Out of the corner of her eye, she saw a colossal oncoming wave. The ocean was reaching high tide. She leapt as the wave crashed down, using the Force to propel herself high and backward.

Rey landed in a crouch before another gun turret. She looked around. No sign of Kylo Ren. Maybe the wave had washed him away.

No, there he was, striding unerringly toward her, ocean water pouring from his hair, his face. He had withstood the wave. The expression on his face said that he could withstand anything.

She attacked, and he countered. But she was tiring, slowing. She hadn't slept in how long? And she was not yet recovered from healing the vexis. Her hand smarted with every blow.

Another attack, another block, and this one knocked her off her feet.

He loomed over her, raised his lightsaber.

Rey stared up at him. She was going to die on this wreck of a space station. But maybe it was better to die now than to give in to the darkness later.

She glared, preparing to dodge, accepting that maybe she wouldn't be fast enough.

Kylo froze, lightsaber held high.

*Leia, there is only one thing left to do.*

Galaxy save us all from big brothers, she thought.

Luke said, *You must try to reach Ben.*

She flashed back to holding her tiny son in her arms, his black hair still wet with birth, the way he'd cried all the time in those early months but settled whenever he sensed that she or Han or Chewie was near. His first steps. His first word. The first time he'd sent a toy flying across the room with the power of the Force, calling on his tiny, toddler rage.

*I never gave up hope for him,* she said.

*Tell him,* said Luke.

With his words came a rush of knowledge, and a vision-memory of Luke sitting cross-legged atop a cliff of Ahch-To, shaking with effort as he projected himself onto the battlefield at Crait.

The effort to reach Ben would take everything she had left.

She couldn't do it. It would be her ultimate failure, to leave behind everyone she loved, everything she'd worked for. Leia *had* to stay. She had to continue fanning the tiny flame of hope, or the Resistance would die.

Her thumb went back and forth across the cool face of Han's medal. Her heart had been so full of hope then, after their first big victory against the Empire. Giving these medals to Luke and Han had been more than a public celebration; they'd been a symbolic awarding of leadership. She'd shared the burden ever since that day.

She sighed with a heavy realization. She'd had it backward. Letting go wasn't giving up. It was the *ultimate* act of hope—hope for her protégés Rey and Poe, faith in the lessons she'd taught them. The last thing they would learn from her was how to go on without her, thus finally embracing their own destinies as leaders.

Bail Organa had been the one to teach her that. Her adopted father had trusted her to find Obi-Wan Kenobi and save the rebellion when she was just a young woman with less experience than any of them.

*Leia*, Luke prompted.

If Vader could become Anakin again, Kylo Ren could become Ben. Her son was tempted by the light; she could sense it. But even if he never turned back the way Anakin had, she still loved him, and her legacy was secure. She was Leia Skywalker Organa Solo. As she caressed Han's medal, she fully embraced *all* those inheritances. And she would pass them all to the next generation. Her Skywalker legacy would go to Rey, Organa to Poe, and she would try one last time to pass her Solo legacy to her son.

So that's how it would be. A final act of hope, and then she would rest.

She reached for the Force, let it surround her, fill her. She thought the effort would exhaust her, but she felt a momentary rush of strength and energy as she connected with every living thing. She reached deeper, and then deeper still. With all the life and love and hope and forgiveness in her being, she called out: "Ben!"

Her last thought washed through the galaxy like a wave. She was vaguely aware of Han's medal clattering to the floor, a whir of sadness from R2-D2, and finally a surge of welcome from Luke, who was not alone . . .

---

Kylo's Ren's gaze suddenly became distant, and he dropped his lightsaber. Rey caught it, exultation filling her. She was going to *win*.

Through the Force came a mighty sundering.

Kylo Ren stumbled.

Rey's stolen blade pierced Kylo, running him through—as incomparable loss washed through her soul, carved her out, left her empty and aching. "Leia!" she cried out.

Kylo collapsed, stared up at her in agony, his chest heaving. He blinked hard, against pain, against whatever he was feeling. Leia's last thoughts had been of her, and Poe, and the Resistance—but mostly Ben. Leia still loved him. She had forgiven him. She had *called him to the light.*

Rey's hands trembled as she turned off her lightsaber, bent and did the same to Kylo's. She knelt before him, unsure what to say. His wound was mortal, that was clear. His eyes searched her face, though she wasn't certain what he was looking for. His cheeks were wet, and she couldn't tell where ocean spray ended and tears began.

"Your mother . . ." she said.

He closed his eyes, as if accepting the inevitable end.

Rey didn't know what to do.

She'd had a chance to kill him before, and she hadn't. With him broken before her, vulnerable, she found she was even less eager to watch him die.

What would Leia do?

Rey reached out, put a hand on his chest.

His eyes flew open. He stared at her in confusion, and maybe . . . longing?

The air filled with a resonant hum. Rey drew on everything around her—so much life in that violent ocean!—but mostly she drew on herself. She *gave.*

Kylo's lips parted. His breathing settled. Muscle and sinew and skin were renewed, rejoined. Even the scar on his face knitted closed, leaving his cheek smooth and perfect.

Rey slumped over, exhausted. She felt his astonished eyes on her, sensed his unasked questions. He was alert, now. Whole. Brimming with life and energy.

But he said nothing.

Between breaths, she tried to explain. "You were right. I did want to take your hand. Ben's hand."

Before he could respond, Rey grabbed Luke's lightsaber. The healing had exhausted her, and she was unsteady on her feet as she ran toward the TIE fighter parked on the wreckage.

She dropped into the pilot's seat. It took a moment to orient herself to the strange controls, but they soon made sense to her, as flight controls always did. She took off, looking back to see Kylo staring after her, still astonished. Finn and Jannah were motes on another island of wreckage, and she was glad to see the *Falcon* approaching. They would be okay.

She didn't know where she was going. She just knew she had to get away. Rey felt like she was being ripped apart, by the truth of who she was, by grief.

Rey let instinct guide her as she punched the coordinates into the navicomputer. She broke atmosphere and entered hyperspace.

# CHAPTER 14

Kylo Ren stood on the wreck of the Death Star, gazing at the ocean. He'd been standing there a long time, watching the tide gradually recede. Physically, he felt better than he ever had in his life.

But his mind was in turmoil. He hadn't known such healing was possible, didn't understand how it had been done. But that wasn't the question that troubled him most. *Why* had Rey healed him? Why would she do such a thing?

*Why* had his mother loved him right up until her last moment? Snoke had lied about that. Snoke had lied about all of it. All those voices in his head, torturing him throughout the years, they had promised him that a moment like this could never happen. *They don't care about you. Just their precious New Republic.* And later, *Just their precious Resistance.*

All lies.

His mother had sacrificed herself to reach him. Then Rey had healed him, at great cost to herself. In spite of everything he'd done.

He had failed to kill the light within himself because it had been all around him all along. In Rey. His mother. Even . . . his father.

"Hey, kid," came a voice. The familiarity was like a lightsaber through his gut. He turned.

Han Solo stood before him, untouched by ocean spray. He looked exactly the way Kylo remembered him last—except his features were calm. At peace.

"I miss you, son," he said.

Kylo blinked. This couldn't be real. "Your son is dead," he said.

His father smiled. "No," he said, striding toward him. Their noses were centimeters apart when he added, "Kylo Ren is dead. My son is alive."

He let his gaze roam his father's face, his jacket, the blaster holstered at his side. Everything felt so real. He could even smell the gear lubricant Han Solo had always used to keep the *Falcon*'s converters running.

"You're just a memory," he said.

"*Your* memory," said his father. His eyes were so full of love. They were like daggers. "Come home," he urged.

"It's too late." It was something the voices in his head had always said. *It's too late for you. They'll never take you back.* But this time it was true, because: "She's gone."

"Your mother's gone. But what she stood for and what she fought for . . . that's not gone."

He stared at his father, afraid to believe his words. Afraid of his own memory. Afraid of what he was feeling.

"Ben," his father said.

"I know what I have to do," Ben Solo admitted, his voice tremulous. "But I don't know if I have the strength to do it."

Han raised his hand to Ben's cheek. Ben remembered it exactly. Rey had been right; he hadn't been able to shake the memory of the warmth of his father's palm, the calluses at his fingertips, the acceptance in his eyes.

"You do," his father said.

Han Solo still believed in him. So had his mother. So had Rey.

Ben raised the handle of his lightsaber, just like he had on Starkiller Base, the last time he'd seen his father. Except this time . . .

"Dad. . .?" he said, suddenly small. Vulnerable. Right.

Han Solo smiled. "I know."

Ben turned, and launched the lightsaber into the air. It sailed in a high arc, far above the wreakage, and disappeared into a haze of ocean spray.

When he turned back, the memory of his father was gone, and Ben Solo was alone in the middle of the sea.

He knew what he had to do. Somehow, he would find the strength to do it.

General Pryde knelt in the dark before the hologram. He was in an area of his private quarters. No one had access to this place but him. Even Supreme Leader Ren didn't know it existed.

It took effort and careful planning to erase all record of these transmissions, but the risk was worth it. Everything had been worth it.

The creature in the hologram spoke. "The Princess of Alderaan has disrupted my plan," said Emperor Palpatine. "But her foolish act will be in vain. Come to me on Exegol, General Pryde."

"As I served you in the Old Wars, I serve you now."

The image sputtered. The transmission was weak and fragile, having made a near impossible journey through the Unknown Regions and anomalous space. But it was enough. "Send the ship to a world they know," Palpatine said, and Pryde's heart skipped. This was the moment he'd been waiting for. "Let it burn. The Final Order begins. She will come. Her friends will follow."

As his master grinned—a slow, centipede crawl across his mouth—Allegiant General Pryde shivered in near-ecstasy. "Yes, my lord."

A flurry of complex coordinate data followed. The way to Exegol. The Emperor was trusting him with his most precious knowledge. "Behold, the fruit of your labor," his master said, as the data streaming toward him revealed another frequency channel.

Pryde's hand shook as he turned the holodisk to the new frequency. A different image sputtered before him—a flat surface, cracked ground, lightning flashes and haze. A colossal fleet hovered in the atmosphere at a staging altitude. So many of them. So beautiful.

The Sith fleet that was his life's work, hidden no more.

As soon as the image settled, indicating he had a good lock, he gave the signal.

He held his breath, waiting.

A single ship separated from the rest. It gradually rose above the others until it had achieved a safe distance, then disappeared into hyperspace. He yearned to go with it.

Everything he had worked for his whole life was finally coming to fruition.

He was a pragmatist, though, and not even the ecstasy of the moment could allay his concerns. The ships were temporarily vulnerable, unable to raise shields in the planet's hellish climate, but there was no choice. Much of the final building, inspection, testing, and maintenance must occur in atmosphere. The Emperor's crews would work triple shifts to get it done.

Pryde could have stayed forever, admiring the sight of the Sith fleet, but he had work to do. He smiled as he ended the transmission. Everything was proceeding as his Master had foreseen.

The Sith Star Destroyer popped out of hyperspace above the white, frozen world of Kijimi. Final Order captain Chesille Sabrond stood on the bridge and watched as a cloud system shifted, revealing the ridged line of a massive mountain range. It must be huge, to be visible from space.

Captain Sabrond had never been outside the Unknown Regions. She'd been raised on Exegol, belowground. It had taken years of hard work and dedication to get this premium assignment, captain of the *Derriphan,* the designated advance destroyer. She'd killed three people, sabotaged two others, and barely slept in twenty years, just so she could be among the first to fly out into their new galaxy.

Their virgin flight had been a success. Now to test the weapon.

She glanced around. The bridge was filled with Final Order officers, many raised on Exegol like her, others from various planets in the Unknown Regions. Several were children of the Empire, following in their parents' footsteps. Many of the crimson-clad stormtroopers had been conscripted by the First Order as children—and then carefully culled and "disappeared" by spies based on their potential. Everyone on this bridge had worked toward one goal: the return of the Sith.

"Kijimi is in range," said one of her lieutenants.

Captain Chesille Sabrond smiled. "Fire!" she ordered.

The deck rumbled as the massive cannon under the ship's belly erupted.

Babu Frik had two more days of work—maybe three—to get this battle droid back online. It would be different, though. More self-aware, capable of higher-level command functions, and of course not quite legal. His client had promised an unholy fee to make it happen, and Babu needed that fee, if he was to get offplanet.

The spice running gang was no more. Everyone he knew had left. The lucky ones, anyway. The rest were dead, killed by the Knights of Ren as they'd swept the city, looking for Zorii's Resistance associates.

"Soon, friend," he said to the droid. It sat on the table, one arm missing below the elbow, occasionally twitching as Babu rewired. He preferred to work on "live" subjects—it was a way to notice and correct any mistakes before they'd done too much damage. "Still, be still!" he ordered.

"Roger, roger," the droid said, then immediately disobeyed by whipping its head to the side, toward the window.

The droid's audioreceptors were more sensitive than his own ears, so Babu dropped down from the table, scampered across the room, and climbed up to the window.

It was night, and the sky had turned the telltale obsidian color that always heralded a thundersnow. He saw nothing unusual.

And then he noticed it. A red glow, barely more than a dot, coming from the northwest.

The dot grew, brightened. Soon the black night was aglow, the icy streets and buildings of Kijimi City awash in crimson.

Babu muttered a prayer. He closed his eyes against the painful brightness and accepted his fate. But then he heard a familiar voice, from someone he thought long gone.

"Babu, hurry! We only have a few seconds!"

The entire planet imploded, sucking in on itself. Then, like an exhale, it exploded into a cosmic mass of ice and rock and magma.

Captain Sabrond wanted to yell her triumph, but that would be unprofessional. Instead, she calmly gave the order: "Contact Imperial Command. Tell them the planet Kijimi is no more. Then set a course for our return to Exegol."

Poe, Finn, Chewie, and the droids hurried down the *Falcon*'s ramp into the jungle base. The place was denser now—more consoles, more people, even a few more ships. The Resistance had been busy while they were away.

Poe was glad to see Commander D'Acy waiting to greet them at the bottom of the ramp. "Poe," she said, her voice heavy with solemnity. "Something's happened. Finn—"

"This can't wait," Finn said.

"We gotta see the general," Poe said.

D'Acy's face was stricken. "She's gone," she said.

Poe froze, staring at the commander, his mind refusing to parse what she'd just said.

Chewie moaned, rolled his head back, dropped to his knees. Finn tried to comfort the Wookiee, but Chewie waved him off, grieving loudly.

After a strange message heralds the return of an ancient evil, the Resistance must endure their most perilous adventure yet to learn the truth. The heroes will face those challenges together.

Rey continues to train in the ways of the Force, enhancing her skills and knowledge as a Jedi, knowing that a final showdown with Kylo Ren is inevitable.

Bent on ruling the galaxy, Kylo Ren has ascended to the role of Supreme Leader within the First Order. He is determined to crush any opposition in his path.

If the Resistance is to save the galaxy, the next generation of heroes, including Rose Tico, Poe Dameron, and Finn, must rise to lead the way.

A year after escaping the Battle of Crait with only a few survivors, the Resistance has been reborn with new allies and old friends.

The enemies of the Resistance use many tools to spread terror and oppression, including the ominous Knights of Ren and terrifying crimson Sith troopers.

After nearly wiping out the Resistance, the First Order has swept across the galaxy seizing power and control with their ruthlessness and military precision.

As the Skywalker saga reaches an end, heroes from across generations come together one last time with the fate of the galaxy at stake.

Poe just stood there, his heart aching, his feet unmoored. He was barely aware as Beaumont grabbed him, began unwrapping the bandages on his arm.

"We came so close," Poe murmured. "I'm sorry."

Beaumont spread bacta gel on Poe's blaster wound, rebandaged it, all the while saying nothing.

A moment later, D'Acy appeared again. "Poe. You need to see this."

He looked back and forth between them—Beaumont, to D'Acy, and back to Beaumont again. How were they still working? Doing anything? How *could* they? Leia was gone, and the Resistance with her.

He allowed D'Acy to lead him and Beaumont to a communications console. She pointed to the message. "Kijimi's been destroyed," she said. "A blast from a Star Destroyer."

"Kijimi . . ." Agony speared him anew. *Zorii.* "How?" he choked out.

"A blast from a Star Destroyer."

He shook his head. "Impossible. It would take . . . No." *No, no, no.* "No way a Star Destroyer—"

"It was from the new Sith fleet. Out of the Unknowns."

Beaumont's mouth dropped open. "The Emperor sent the ship from Exegol. Does that mean all the ships in his fleet—"

"Have planet-killing weapons," Poe finished with dawning horror. "Of course they do. Every one . . . This is how he finishes it."

Something beeped on Rose's console, and she hurried over. "Listen," she said. "It's on every frequency."

The console crackled and popped, and a voice began speaking in a language Poe didn't recognize.

But Beaumont's eyes flew open. "The Resistance is dead," he translated. "The Sith flame will burn. All worlds, surrender or die. The Final Order begins."

And then the message repeated on a loop.

Everyone turned to Poe.

"Leia made you acting general," Rose said. "What now?"

Commander D'Acy put a hand on his shoulder and looked him straight in the eye. She said, "We await orders."

His first impulse was to refuse. He'd never run from anything in his life, but he wanted to run now. He couldn't accept that Leia was gone, much less take on her job. He wasn't ready. Maybe he'd never be ready. He'd made terrible mistakes, gotten so many people killed. He thought he'd have more time to learn. To atone for what he'd done. What had she been *thinking,* naming him acting general?

He'd thought he was past this. She'd told him as much. But maybe forgiving yourself was a longer, harder process than a fellow realized.

Suddenly, a memory of Leia popped into his mind, clear as day, and he imagined her voice so deeply and profoundly it was almost like she was standing right there. *Failure is the greatest teacher,* she said.

Finn sat on Rey's cot. He couldn't believe Leia was gone. She had accepted him so readily, hadn't even blinked when she'd learned he was a First Order deserter. In fact, she'd called him *brave,* considered him one of her most valuable assets. She'd set up training and education opportunities for him. Pushed him to learn, to always do better. Leia hadn't spent nearly as much time with him as with Poe or Rey, but it was clear that she'd expected great things from him.

The tiny droid they'd rescued from Ochi's ship toddled toward him and began poking around Rey's things. He noticed Rey's half-built lightsaber and inclined his pointy nose cone toward it.

"Hey, don't touch that! That's my friend's."

The tiny droid recoiled, cocked his head. "So-so sorry," he said. "She is gone."

"Yeah, she's gone," Finn answered. "I don't know where."

The droid rolled back and forth. "I miss her."

"Yeah, I miss her, too."

He'd give anything to be sitting beside her now, sharing grief. Not necessarily saying anything, just . . . being.

If he knew where Rey was, nothing in the galaxy would prevent him from going to her. He and Rey had been saving each other since the moment they met. That's what friends did.

No one quite understood his single-minded devotion to Rey, except maybe Leia. Even Rose—though she accepted it—thought it was a bit strange. But it wasn't strange at all. Rey was Finn's friend, yes, but she was also *important*. He sensed it. It was that same undeniable feeling he'd told Jannah about. If anything happened to Rey, the Resistance didn't stand a chance.

The droid whirred again, a lonely sound. Finn realized he'd been so caught up in everything that was going on, he'd never bothered to get to know the little fellow. Rey mattered, but so did everyone else. The only way they were going to make it through this was together.

"So," he said. "What's your name?"

C-3PO wandered the base, disoriented. The place was a disaster, with cables strewn everywhere, jungle vines invading everything. Mud was starting to clog his joints. An oil bath would be just the thing, but he had no idea who to ask. This ragtag group of beings included humans, Mon Calamari, a Wookiee, and a dozen other species—not to mention several droids. No one culture or language seemed to dominate, which meant C-3PO had no idea what the protocol was.

An R2-series astromech spotted him and rolled in his direction. He was white with blue markings, and he bore the scars of battle. An uncouth little thing, but it paid to be polite in these circumstances.

"Hello," C-3PO said. "I am See-Threepio, human–cyborg relations. And you are?"

The astromech rolled back as if struck. Then beeped insistently.

"My memory backup? Why would a stubby astromech droid have my memory stored?"

The little droid beeped again, irritated.

"Well, I'm quite certain I'd remember if I had a best friend." C-3PO turned away. There was nothing worse than an astromech with delusions of grandeur.

The astromech warbled insistently.

"You want to put *what* in my head? Under no circumstances—"

The blue droid extended his transfer arm and began to chase after him.

"You stay away from me with that!"

More warbling, almost too fast to keep up with.

"Whatever are you referring to? What history together?"

The astromech whistled, more gently now. His words stopped C-3PO in his tracks. The golden droid looked up at the ship looming over them.

"On a ship like that?" C-3PO said. "With a princess? You're malfunctioning!"

But he let the little droid approach.

Poe sat in the dark, beside Leia's covered body.

"I gotta tell you," he told her. "I don't know how to do this. What you did . . . I'm not ready."

"Neither were we," came a voice from the shadows, and Poe turned. It was Lando Calrissian.

The former Rebellion general had flown to Ajan Kloss on his ship, the *Lady Luck,* almost as soon as they'd left Pasaana. Something Rey had said convinced him, and Poe was so glad he was here.

"Luke. Han. Leia. Me," Lando said. "Who's ever ready?"

Poe stepped toward him. According to Connix, Lando had been overcome with grief when he arrived just a little too late. He'd missed his chance to say goodbye.

Lando looked as sad as Poe felt, his brow knitted, his shoulders slumped. He kept eyeing Leia's shroud. He'd probably regret not coming sooner for the rest of his life. Poe understood what it was to regret.

"How did you do it?" Poe asked. "How did you defeat an Empire with almost nothing?"

Lando was silent for a long moment. Then: "We had each other. That's how we won. We were *friends.*"

A light dawned in Poe's mind. For the first time since his return to Ajan Kloss, he smiled.

Poe went searching for Finn. Finn found him first. His friend rushed toward him, the tiny conical droid lapping at his heels.

"I gotta tell you something," Finn said, his voice urgent.

"I gotta tell *you* something," Poe returned. "I can't do this alone. I need you in command with me. Tell me yours."

"This droid!—uh, that's really nice, I appreciate that. . ."

"General," Poe said, saluting.

"Uh, General, this droid has a trove of data on Exegol."

"Wait, *what*?" Poe said. "Cone face?"

"I am *Dee-Oh*!" the droid said.

"Sorry. Dee-Oh," Poe said.

"He was going to Exegol with Ochi of Bestoon," Finn said.

Poe looked at the droid, back at Finn. "Why was Ochi going *there*?"

Finn took a deep breath. "To bring a little girl he was supposed to take from Jakku. To the Emperor. He wanted her alive."

Poe gaped. Finn just stared at him, waiting for him to put the pieces together.

The coral sun set over the ocean of Ahch-To as flames engulfed Kylo Ren's TIE fighter. Rey watched the ship burn, tears in her eyes. She chucked bits of driftwood at it. Not that they could do any damage, but it felt good to throw things.

She finally understood why Luke had come here, why he'd given up everything and taken up the life of a hermit. Rey was never going back. She would never put her friends in danger again. She would never face Kylo again. She would live out whatever years she had right here.

For she was the granddaughter of the most evil despot ever known, and his darkness was rising within her. Without Leia, she had no chance of pushing back the tide. The galaxy was better off without her.

Belonging had been a fleeting fancy. She was meant to be alone.

She pulled out Luke's lightsaber and stared down at it. The weapon of a Jedi. But she was no Jedi.

Rey threw it with a vengeance into the fire.

A hand reached out and caught it. A robed figure emerged from the flames, limned in ghostly light, almost transparent.

"A Jedi's weapon deserves more respect," he said.

"Master Skywalker!" she breathed.

His eyes narrowed in consternation. "What are you *doing*?"

They stared at each other. Rey wasn't sure what to tell him. Maybe he already knew.

Beside her, a ragged porg shook its feathers, cawing at her in irritation.

She sat by the firepit—she *had* to sit; she was so exhausted from battling Kylo and healing him.

Luke stood over her, unbothered by the proximity of his robes to the flames. "I did everything I was trained not to," she told him. "I drew my saber first, attacked Ren, blind with anger."

"But then you healed him."

Rey said, "I gave him some of my life. In that moment I would have given him all of it . . . died if I had to."

"Your compassion saved him," said Luke.

Rey didn't feel like fielding anything resembling a compliment. She didn't deserve it. "I saw myself on the dark throne," Rey told the Jedi Master. "I won't let it happen. I'm never leaving this place." She looked at him in challenge. "I'm doing what you did."

The fire popped. A spark landed on Luke's robe, but he didn't react, and the spark winked out as though it had landed on nothing.

"I was wrong," Luke said. "It was fear that kept me here. What are you most afraid of?"

The answer was easy. But saying it was hard. "Myself."

"Because you're a Palpatine."

She gasped. He'd said it so casually, as though not impressed in the least.

"Leia knew it too," he added.

Rey had guessed as much, but it was still startling to hear him say it. "She never told me," she whispered.

Luke moved to sit beside her.

"She *still* trained me," Rey said.

"Because she saw your spirit," Luke said. "Your heart."

Rey had always assumed that Leia agreed to train her because she saw her as a weapon. An asset in the fight against the First Order. Could it be true that she'd also seen something else in her? Something *good*?

Rey looked down at her hands, feeling foolish. "I wanted Leia to think I was as strong as she was. I'm not."

"Leia was stronger than all of us," Luke said.

Which made Rey wonder: Had Leia *ever* been tempted by the dark side? In all the stories she'd heard, in reading Luke's journals, studying with Leia, she had never once heard of anyone even *trying* to turn her, the way Vader and the Emperor had tried to turn Luke. The way Kylo had tried to turn her. Maybe, of all of them, Leia had been unturnable.

Finn would be like that, she realized with a jolt, if he could touch the Force. He was special that way.

She was shaking her head, and tears threatened once again. "I don't think I can do it without Leia. I'm descended from such dark—"

"Rey," Luke said. "Some things are stronger than blood."

The rightness of his words sparked inside her. The Force was stronger than blood. And friendship. And love.

"But I'm afraid," she confessed.

"Confronting fear is the destiny of a Jedi," Luke went on. "*Your* destiny. If you don't face Palpatine, it will mean the end to the Jedi. And the war will be lost."

"Like you had to confront Vader," she said, remembering the notes in his journals.

"It's okay to be afraid. I was."

She gave him an arch look.

"You think it's an accident we found each other?" Luke continued. "Two orphans from the desert . . . The Force brought you to me and Leia for a reason.

He rose. Though island wind whipped at the strands of Rey's hair, Luke's seemed unaffected. "There's something my sister would want you to have" he said. "Follow me."

Luke led her inside his old hut. It was still in good condition, maintained by the Lanai caretakers in his absence. He pointed toward a loose brick in the wall.

"In there," he said.

Rey removed the brick and reached inside. Her fingertips encountered a hard object wrapped in soft leather. She pulled it out. Unwrapped it.

It was a lightsaber, shining with relative newness. As soon as her hands gripped it, she sensed its owner, and she smiled.

"Leia's lightsaber," she said.

"It was the last night of her training," Luke said.

Rey caught glimpses of his memory—*lightsabers clashing, their blades lighting the jungle around them in soft blue and green. Their fight was fierce, but Rey felt a sense of fun. Of joy. Luke had* loved *training his sister.*

*Luke found himself toppled to the ground, his fall cushioned by a bed of ferns. He looked up at his twin—a much younger version of the woman Rey had come to know—who grinned, but her face held sadness too. Resignation.*

"Leia told me that she had sensed the death of her son at the end of her Jedi path," Luke said.

"Oh," Rey breathed. That was it. The thing Leia had been holding back.

"She surrendered her saber to me and said that one day, it would be picked up again by someone who would finish her journey."

Rey stared at it. Was she *meant* to have this?

"A thousand generations live in you now," Luke said. "But this is your fight." He glanced down at the lightsaber in her hand. "You'll take both lightsabers to Exegol."

Her heart sunk. By trying to do the right thing, she had ruined everything. "I can't get there," she said. "I don't have the wayfinder. I destroyed Ren's ship."

The Jedi Master's smile held so much fondness it made her heart ache. "You have everything you need," he said gently.

On Luke's orders, Rey had laid down in the hut and closed her eyes. She'd given away too much of her life force during the healing, and she needed a brief rest, or she would get nowhere fast. Luke hadn't pushed her, or told her how he expected her to get to Exegol, just given her space to think. It was exactly what Leia would have done.

*What Leia would have done.*

Rey flipped onto her back, sighing. She'd been asking herself for months: What would Leia do? This time, the answer was easy: Leia would leave Ahch-To and get back in the fight. In fact, she wouldn't have come here in the first place. Even though, like Rey, Leia was descended from unspeakable evil.

Luke, too, when given the choice, had left to face his fears. How could she do any less?

Rey gave up resting and exited the hut, entering a damp, foggy morning. Clouds shrouded the island, and a low tide revealed wet, kelpy shoals.

One of the Lanai caretakers immediately stood up from a stone bench, giving Rey a disapproving glare over her beaklike nose. Rey glared right back, as the caretaker went inside the hut she'd just vacated, no doubt to clean and straighten. Had she been outside the doorway all night? The caretakers probably couldn't wait for Rey to be gone, just like last time.

The TIE was now a smoldering wreck. A few porgs huddled nearby, as close to the warmth of the dying fire as they dared.

Something twinged inside her, called to her, and she stepped forward. A night drizzle had cooled the wreckage. Following her instincts, she reached down and shoved the detritus aside.

A wayfinder sat there, smokeless and pristine. *Vader's* wayfinder.

Rey whispered, "Two were made . . ."

The noise of the sea was ever-present here on Ahch-To, but compared with what she'd just experienced on Kef Bir, it was a gentle, peaceful rhythm of waves against cliffs, diving porgs, crying gulls. So when something happened, it was noticeable.

Behind her, the sea churned violently, and wet spray hit her back. She turned. Peered over the cliffside.

Water was boiling up in the cove below. Luke's submerged X-wing began to rise—first came the laser cannons on the wingtips, shedding water and seaweed. Then the fusial thrust engines, the cockpit canopy, the nose cone. Soon even the landing gear was clear, and Rey watched, awestruck, as the fighter drifted with perfect precision and control to an area of flat ground, where it landed with a tiny thump.

Her gaze was drawn to a figure nearby. Luke, eyes closed, shining blue against the cliffside, reaching out his hand.

He opened his eyes, saw her, and smiled.

She smiled back. Luke was right. She had everything she needed.

# CHAPTER 15

D-O was hooked into a console, and Finn stood with Poe and Rose, staring at it, waiting for the information he knew would come. D-O twittered a question, and BB-8 beeped encouragement, assuring the little droid that all was well, that this was his *mission.*

Finn found himself fidgeting with impatience. A few strides away, C-3PO was similarly hooked up to R2-D2.

"Artoo, have you heard?" C-3PO said suddenly. "I'm going with Mistress Rey on her mission!"

R2-D2 chirruped in clear frustration.

"What do you mean, I already have?"

"There!" Poe pointed. Information flashed across the console screen: diagrams, maps, navigational codes, atmospheric data, asset distribution, tower logistics . . .

Finn exchanged an excited glance with his friend. "Everything you ever wanted to know for an air strike on Exegol."

"Except how to get there," Poe said, frustrated. "You see these atmo readings?"

Finn nodded. "A mess. Look at those magnetic cross fields."

Rose leaned closer. "Gravity wells? Solar winds?" she said in a disbelieving voice. Which worried Finn. If their top engineer thought Exegol's atmosphere presented an insurmountable obstacle, their mission was doomed before it had begun.

"How can their fleet even take off in that?" Poe said.

Which begged the question: How could they land in that? Fight in that? There had to be a way . . .

"I'm terribly sorry," came C-3PO's voice. "But he insists!" The golden droid waddled toward them, gesticulating with his arms, the little astromech following behind. "I'm afraid Artoo's memory bank must be crossed with his logic receptors."

Finn was glad the real C-3PO was back, but this was not the time—

"He says he's getting a transmission from Master Luke!"

R2 was practically singing as he plugged into one of the console's dataports. A subspace radar map appeared on the display. A blip showed as IN FLIGHT, bearing an X-wing signature.

Poe called up the identification. "That's an old craft ID. AA-589." He stepped back, blinking. Turned to Finn. "It *is* Luke Skywalker's X-wing."

Finn gaped.

"It's transmitting course-marker signals," C-3PO said. "On its way to the Unknown Regions!"

Finn was nearly overcome—with relief, with joy, with hope. "It's Rey," he said, with absolute certainty. "She's going to Exegol." He gripped Poe's shoulder. "She's showing us how to get there!"

Poe considered. Finn watched as his friend came to a steady conclusion. "Then we go together."

Pilots and ground crew, mechanics and officers, all rushed toward the *Tantive IV.* Poe had called a briefing, and Rose had quickly rigged a holodisplay under the blockade runner's giant belly. It sat atop cargo cases, and the image flickered in and out, but it would do. Finn had the floor, and Poe was happy to give it to him. Leadership was much easier when shared.

"As long as those Star Destroyers are on Exegol, we can hit them," Finn was saying as Chewie joined the meeting, along with Lando and the droids.

"Hit them how?" Tyce asked. The pilot stood beside her wife, Commander D'Acy. The two were not prone to public displays of affection, but it was obvious to Poe they took courage in each other's presence.

"They can't activate their shields until they leave atmosphere," Rose explained.

"Which isn't easy on Exegol," Poe added. "Ships that size need help taking off; nav can't tell which way's up out there."

Tyce asked, "So how *do* the ships take off?"

"They use a signal from a navigation tower. Like this one." Poe flipped the holodisplay to a new image: an obelisk-like tower jutting from the flat ground, spreading its array like a metal flower opening its petals.

"Except they won't," Finn said. "Because air team's gonna *find* the tower, and ground team's gonna *blast* it."

"Ground team?" Vanik asked. He was an A-wing pilot and one of Poe's personal recruits.

"I got an idea about that," Finn said.

Poe gave him a nod. Finn's plan for the ground team just might work, though it was a bit unconventional. It would definitely take the enemy by surprise. "Once the tower's down, their fleet is stuck in atmo. For just minutes. No shields, no way out. And Rose has an idea about *that,*" Poe said. "Rose?"

"My team's been analyzing the Sith Star Destroyers," Rose said. "In order to kill a planet with those cannons, they need an enormous power source."

"They're drawing on the main reactors!" Vanik said.

Rose nodded. "We think hitting a cannon might take down the whole ship."

"That's our chance," said Lando. He'd changed his Aki-Aki garb for bright clothing and a knee-length cape. Poe *really* liked his cape. He'd have to ask about it when all this was over.

"Shields or no shields," Wexley cut in. "Star Destroyers aren't target practice. Not for single fighters."

"We'd be no more than bugs to them," Connix agreed.

Snap and Connix had a point.

Beaumont leaned forward. "We need to do some Holdo maneuvers," he said. "Do some *real* damage."

Before Poe could answer that they couldn't afford to sacrifice anyone, Finn jumped in with "C'mon that move was one in a million. Fighters and freighters can take out their cannons if there are enough of us."

What kind of galaxy had it become, Poe marveled, if freighters were considered war-class ships? He supposed it didn't matter. Getting their fleet ready was his job, now that Leia was gone. He would do whatever he had to do to get them all ready to fight.

"There aren't enough of us!" Nien Nunb protested, in his native Sullustese.

Poe nodded at the pilot, saying, "That's where Lando and Chewie come in. They're going to take the *Falcon* to the Core systems. Send out a call for help to anybody listening." Under Leia's direction, Poe had been laying the groundwork for months. Allies were out there. And if anyone could smooth-talk them into helping now, it was Lando Calrissian, friend to General Leia, hero of the Rebellion.

Poe continued: "We've got friends out there. They'll come if they know there's hope." Everyone started to protest; they all remembered Crait as painfully as he did. Poe thought of Zorii's words and said, "They will! The First Order wins by making us think we're alone. We're not alone. Good people will fight if we lead them."

"Leia never gave up," Finn said. "And neither will we. We're gonna show them we're not afraid."

"What our mothers and fathers fought for," Poe said, thinking of his own parents, Shara Bey and Kes Dameron, who had sacrificed so much to fight for the Rebel Alliance. "We will not let it die. Not today. Today we make our last stand. For the galaxy, for Leia. For everyone we've lost."

"They've taken enough of us," Finn added. "Now we take the war to them."

Around Poe and Finn, people were nodding. Rose's face was rapt. "May the Force be with us," she said, with feeling.

"May the Force be with us," Connix repeated.

Then several called out at once: "May the Force be with us!"

Lando Calrissian watched as everyone prepped for battle. It was like plucking the sweet strings of memory to see it all happen again. Ground crew moving fuel lines from ship to ship. *Pluck.* Droids loading into fighters. *Pluck.* Comm officers making console adjustments and testing frequencies. *Pluck.* Commander D'Acy kissing Tyce. *Pluck.* Wedge's stepkid Snap Wexley, hugging his wife Karé goodbye. *Pluck.*

More impossible odds. Another cause he unexpectedly found himself willing to die for.

Chewie hollered down to him that the *Millennium Falcon* was ready to go, and he realized he'd been observing the Ajan Kloss preparations because he was putting off the inevitable. Stepping foot inside the *Falcon* again was going to *hurt.*

Lando took a deep breath, gathered his cloak, and climbed the ramp.

He entered the curved corridor. At his feet were secret compartments, lined with a sensor-confusing amalgam of rare metals and conductive mesh. He'd smuggled a lot of stuff in those compartments—jewels, weapons, Imperial identichips, himself. His buddy Han had smuggled even more.

To his right were the cockpit and lounge, to his left was the cargo hold. He loved that hold. Lando had transported legal cargo, too, though it had most often been cover for more valuable, less legitimate goods. Often, though, his cargo hold had remained empty. Or at least not quite full. He'd thrown a lot of great parties in that hold.

He turned right and headed toward the lounge. Chewbacca

seemed to understand that Lando needed to take his time, so he motioned that he'd be waiting for him in the cockpit.

"Thanks, Chewie."

The hologram board and lounge seat were exactly the way he remembered them, though the stuffing in the seat was starting to come out at one seam. An easy patch.

He smiled. Han and Chewie had always had too many things on their minds to notice something so inconsequential. Back when he owned the *Falcon,* he would have fixed it right away.

Behind the lounge was the guest bunk, a place he'd slept often in the days of the New Republic, and he felt a pang so sharp it was like a stab to his chest. Leia had always managed to find some essential errand for him, and Lando had ended up an unofficial second mate on a ship that used to be his.

He missed them both so much. It had been a manageable sorrow, when he'd been on Pasaana with the Aki-Aki, knowing that his friends were out there somewhere, alive. But now that they were gone . . .

Lando passed the galley and headed toward the captain's cabin. When he had owned the *Falcon,* the ship could only sleep four comfortably, two in the guest bunk, and two in the captain's cabin. Then that cheater Han had won the ship from him in a fateful game of sabacc, and the first thing he'd done was retrofit the cape closet to create a first mate's bunk for Chewie and a hidden compartment.

Lando had been outraged. It seemed so silly now.

He peered into the captain's cabin. The *Falcon* had endured a rotating crew for the last few months. He had no idea who slept here, if anyone. The room contained a triple bunk now, because Han wanted to squeeze more people in. For a while, he'd thought he'd take his new family on a run or two.

Lando understood. He'd have given anything to have his little girl by his side as he traveled the galaxy on the *Lady Luck.* But it was not to be, for either of them.

He stepped toward Chewie's bunk and the compartment it was hiding for a closer look, but then he hesitated. The Wookiee was waiting for him in the cockpit, but surely he wouldn't begrudge his old buddy a peek inside? It used to be his cape closet.

Lando reached across the bunk for the rivet that was really a button, and the panel whisked open. The first thing that hit him was the smell of Wookiee fur. Not unpleasant, once you were used to it, but a little surprising just the same. The compartment was small, with a grate for ventilation; Han must have used this hidey hole to smuggle live cargo. No trace of Lando's closet remained.

Inside was a small metal shelf. And on the shelf was a hologram disk, the edges worn with use. It was none of his business. Probably a treasured memory from his homeworld of Kashyyyk. Chewie was over two centuries old, with a long history of family and friends Lando knew nothing about.

He started to leave, but stopped. He couldn't resist. He was a scoundrel, after all.

Lando reached forward and flicked the hologram switch.

An image of Chewbacca himself was projected onto the disk in soft blue. He held a small human child in his arms. Lando leaned closer.

It was Ben, dark-haired, chubby-fisted. He kicked his legs and yanked on Chewie's fur, shrieking in delight. Chewbacca just cuddled him close, making a sound that was almost like a purr.

Lando flicked off the hologram. He couldn't watch anymore. The First Order had taken so much from them. From all of them.

It was time for Lando to fight back. He left Chewie's quarters, going over their plan in his head. He couldn't rally their allies individually in the short time they had. So Beaumont and Connix had plotted a course that would take them past First Order jammers, where they could transmit a call for help at strategic coordinates. A few key figures, like the former Mon Calamari ambassador, would be contacted directly and given the special Calrissian touch, but mostly their goal was to jump, transmit, jump, transmit, over and over again until time ran out.

He ducked under the bulkhead and entered the cockpit. Chewie greeted him, and Lando spent a precious moment staring at his friend. Leia had held out hope for Ben until the very end. Turned out, Chewie felt the same way.

He settled into the pilot's seat.

Chewie moaned loudly.

"You said it, Chewie," Lando agreed. "One last time."

Poe's X-wing was almost ready. He watched as a crane lifted R2-D2 into the ship's astromech compartment. He'd miss having BB-8 with him, but his buddy had another assignment. Besides, R2-D2 had logged more X-wing hours than any other droid on the base, and he and Poe made a good team.

"I don't know of any droid ever returning from the Unknown Regions," C-3PO said tremulously. "But you're no ordinary droid."

Poe was about to climb into the cockpit when he saw Finn hurrying off toward the lander. He jogged over to intercept, Finn saw him and paused, and then they clapped each other on the shoulders.

Poe wasn't sure who moved first but all of a sudden they were hugging like the brothers they were.

They stepped apart, and Poe became keenly aware that one of them was missing. He frowned. "What's waiting for her out there?" he asked Finn.

Finn's face was grim. But he said, "We'll see her again. I know we will.

"You know . . ." Finn hesitated.

"I know a lot of things."

"You're a general now, *the* general—should you be, uh, flying a fighter?"

Poe took a deep breath. He'd expected this, but he hadn't known who would be the first to bring it up. He was glad it was Finn. "I'm a pretty good pilot," he reminded his friend.

"Pretty good," Finn shrugged.

"If we're going to have any chance on Exegol, we need every pretty good pilot we have inside a fighter. That's a decision that I've made as general. But come talk to me about it again after the battle's over."

Finn mock-glared. "I will."

Poe gave Finn's shoulder one last squeeze, and they both hurried off.

He passed C-3PO on his way to the cockpit. Come to think of it, the golden protocol droid wasn't so bad. It had been hours, maybe a whole day, since Poe had found him irritating. Poe patted the droid on the shoulder. In his own strange way, C-3PO was his brother, too.

He reached for the ladder. His arm still smarted from the blaster burn he'd received on the *Steadfast*. But he was Poe Dameron, ace pilot, acting general of the Resistance, and he could fly anything, even one-handed.

He climbed the ladder into the cockpit.

Allegiant General Pryde stared out the viewport, hands clasped behind his back. They'd made it through red space without incident and had entered normal hyperspace. Streamers of light rushed by, illuminating the beautiful, perfectly ordered bridge and the faces of its officers.

Pryde loved this ship. The *Steadfast* was officially the mobile command center of Supreme Leader Kylo Ren, but Ren didn't know it like he knew it. The Supreme Leader had no idea the modifications that had been made, no idea how *special* it was.

Admiral Griss approached. "Entering the Unknown Regions, sir." A simple announcement. It used to be Hux's job to inform Pryde of such things, except Hux wouldn't have been able to resist adding something ingratiating. *Would you like me to prepare your personal shuttle? Shall I have a ground team waiting? May I fetch you a hot beverage?* Pryde smiled unkindly. He'd been so glad for an excuse to kill the sniveling rat.

The ship came out of lightspeed. Exegol loomed before them, dark and hazed, crackling with power and ferocity.

Pryde's hands began to shake, and he clasped them even tighter. His life's work had led him here. He took a deep breath to steady his voice and said, "Soon worlds will burn. Our lord will rise again."

Rey exited hyperspace. The planet Exegol was finally before her, shrouded with dark clouds that flashed bright with lightning. The instruments on her console beeped warnings about the approaching atmosphere.

She ignored them, angling downward into the clouds, grateful to be piloting Luke's X-wing. It was old tech, and it had taken some fast thinking and even faster fingers to get it flight worthy—the wing patched with the door to Luke's hut, shield panels scavenged from the TIE wreckage, and a hefty amount of rewiring. It might never fight again—not without help from Rose and her parts-requisition channels. But it was still fighter-class, and its transition from vacuum to atmo was seamless. Rey had needed its added stabilizers to fly Exegol's unfriendly skies.

Her ship dipped below the cloud line and she gasped. The Sith fleet spread out before her, even more vast than her vision had led her to believe, shining bright in relief against the perpetual storm, stretching as far as her eyes could see. The vessels were based on an older model, from the days of the Galactic Empire, but they were so much bigger than those. Extra gun turrets and laser cannons attested to a much greater ordnance capability than her Resistance friends were expecting.

Her ship wobbled a little—gravity well! She compensated quickly, and cruised to an altitude considerably below the Sith fleet. Exegol was a horror of a planet, but its atmospheric anomalies might confuse the Destroyers' sensors and keep them from noticing her tiny ship. In fact, she was counting on it.

Moments later she was on the ground. The air was hot, the soil fissured with dryness. A dark building breached the clouds ahead of her, and for the briefest moment she considered giving in to terror. Such malevolence radiated from the building that she knew exactly what—who—she would find inside. Even more terrifying was the fact that the presence was familiar. As though some form of it had been watching her, maybe her whole life.

*Confronting fear is the destiny of a Jedi.*

Rey pressed on.

She stepped beneath a massive monolith that seemed to hover in the air. She would trust Luke and his lightsaber to light her way.

Rey removed the lightsaber from her belt and ignited it. She startled a bit when the section of floor she stood on detached from the rest, began to descend. She looked around, alert to any sight or sound, but all was as silent as death.

Then a rumble sounded, too distant to identify.

The lift settled, and Rey stepped off. She raised her weapon, and its blue light snagged on huge stone faces, sparking with electricity. She knew, without knowing how she knew, that the statues commemorated Sith Lords who had come before. This place of evil must have been here for centuries, maybe millennia, for the air was heavy with the weight of time and dark secrets.

Rey was suddenly aware that she was not alone. Figures scurried in the shadows, but she sensed no immediate threat from them, so she continued on. A few more steps took her past a dizzying array of lab equipment—monitors, tubes, some kind of tank, all empty and abandoned.

Just like the planet's surface, the floor here contained fissures, and light flashed deep down—Rey couldn't tell how deep—as though Exegol's entire crust had formed around a core of electricity.

She came to a narrow stone corridor, and her gaze was pulled forward. A chill pimpled the flesh of her arms, because resting upon a dais was the shape from her vision. A chair with spikes curving up and around it, like a halo of giant thorns. The throne of the Sith.

Rey stepped toward the dais. The rumble grew louder.

The corridor broke open into an an amphitheater as big as a hollowed-out mountain, brimming with robed figures. There were thousands of them, faceless in the dark distance, but pulsing with zealotry. Religious disciples, awaiting the return of the Sith. As she approached, the rumbling swelled, became a collective, worshipful welcome.

"Long have I waited," came a voice from her nightmares, deep, resonant, and slow, as though he had all the time in the galaxy.

Rey turned toward the voice. A robed figure materialized, suspended from strange machinery. Her grip on the lightsaber tightened when she saw his face. He was monstrous, repulsive, with red-rimmed eyes, skin barely clinging to his skeletal form, disintegrating into oozing sores. One of his hands had half rotted away.

It was her grandfather, his spirit trapped in an artificial form, his power too devastating to contain.

"My grandchild has come home!" he added triumphantly.

He radiated evil, but her feet twitched toward him. She could not look away. There was something oddly compelling about him.

"I never wanted you dead," he said. "I wanted you here, Empress Palpatine."

This was nothing she wanted, she reminded herself, even as her feet threatened to step forward.

"You will take the throne," he assured her. "It is your birthright to rule, here. It is in your blood. Our blood." Several figures stepped forward, draped in crimson, similar to Snoke's guard, which she and Kylo had defeated together. Rey had a feeling these guards would prove more formidable adversaries.

She forced herself to sound strong, to back away from the Emperor. "I haven't come to lead the Sith. I've come to end them."

"As a Jedi," the Emperor said, his voice oozing contempt.

"Yes."

He smiled. "No. Your hatred. Your anger. You want to kill me. That is what I want. Kill me and my spirit will pass into you. As all the Sith live in me. You will be Empress. We will be one."

Poe's X-wing exited hyperspace, and he finally caught his first sight of Exegol.

What a dung heap. It was the deadest, ugliest thing he'd seen in a long while, and he wondered if it had always been this way, or if building a colossal fleet of Star Destroyers here had killed the place.

Beside him, his tiny squadron popped into view—the *Tantive IV*, Finn's lander, several more fighters. "Welcome to Exegol," Poe said drily.

They dived into the cloud cover, and nearly collided with the Sith fleet. Someone gasped into their comm. Their triangled hulls were enormous, but they grew ever smaller as their number stretched into seeming infinity.

"Great dark seas," Ackbar said. "Look at that!" He angled his Y-wing closer to Poe, determined to keep his new acting general alive at any cost.

"No sign of the *Falcon* or allies," Tyce said from her own Y-wing.

"Just find that navigation tower," Poe ordered. "Help will be here by the time we take it down!"

*Please be here by the time we take it down.*

Captain Chesille Sabrond stood on the bridge of the *Derriphan*, looking through the viewport at the rest of the Sith Fleet.

They held formation slightly above everyone else, as the only Destroyer to have already made the climb. Allegiant General Pryde had tasked her crew with observing the ascension and reporting any anomalies.

The fleet was a beautiful sight to behold. Together, they were going to conquer an entire galaxy, and Sabrond was going to play a major role in the Final Order.

She'd have to continue distinguishing herself. Sabrond was under no delusion that captaining a Star Destroyer would be enough. There were thousands of captains. Tens of thousands. Somehow, she'd make sure that Allegiant General Pryde and the reborn Emperor saw her as one in ten thousand.

Sabrond could do it. Somehow. She had come this far. And she was just getting started.

"Incoming transmission on a fleetwide frequency," said her comms officer, flicking a switch to open the channel.

Allegiant General Pryde appeared on the bridge holo. "All ships rise to deployment altitude," he ordered. He'd been out in the galaxy for his whole career, only communicating with Exegol rarely. She wondered what that must be like, wondered about the marvels he'd seen. Maybe she'd get a chance to ask him.

"Captain!" said one of her technicians. "We have Resistance craft incoming."

Chesille Sabrond smiled. She'd been drilling for this moment for years. "Allegiant General?" she asked, though she knew what he would say.

"Use the short-range defense cannons," Pryde said. "Scatter-fire pattern."

"Yes, General." She turned to her crew. "Ready the defense cannons!"

# CHAPTER 16

Pryde frowned as more spacecraft popped out of hyperspace all around them, even more than the *Derriphan* had initially reported. The Resistance had managed to cobble together a small fleet, one he wouldn't underestimate. Their ships were like bloodsucking insects. Tiny and annoying, but relentless until they'd been properly squashed.

"How did they manage to get here?" Admiral Griss said.

Pryde muttered under his breath, considering. The short-range defense cannons wouldn't be enough against this swarm of flies. Then he addressed the bridge. "I need another transmission channel to the fleet!"

It took a few seconds. Exegol's atmosphere made fleet-wide transmissions tricky. It also messed with their sensors, which meant they'd need visual confirmation to eliminate the Resistance threat. And *that* meant scrambling fighters.

He would do whatever he had to, use whatever resources at his disposal, to end this final, futile act of rebellion.

"You're on, General," said his communications officer.

Pryde cleared his throat and said, "Nothing will stop the Final Order fleet from ascending! Scramble fighters! Cannons: Fire at will!"

Poe banked hard as thousands of simultaneous cannon blasts lit up the sky like a nova. To his left, a fighter was stripped of its hull, debris flying off in all directions, until it finally exploded into a fireball.

A quick glance around showed that they'd lost several fighters in just that first volley, and with sensors so unreliable, he had no idea who. This was the price of leadership.

Poe did not have the luxury of grief or regret. Finishing this mission was all that mattered. "Stay at their altitude!" he yelled into his headset. "They can't fire on us without hitting each other."

Following Poe's lead, the squadron dived hard, dodging blasts all the way, toward the endless sea of Destroyers. They swooped into the corridors created by the ships' hulls, almost daring them to fire.

"Incoming TIEs!" Snap Wexley warned, and Poe was glad to hear his voice. That was one survivor confirmed.

His relief was short-lived. Hundreds of Sith TIEs screamed toward them like giant predator birds, with wicked red and black lines across razor-sharp wings.

Finn stared through his quadnocs as his team piloted the lander *Fortitude* toward the planet's surface. He'd used this ship for a few missions before; it was sturdy with decent shields and lots of space for quick crew transport—even if that crew was a bit unconventional.

A TIE dived toward them, and Finn flinched, but the *Fortitude*'s guns blasted it out of the sky.

He glanced across the crowded cabin at Rose, and their eyes locked. "I'm sure glad someone made time to add a defensive arsenal to this troop carrier," he said.

"Only because I knew I'd be on it too, as part of the ground team," Rose said, completely deadpan. "I mean, if it were just you . . ."

Finn laughed in spite of himself. "Uh huh."

Rose turned away to hide her smile.

Truth was, Finn had a *lot* of friends on board, and Rose had just saved all of them.

"Heads up," shouted the pilot.

A structure rose before them in the distance, tall, silvery, and imposing.

"I see it!" Finn yelled. "I've got a visual on the nav tower!"

"Lander," Poe responded from somewhere high above. "Prep to unload the ground team at the base of the tower."

Pryde was pleased. They'd already destroyed numerous Resistance fighters. The remaining ships were a skeleton squadron, incapable of mounting any real offensive.

"General," said his comm officer. "They're targeting the navigation tower. So the fleet can't deploy."

Admiral Griss gasped. "We need to get those Destroyers out of there."

Fortunately, Pryde always had a backup plan.

"Switch over the source of the signal," he ordered. "To this ship." His modifications were going to come in handy even sooner than he'd hoped. "We'll guide the fleet out ourselves."

A light flashed atop the tower as Finn and his crew approached in the lander. Then the light went off and stayed off. Watching it through his quadnocs, Finn got a bad feeling.

Jannah approached his shoulder. "Finn, we're good to go," she said.

"Thanks for doing this," he told her.

She started to say something, but an alarm beeped in the cockpit.

Tyce's voice filtered in over the comm. "The navigation tower," she said. "It's been deactivated!"

"What?" Finn exclaimed.

"They're not transmitting from that tower anymore," she clarified.

"The ships need that signal," came Snap's voice. "It's got to be coming from somewhere."

Finn's gaze was inexplicably drawn upward, to the side. The First Order Star Destroyer, the only one not part of the Sith fleet. The *Steadfast*.

"Call off the ground invasion!" came Poe's order, which was a smart move, because if the fleet had transferred the signal, it meant they knew Finn and his team were coming. Except . . .

"No," Finn said. "The signal's coming from that command ship."

"How do you know?" asked Jannah.

They locked eyes, and Jannah nodded. "A feeling," he confirmed.

Finn spoke into the radio: "The nav signal's coming from the command ship! That's where we drop!"

"You wanna launch a ground invasion on a Star Destroyer?" said Tyce, unbelieving.

Finn would have atmosphere, gravity, and a plucky unit of former stormtroopers ready to take the fight back to the bullies. What more did a fellow need?

Luck, he supposed. Or maybe the Force. "Well, I don't *want* to," Finn said. "But that ship's nav system will be defended from air attacks. If you give us cover to land, we can get to it. And take it out. We gotta keep that fleet here until help arrives!" He leaned over the pilot's shoulder and pointed. "The command ship. That's our landing zone."

As he and Jannah hurried toward the rear hold to explain the plan to the rest of the landing team, he heard Poe's voice over the comm: "You heard him. All wings, cover that lander!"

General Pryde watched through the viewport, perplexed, as the bulky Resistance craft dived toward the ship. Was this a suicide maneuver? If so, it was folly. An impact would avail them nothing.

The Resistance ship careened into their hull and kicked up sparks as it screeched across. It came to a rough stop against a communications array. The ramp began to descend.

"Sir," hollered Admiral Griss. "They're invading our ship; they've landed a troop carrier!"

"Jam their speeders!" Pryde commanded.

"I can't, sir," said his comm officer, even as his fingers flew across the console, trying everything he could think of. He looked up at Pryde, confusion writ on his face. "They're . . . not using speeders?"

Finn and Jannah led the cavalry charge of nearly two dozen orbak riders down the ramp of the lander and onto the hull of the *Steadfast.* The orbaks had been cooped up for hours, and they ran with joyful abandon, eating up distance at a dizzying speed.

BB-8 kept pace, rolling so fast his markings were a blur, head canted forward with determination.

"Doing great, buddy!" Finn called down to him.

He tossed a quick glance over his shoulder to check on his team. Behind Jannah's company of riders came the rest of his friends, pouring from the lander on foot: Rose, Connix, Beaumont—anyone who could hold a blaster. So far, so good.

Ahead of them, a Sith troop carrier landed and spit out dozens of crimson-clad troopers. They spread out in formation and began firing.

Finn's rear team fired back, providing them some cover. One stormtrooper went down right away—Connix, no doubt, who was a crack shot.

He reached into the munitions bag hanging from the saddle. Homemade explosives, cobbled together with what the company could find on Kef Bir, but effective nonetheless. Finn sighted a squad of troopers, took aim, and tossed the bomb, allowing it to arc just as Jannah had taught him.

It exploded into fire and black dust, knocking several stormtroopers backward.

"One lesson!" Finn shouted to Jannah. "Did you see that?"

"You had a great teacher!" she hollered back.

They were almost to their destination. Finn and Jannah grabbed their bags of explosives, jumped from their orbaks, and sprinted along the hull. BB-8 kept pace at their heels.

Another Final Order troop lander touched down on the surface nearby. The ramp descended and out poured a company of crimson stormtroopers, who immediately began firing. Several of them engaged red jetpacks, which lifted them into the air so they could fire from a superior vantage.

Finn was *really* tired of jet troopers. He fired back, most of his shots going wide, as he and Jannah pressed forward. They had to make this happen fast. More trooper carriers would come. They would be overwhelmed in minutes.

Or worse, the ship would simply leave atmo, instantly killing them all. The orbak riders deployed around them and aimed a barrage of covering fire at the jet troopers.

Finn and Jannah reached the nav deck. Ahead was a bunkerlike structure, built out from the hull to prevent interference from interior ship frequencies.

"This is it," Finn yelled.

"Beebee-Ate, do your thing!" said Jannah, whipping up her makeshift bow.

The little droid extended a pilex driver and unscrewed a panel. Finn began placing explosives as Jannah fired shot after shot with her bow and arrow, covering them. One shot hit a jet trooper, who spun up into the air, missiled into an oncoming TIE, and sent it crashing onto the Destroyer's surface.

"Almost there," Finn said, working as fast as he could.

The Emperor said, "The time has come!"

As one, thousands of disciples fell to their knees, chanting something in a language Rey had never heard.

Palpatine's eyes widened with zeal. "With your anger, you will take my life, and you will ascend. As I did, when I killed my master, Darth Plagueis." He grinned, showing gray teeth and oozing red gums. "Now. Raise your saber and strike me down."

Rey frowned. Luke had warned her about this. "All you want is for me to hate. But I won't. Not even you."

"Weak! Like your parents."

She shook her head. "My parents were strong. They saved me from you."

As if reading her thoughts about Luke, the Emperor said, "I've made this very proposal before. But on that unfortunate day Luke Skywalker had his father to save him. You do not."

The cavernous room shook. Light poured down as a vast stone ceiling opened, revealing Star Destroyers silhouetted against a furious sky. The Resistance fighters were gnats in comparison, darting in and out, dodging fire from monstrous cannons and Final Order TIEs. Explosions lit up the sky. Her friends were dying.

"They don't have long. And you are the one who led them here," the Emperor pointed out.

Tears filled her eyes. The Resistance fighters were losing badly. The Emperor was manipulating her, yes, but he was doing it with the truth. This was her fault.

"Strike me down. Take the throne as Empress. Reign over the new Empire and the fleet will be yours to do as you wish. Only you have the power to save them all. Refuse and your new family dies."

The thought swelled in her head, until she was giddy with it. *Empress.* Would that be so bad? Maybe taking on this mantle would be worth it. To bring peace. To save her friends. The whole galaxy would have *no choice* but to be saved.

Rey stared, agonized, at the battle above her.

"Very well," Palpatine said. "Finish them."

"Wait!" she said. "Wait."

He paused, thinking she was nearly his. But a presence was making itself known to her, even through the cloud of evil and rage and terror. She gazed off into the distance for a moment, probing, all the while shielding her thoughts.

Kylo Ren had given her lots of practice at shielding her thoughts.

She turned back to the Emperor, filling her mind with thoughts of surrender. With resignation.

Her grandfather smiled indulgently. "Good," he said. "It is time for a scavenger to rise as an empress. Strike me down and pledge yourself as a Sith."

It had taken Ben Solo too long to climb through the ruins of the Death Star in search of a hangar bay, even longer to find an old scout-class TIE and coax it into flying for him. He'd then followed Rey's transmitted tracking markers toward Exegol, but the scout's barely functioning navicomputers had taken a wrong turn, and he'd found himself grinding through unknown rough space. It had taken all his concentration to correct his course and get back on track.

All that had been the easy part.

He landed his TIE scout beside an old Rebellion X-wing. He couldn't help pausing to stare at the two ships. Old enemies, parked side by side.

Something tingled at the base of his skull, a familiar awareness . . . Rey! She sensed him. She understood that he was Ben again. He caught a wave of relief from her, of joy. Then, abruptly, nothing.

She was in trouble.

He was unencumbered by helmet or cape, and he sprinted for the monolith, ducked beneath it, launched himself into the shaft. Nothing would stop him from reaching her.

He caught himself on one of the massive chains dangling from the ceiling and looked down. The floor was so far below him that it was lost in shadow. Too far to climb down quickly, probably too far to jump down safely.

Probably.

Rey had healed him. He had accepted his father's forgiveness. He might even forgive himself someday.

He would find the strength to make everything right, no matter what.

Ben Solo called on the Force, and dropped.

# CHAPTER 17

Finn was not so caught up in rigging the nav bunker to explode that he did not notice how, one by one, the Star Destroyer thrusters began to glow bright blue.

"Those thrusters are hot!" said Poe over the comm. "Finn, how we doin'?"

*Almost there . . . Just one more bit of putty . . .*

Finn gave Jannah the signal, and they both ducked, hands over their heads, as Finn triggered the explosion.

*Boom!* His ears rang with the blast, and pressure hit his back. Lights across the surface of the Destroyer went dark.

"Navigation beacon's shut down," a technician yelled. "Repeat, navigation beacon down. Final Order fleet, hold position. No deployment! Resetting all systems!"

Now Pryde was angry. These gnats were proving unexpectedly vexing.

The Star Destroyers all powered back down to standby mode. They were vulnerable now, but only for a few minutes. Their hulls were strong; the gnats' mission was futile.

The *Steadfast* would have to reset its nav systems to regain comms, but it wouldn't take long. The gnats had bought themselves so little time, he couldn't see why they'd bothered.

Allegiant General Pryde was going to enjoy destroying the last remnant of the Resistance.

R2-D2 beeped in celebration as engine lights dimmed all across the fleet.

"Nav beacon's down!" Poe yelled. "They did it!" He swooped toward the *Steadfast,* catching a glimpse of Finn and Jannah racing toward their orbak mounts, BB-8 at their heels.

"You got three minutes," Finn said, "until the command ship resets the nav and the fleet can escape."

"Still no *Falcon* or backup," came Snap Wexley's voice.

R2 beeped a question to Poe. Off comm, he answered, "I don't know, Artoo. Maybe they didn't find any allies. Maybe nobody's coming."

He stared out at the fleet, his own words echoing in his head. *Maybe nobody's coming . . .*

What would Leia do?

He turned his comm back on and said, "We gotta hit them ourselves."

"What can we do against those things?" Tyce asked.

"Whatever we can! Be fast, be precise, hit those cannons. You with me?"

"We're with you," Tyce responded without hesitation.

"Right behind you, General," said Snap.

Poe started flicking switches. "All wings, arm torpedoes! Attack formation!" He paused. Took a deep breath. "May the Force be with us."

Led by Poe, their tiny squadron phalanxed toward a stalled Destroyer, firing on its vulnerable underbelly cannons. The hull lit up with explosions.

---

Finn, Jannah, and BB-8 raced after the orbak company toward the lander. Blasterfire erupted all around them. But Finn came to a halt, realizing that every shot aimed at them was coming from a blaster. The deck cannons had gone silent with the reset.

BB-8 kept rolling after the orbaks, but Jannah turned. "Finn! Let's go!"

"The surface cannons stopped," he said. "They're resetting their systems."

"So?" She looked toward the lander, back at Finn.

"So before they do . . ." Finn stared at the cannon. This had to be the worst idea he'd ever had. "Maybe we can do some shifty stuff." Yep, definitely the worst. He turned back to Jannah and said, "Jannah, go. I gotta do something."

"No. I'm staying with you."

He'd learned better than to argue with a determined woman. He nodded his thanks, and together they sprinted for the cannon.

Framed by the *Steadfast*'s viewport window, the designated advance Destroyer *Derriphan* turned into a ball of fire as a trio of A-wings swooped out of range of the blast they'd created.

Pryde grimaced. There were bound to be casualties, and the *Derriphan* had been commanded by a mediocre captain with no real potential—that ship had been designated expendable after all. But he hated for the gnats to claim any sort of victory.

"How much longer?" Pryde demanded.

"Ships coming back online in just a few seconds," said a technician.

"Then reset the navigation signal!" he commanded. "I want the fleet *deployed*!"

Finn and Jannah arrived at the cannon, began circling cautiously, like it was a wounded animal, ready to attack.

"This is the command ship," Jannah said. "We take it out now, the whole nav system goes down for good."

"Every Star Destroyer in this fleet!" Finn said.

"All of them without shields! This could end them."

"Finn!" came Rose's voice on comm just as he began climbing up the cannon.

"Rose!" he said. He hoped she and the rest of the ground team were safely back on the lander.

"Lander's leaving," Rose said. "Where are you? What are you doing?"

He reached the massive gun barrel. Finn said, "I'm saving what I love."

A long pause. Jannah whipped up her bow to take out a jet trooper winging their way, then pivoted quickly and did the same to a ground trooper.

"Go without us," Finn urged. "We're taking this whole ship down."

Rose finally found her voice. ". . . What? How?"

"You'll see from the lander. Rose, *please.* Go. And . . . take care of yourself."

"The ritual begins!" the Emperor cried out, and the mass of followers surrounding them responded with a ceremonial chant so loud and deep it shook the very ground. "She will strike me down, and pledge herself as a Sith."

The lightning in the cavernous cathedral intensified, reflected against her grandfather's milk-blind eyes. She took one step forward. Another.

Thoughts shielded from the Emperor, she sent out her awareness, searching. *There!*

She just had to stall a little bit longer.

---

The robed figures had not bothered Ben at all when he was here last, but this time they launched themselves at him with fury. He blasted them easily, one shot for every kill. Not long ago, he would have taken pleasure in this, but now he had only one consuming desire: *Help Rey.*

He reached the end of the Sith monoliths and rounded a corner. Familiar figures manifested in the flashing dark. First Vicrul and his scythe. Then Kiruk and his plasma blaster. And suddenly all six were arrayed before him. His Knights.

For the briefest moment, Ben actually thought they'd come to help.

But hate rolled off them in waves like fetid air. The Knights of Ren had never been his. They had belonged to the Emperor all along.

A final betrayal.

Snoke had been nothing more than a pawn. The Emperor had whispered poison to Ben his whole life. Now even the Knights, those whom he thought his faithful brothers, were raising their weapons for the kill.

They surrounded him slowly, like predators stalking their prey. He could take two or three at a time, but these were his very own. He'd trained with them. They could even touch the Force in a small way. He didn't stand a chance against all of them at once, not armed with just a blaster.

Maybe it had been premature to throw his lightsaber into the sea.

An image lit up his mind, another lightsaber, flashing blue. It was a message from Rey.

"She will draw her weapon," the Emperor intoned.

Rey made her face blank. She unhooked Luke's lightsaber and ignited it.

"She will come to me!" he said, and the crowd responded with a collective yell.

Rey stepped closer still. Her grandfather smelled like rotting meat.

Ben blasted one attacker, thrusted away another with the Force, spun to face a third . . .

. . . as something cracked the back of his skull, sending him to his knees.

Another blow crushed his abdomen, robbing him of air, and he bent over gasping.

The Knights, in their supreme arrogance, backed away, allowed Ben to gain his feet. He seemed defenseless to them. They must have never really respected him, or even his abilities, to give him ground now.

Ben sucked in air as they circled for another attack.

"She will take her revenge," Palpatine boomed.

Rey continued to approach. His power was intoxicating. She found herself raising her weapon, almost against her will. If not for the other presence in her mind, bright and shining with *light,* she would not have been able to resist him.

"And with the stroke of her saber, the Sith are reborn! The Jedi are dead!"

Wave after wave of triumph emanated from him, and along with it came knowledge, memories. Maybe it was their shared blood that enabled her to see his thoughts, but somehow she could, and Rey saw it then, how he'd done it, what he was about to do again:

*Falling . . .*

*falling . . .*

*falling . . . down a massive shaft, the betrayal sharp and stinging, a figure high above, black clad and helmeted and shrinking fast. His very own apprentice had turned against him, the way he himself had turned against Plagueis . . . whose secret to immortality he had stolen.*

*Plagueis had not acted fast enough in his own moment of death. But Sidious, sensing the flickering light in his apprentice, had been ready for years. So the falling, dying Emperor called on all the dark power of the Force to thrust his consciousness far, far away, to a secret place he had been preparing. His body was dead, an empty vessel, long before it found the bottom of the shaft, and his mind jolted to new awareness in a new body—a painful one, a temporary one.*

*It was too soon. The secret place had not completed its preparations. The transfer was imperfect, and the cloned body wasn't enough. Perhaps Plagueis was having the last laugh after all. Maybe his secret remained secret. Because Palpatine was trapped in a broken, dying form.*

*The heretics of the Sith Eternal toiled, splicing genes, bolstering tissue, creating unnatural abominations in the hope that one of these strandcasts would succeed and become a worthy receptacle. The heretics would do anything, risk anything, sacrifice anything, to create a cradle for their god-consciousness.*

*Nothing worked. But their efforts were not entirely in vain.*

*One genetic strandcast lived. Thrived, even. A not-quite-identical clone. His "son." But he was a useless, powerless failure. Palpatine could not even bear to look upon such disappointing ordinariness.*

*The boy's only worth would lay in continuing the bloodline through more natural methods.*

*And it was through that eventual union, unexpected as it was, that Rey was born. The perfect vessel. Strong enough to contain all the power of the Sith. His granddaughter . . .*

The vision shifted. It was Luke, sitting crosslegged on the island of Ahch-To, trembling with effort as he projected himself onto the battlefield of Crait.

And yet another flash, this time of Leia in her jungle quarters, giving everything she had to send a final thought to Ben.

They were all manifestations of the same power. And now Rey would use it in her own way.

She lifted her saber as if to strike—

—and reached for the connection she shared with Ben. Showed him.

He acknowledged her, and Rey's lips parted in surprise. It felt different now. The connection was . . . right. Good. Like coming home.

Ben was similarly stunned, and together, they wasted a precious moment reveling in this new sharing. This is how it should have been all along. A true dyad.

The Emperor and Snoke had robbed them of this.

"Do it!" Palpatine screamed. "Make the sacrifice!"

Rey lowered the lightsaber behind her back, as if readying for a massive blow. She reached for the Force. The effort made tears sting in her eyes.

The Emperor leaned forward with gleeful anticipation.

She raised her hand . . . which was now empty. She had projected her weapon away.

Rey watched her grandfather's dawning horror as he finally realized his mistake, allowing Rey and Ben to come together. Their bond—refined in the fire of mutual searching, shared grief, rage and hate, but also of compassion and empathy—was the one thing he had not foreseen.

The moment Ben felt the grip of Luke's lightsaber in his palm, he knew it belonged to him, an extension of his very own self. He raised it slowly, relishing the feel of it.

The Knights startled backward a few steps.

*Surprise,* he imagined his father saying.

He attacked.

Rey grabbed Leia's lightsaber from where she had hooked it to her belt, behind her back. Ignited it.

Suddenly, she was surrounded by the crimson-clad guards. They raised their blasters and fired. She deflected one blast with her hand, sent it careening into the abdomen of one of the guards, while whipping her lightsaber around to block the rest.

She drew on Ben's strength, and he drew on hers, and just like before, they were separate but also together, Rey battling guards, Ben battling the Knights.

*Behind you,* she warned, and he brought up his saber to block his back, whirled, impaled Trudgen, flipped over his falling body, spun, and did the same to Ushar.

He stared at the bodies of his fallen former comrades. Then he sprinted for the throne room—

—as Rey used the Force to collapse a guard under his own weight, and then throw him back into the darkness. She deflected another blaster bolt, dodged another. She spun to face the final guard, but Ben got there first and tossed him aside like a piece of garbage.

They stood facing each other for the space of one breath, two . . . together at last. Ben was different. Relaxed. Unguarded. How had Rey not noticed before that he had the long face and posture of his father, the warm brown eyes of his mother?

As one, they turned to face Palpatine, dropped into fighting stances, raised their lightsabers.

The Emperor snarled. "Stand together, die together," he said. Then he raised his rotting hand and impaled them with the Force.

Their backs arched against their wills, and the pain was breathtaking. Their lightsabers dropped from their hands and clattered to the ground.

The Emperor yanked them toward himself, and they slid across the floor, helpless against his power, as he took, and took, and took.

The Emperor gasped. Stared at his hands, which had begun knitting themselves back together, bones regrowing, pale flesh closing over them. "The life-force of your bond," he said, his voice tinged with wonder. "A dyad in the Force!"

His gleeful triumphant thoughts washed over Rey, as she struggled against his grip, unable to move. He had won. At last. All those years, all that searching. He'd tried to create a dyad with Anakin, as his master had tried to create one with him. The Rule of Two, a Master always in desperate search of a yet more powerful apprentice, was a pale imitation, an unworthy but necessary successor to the older, purer doctrine of the Dyad.

"Unseen for generations," he crowed. "And now the power of two restores the one true Emperor!"

He raised his perfect, healed hands, and called on all the dark power of the Force and the Sith who had come before him, and pulled their life from their very bodies. It poured from them like a river of light, leaving them weaker and weaker.

The Emperor laughed as his body strengthened, became whole. The milky film faded from his eyes, revealing golden irises around obsidian pupils.

"This is it!" Snap Wexley called from inside his X-wing. He fired, and felt a surge of exhultation when the belly cannon lit up like a fireworks display. He'd gotten pretty good at this. All those lessons with his stepfather, Wedge, had paid off.

Snap's console beeped.

"Fleet's locking onto a navigation signal," he warned anyone who was listening. "They're gonna split!"

"Watch your starboard, Wexley," yelled Vanik.

He looked over. "Yeah, I see 'em."

But he didn't see the other TIE, the one that came out of nowhere.

"Snap!" Poe yelled. "Snap, *Snap!*"

A blast rocked his cockpit, and he heard Poe yell, "No!"

He had just enough time to reach down for the tiny holo he kept on his dash, whisper, "Karé," before everything exploded with unbearable light.

Poe stared in despair as the wreckage of Wexley's ship peppered down against the Destroyer's hull.

Cries of terror and despair were lighting up his comm. They were getting torn apart.

"General!" Tyce called. "Do we retreat?"

"What now?" Someone called.

"What's our next move?"

His people—his friends—were dying all around him. "My friends," Poe said, his voice tremulous. "I'm sorry. I felt we had . . . a shot . . . There's just too many of them." He'd learned nothing from Crait. Instead, he'd just gotten people killed ag—

A familiar voice broke through on comms: "But there are more of us, Poe. There are more of *us*."

It was Lando. He was back! But had he brought anyone with him?

Poe's heart leapt in his chest as he flipped his fighter around, swooped over the hull of a Destroyer to get a visual on the atmosphere above.

He gasped. Ships were popping into sight all over the place. Freighters, fighters, medical frigates, longhaulers, from every sector of the galaxy, from every era Poe had ever heard of. Hundreds. No, thousands. A fleet of fleets.

"Look at this!" Poe hollered, *"Look at this!"* as Lando laughed and laughed.

"The allies," Aftab Ackbar said. "They're here!"

"The whole galaxy's here!" Poe exclaimed.

"Lando, you did it," Finn yelled. "You did it!"

The comms erupted, as ship after ship began calling in. Thousands of resolved voices, crying out, refusing to be silenced.

"*Millennium Falcon,* standing by for orders," said Lando.

"Mon Calamari fleet, standing by," came another voice.

"Phantom Squadron, standing by."

"*Ghost,* standing by."

"*Anodyne Two,* standing by."

Poe was not the crying type, but as everyone called in, one after another after another, liquid pooled in his eyes. They had done it. The spark of the Resistance had become a fire.

"Alphabet Two, standing by."

"Zay Versio with Inferno Squad, standing by. Look at all these ships!"

"*Fireball,* here. Hi, everyone!"

"Cut the chatter, Kaz," a deep voice responded.

"Okay, okay!" Poe interrupted, because they had no time for a hundred thousand ships to call in! "Just . . . go shoot stuff! Uh, I mean, hit those underbelly cannons with all you've got. Every one we knock out is a world saved."

Lando whooped as he and Chewie charged ahead, and a thousand fighters, frigates, and even well-armed freighters swooped after them.

Within seconds, the *Millennium Falcon* had taken out a cannon. That ship made everything look easy.

"Nice flying, Lando," came Wedge Antilles's voice, and Poe realized the old Rebellion captain, and his former flight instructor, was operating one of the *Falcon*'s turret stations.

He wished Leia could be here to see this.

Finn threw his fist into the air. I knew Lando would do it. I knew it!"

Jannah was gaping at the sky, forgetting for a moment that she was supposed to be laying cover fire.

"Finger to trigger, Chewie," came Lando's voice on the comm.

People had come from everywhere to help them. The whole galaxy was here. Finn watched as they swooped among the Destroyers, laying waste to the hapless ships.

He shook off the moment of triumph with effort.

Jannah resumed firing, while Finn got back to work on his shifty stuff.

For this, Pryde had no backup plan.

"Where did they get all these fighter craft?" Allegiant General Pryde demanded. "They have no navy."

Admiral Griss was gaping. The light had gone out of his eyes. "It's not a navy, sir," the admiral said, and his voice shook a little. "It's just . . . people."

The tide was turning. Poe's patchwork navy pummeled the defenseless fleet. One Destroyer listed sideways, smoke rising from its hull. It collided with another, and both dropped to the surface, helpless in Exegol's gravity. Another dropped after a pair of proton torpedoes hit it in the gut. Soon Destroyers were falling away all over the place.

But the TIEs remained viciously relentless, and they were still targeting Poe specifically.

One threatened him head-on, but he was hemmed in between hulls. He gunned the accelerator, firing. Poe wasn't sure if he'd destroy it in time, or if he should wing away . . .

A Y-wing slipped into the assist position beside him—a precision move. Together they gunned the TIE, which exploded into a satisfying fireball.

"So long, sky trash!" came a familiar female voice.

He turned in his cockpit as the Y-wing screamed past. "Who's that flier?" he muttered.

"Take a guess, spice runner."

It *was* Zorii!

Poe's relief was so huge he almost choked on it. "Zorii, you made it!"

Someone warbled at him in Anzellan, then added, "Hey, heyyyyy!"

"Babu?" Poe said, disbelieving.

This day just kept getting better and better.

Rey and Ben lay collapsed on the floor as Emperor Palpatine released himself from the Ommin harness and drifted down. He stood straight and strong now. Invincible.

The Emperor raised his voice to the throng. "Look what you

have made," he said. Their chanted response was thunderous, and he stood, hands slightly raised, as if absorbing their worship as power.

Ben forced his near-lifeless body over onto his hands and knees. Rey remained limp beside him as he struggled to his feet and faced his enemy.

The Emperor was not impressed. "As once I fell, so falls the last Skywalker."

He lifted Ben with no more than a thought, thrust him away with such force that he tumbled end over end through the length of the cathedral, then disappeared into a flashing abyss.

Rey would have screamed, but she could barely draw breath.

"Do not fear their feeble attack, my faithful!" the Emperor said, Ben already forgotten. His lips spread apart into a nightmarish grin, and he lifted his face to Exegol's sky. "Nothing will stop the return of the Sith!"

He raised his hands as though reaching toward the battle overhead. Even through her haze of weakness and exhaustion, Rey could sense him draw on the Force. The Emperor's power was staggering now. No, *their* power. Hers and Ben's.

Tears streamed down her face as he used their stolen power to create a conduit of Force lightning. Writhing, crooked tendrils of light shot from his fingers, coalesced into a thick stream of light that burst into the sky, flooding the Resistance ships. They sparked helplessly against the onslaught, tilting on their axis.

# CHAPTER 18

Poe watched in horror as raw power shot up from the planet like a massive geyser, devouring everything in its path. Several fighters were suddenly adrift, their controls no longer responding. The *Tantive IV* trembled, as if fighting a tractor beam. It listed to the side, began to drop.

Poe wanted to look away. *Leia's ship* . . . he clenched his jaw and stared anyway. He would bear witness to this.

The trembling intensified. One of the engines detonated. Explosions spread out along the hull, and suddenly the *Tantive IV* was dropping like a meteor, past the Final Order fleet and out of sight.

Poe had just lost a lot of friends. He'd known Nien Numb his whole life.

Suddenly, the console of his own fighter was sparking, shocking his hand even through his flight gloves. "Artoo, my systems are failing . . ."

From the droid socket of his X-wing came the sound of an astromech screaming.

Poe punched his comm. "Does *anyone* copy?"

No response. Beside him, a sleek Nubian yacht trembled in the throes of wicked lightning, then dropped out of view.

---

The Emperor would not stop laughing as he took his throne, light still shooting upward from his fingertips. Rey hated the sound—grating, smug, oddly familiar. She was near death; she knew it with certainty. She didn't want his laugh to be the last thing she heard.

She could hardly move, but she managed to roll over onto her back. Her vision blackened with the effort.

She reached for Ben—nothing. Their connection had weakened when the Emperor stole their life-force. She'd vaguely sensed Ben falling, but it was like he'd fallen out of existence itself, leaving her carved out and broken.

Rey's limbs refused any order to move, much less stand, so she stared at the battle above. Not that it was a battle anymore. Explosions peppered the sky. Black debris rained down everywhere, trailing smoke and fire. The *Tantive IV* listed, then plummeted.

She had failed so utterly.

The Emperor's power was beautiful to behold, reaching ever higher, spreading out like a flower of light. In a way, she and Ben had made that. But the Emperor was using it for unspeakable evil. And now she was helpless. Dying.

*What would Leia do?*

The answer came to her gently, like a soft morning breeze.

She had to give. She had to give *everything.*

Rey remembered her training, and she reached into the Force. Steadied her mind. "Be with me," she whispered.

Her true power would always come from *oneness.*

"Be with me. Be with me."

The battle above disappeared. Instead, Rey saw a perfect sky, vast with stars. Peaceful. Light-filled. It was like she was staring through a window to somewhere else, a place between places.

"Be with me."

Her body relaxed. She embraced peace and calm, the way Leia had taught her.

Through the calm, came a voice. *These are your final steps, Rey. Rise and take them.*

Then others joined.

*Rey,*

*Rey,*

*Rey.*

She didn't recognize them all, but somehow, she *knew* them the moment they made themselves known to her. They'd been with her all along; she just needed to learn how to hear them. Like Leia had promised.

More voices came at her fast but gentle, as though she lay at a confluence of the Force, possibilities, futures and pasts all stretching away from her, or maybe leading toward her. The cosmos, time, energy, *being*—nothing was the way she'd thought it was.

*Bring back the balance, Rey.*

*In the night, find the light, Rey.*

Presences filled her awareness, some recent, some ancient, some still anchored to the living in a strange way. Rey didn't understand. But she accepted.

*Alone, never have you been.*

*Every Jedi who ever lived, lives in you.*

*The Force surrounds you.*

*Let it guide you.*

*As it guided us.*

Palpatine had wanted Rey for himself. But she chose to be *their* conduit. *Their* vessel. She was a *Jedi.*

Rey moved an arm. Then a shoulder. She let the voices surround her, fill her, strengthen her. She turned over, placed a palm to the ground, pushed up.

*We stand behind you.*

*Rise in the Force.*

She got a knee beneath her, leveraged herself up onto her toes. Rey paused, crouched, gasping for air. Her muscles didn't want to obey. Every movement turned her very bones to knives of pain.

*In the heart of a Jedi lies her strength!*

The voices were becoming louder, even more powerful.

*Rise.*

*Rise!*

Luke's voice became deep and insistent, rising above all the others. A well of power from which to draw: "Rey, the Force will be with you. Always."

She rose. Summoned Luke's lightsaber, which skidded across the stone and smacked into her hand. The blade ignited, and Rey stood, full of strength freely *given* to her by those who had come before.

The Emperor gasped. The avalanche of light from his fingertips ceased.

He rose from his throne and stepped forward. His eyes glowed with lingering power. "Let your death be the final word in the story of rebellion." Palpatine reached with his arms, sent Force lightning zagging toward her.

She whipped up her lightsaber and blocked it. The impact nearly knocked her from her feet, but she reached for the Force, and stood her ground.

His attack intensified. "You are nothing!" he yelled. "A scavenger girl is no match for the power in me. I am all the Sith!"

Her wrist felt like it was going to break. But it wouldn't. Not today.

"And I," she said, reaching for more strength, for Leia's lightsaber. It clicked into her hand. "I am all the Jedi."

She brought the second lightsaber to bear, crossing its blade with the first, creating an impenetrable shield.

Rey stepped forward, pushing back against his onslaught. Then again. Every step was anguish. It was taking everything the Jedi had given her, everything she had.

The lightning began to feed back on the Emperor. It ravaged his face, and he tossed back his head in agony, and in denial of what was happening. Rey pursued mercilessly, one foot in front of the other, absorbing power from the Force. Finally, she was ready. She gathered her strength, her faith in the Jedi past, her love of her friends, and she thrust it all at the Emperor.

He staggered backward, his own power reflected against him. It devoured him completely, ripping away his newly healed fingers, searing away the skin of his face, his very bones, until he disintegrated.

And like collapsing stardust, what remained of him coalesced into a single point, which then exploded with a massive shock wave that threw Rey to the ground. The Sith throne shattered. The ceiling bouldered down around her, crushing thousands of disciples in the amphitheater.

Poe's nav screen cleared suddenly. He looked around. The strange power coming from the planet's surface had stopped. Or maybe only paused. Whatever. It was time to work.

"We're back on!" he yelled. "This is our last chance. We've got to hit those cannons now!"

He winged toward a Destroyer, aiming for the belly cannon. Thousands of ships corrected, some even lurched out of free fall, as everyone brought their weapons to bear.

They all understood what he did: the impasse might be temporary. They might have only seconds to act.

The red jetpack troopers were not letting up. Jannah was doing a great job of keeping them off his back, but Finn couldn't help getting distracted. *Focus, Finn.* Rey or Rose would have had this thing rewired in half the time.

One more splice . . . there. "Okay, we're hot!" he yelled to Jannah. He jumped down from the cannon, yanking a handful of wires with him. He was *almost sure* he had the right ones.

He handed two of them to Jannah. He would aim; she would fire.

Finn touched his wires together, and the giant cannon barrel swiveled until it was pointed directly at the deck.

He looked up at Jannah one more time. This was it. They weren't coming back from this one. "Never another kid," he said.

"Not even one," she agreed.

And with that, she touched her wires together. They sparked, and a split second later the cannon fired a massive pulse blast. Finn and Jannah waited, breathed. Had it worked? Maybe Finn should have aimed for a different—

The hull came apart beneath them.

Pryde wasted the few precious seconds he might have had to reach an escape pod in frozen disbelief. The floor of the bridge shuddered as though urging him to run. And he did, finally, only to discover that the corridor leading away from the bridge was buckled and impassable.

Admiral Griss met him at the door that led nowhere. They exchanged a panicked look as an officer rushed toward them. "Comms are down everywhere!" he said.

"There are attacks on Destroyers in all occupied systems," said another bridge officer. "Overwhelming numbers of small craft!"

This wasn't happening. It wasn't possible. His Emperor had foreseen everything.

The floor began to slant sideways. Several explosions drew Pryde's gaze to the viewport. He dashed forward, as though getting a better look might present him with a solution.

The hull of the *Steadfast* was dangerously tipped, and the Resistance ships were recovering from the strange energy that had held many of them in its grip. It seemed as though all was lost. For the first time, Pryde considered that maybe the Emperor would *not* restore the glory of the former Empire.

He let that possibility wash through him, absorbed it, examined it. He was forced to conclude that he didn't care. It didn't matter to him one bit.

In his last moment, Allegiant General Pryde finally understood that the return of Emperor Palpatine was meaningless if he were not alive to see it. All his efforts, his sacrifices had *not* been worth it.

The bridge exploded. Pryde fell.

---

Finn and Jannah clung to the hull together, ducking as flaming debris from the bridge tumbled past them. They couldn't hold on much longer. They'd lose their grip and missile to the planet's surface—if the *Steadfast* didn't come apart first.

He looked to Jannah. He was so glad they'd found each other. Two former stormtroopers, together and doing the right thing in the end. "You know what?" he yelled over the sounds of destruction.

A smile like the sun broke out on her face. "I'm not sorry, either!" she hollered.

The ship jolted. Pieces of the hull broke away, and suddenly they were sliding down the length of the Destroyer. How long could you slide down a ship this size before finding open air? A couple minutes, maybe.

As Finn slid, he held Jannah and *breathed.* He had no regrets. It had been worth it.

Someone tried to patch through to Poe from below, and he flipped his frequency to take the comm.

"Finn didn't board the lander," came Rose's voice.

"What?"

"They're still on the command ship!"

All his relief at getting the fleet back online ebbed away. He could not lose Finn. He *would not.* He peeled his X-wing away from the attack and dove for the *Steadfast.* The command ship was now pointed tip-downward, ready to spear the planet's surface.

His buddy had done that.

Scanners were near-useless in this atmosphere, so he could only do visual sweeps. There was a good chance the bridge explosion had taken Finn with it. But Poe wouldn't give up, not until he had to. He'd just lost the *Tantive IV* and everyone on it. He needed to save as many of his people as he could.

He buzzed by a comm tower, now thrusting parallel to the

ground, and he almost missed the two figures huddling together on top of it.

"I see them!" he said. "I'll double back."

"You won't make it," Tyce warned.

"Trust me, I'm fast!" he insisted, already turning his fighter around.

"Not as fast as this ship," came Lando's voice. "Hold on, Chewie!"

The *Falcon* meteored toward the Star Destroyer, then angled to come up from below.

Finn almost lost his grip when he saw the *Falcon*'s hull rise below him.

"Jannah!" he yelled, surging with hope.

"I know!"

They would have to time this just right. They'd have a few steps of running room along the side of the comm tower, and then nothing but air.

They gripped hands. Not just yet . . . Now! They took off running as Lando guided the hull closer. With all their might, they leapt . . . just as the *Steadfast* finally succumbed to gravity and dropped toward oblivion.

They landed hard on the *Falcon*'s hull; Finn's ankle twisted. A hatch opened revealing Chewbacca, who waved at them to hurry. They sprinted across the top of the *Falcon,* Finn's ankle screaming with each step, and finally dropped into the hold.

"Chewie, you got the kids?" Lando hollered from the cockpit.

Chewie roared confirmation, and the *Falcon* sped away.

Finn collapsed against the wall. He couldn't believe they'd survived.

The Emperor was no more.

Rey gazed at the tumbled wreckage of the cathedral around her. She couldn't feel her arms and legs. Vaguely, she heard the clink of her lightsabers hitting the ground—when had she let go of them?

She reached for the Force one last time . . . Some of her friends were surely still up there somewhere. She sensed . . . Finn! And . . . Jannah?

Giving absolutely everything was no big deal at all—compared to saving her friends.

She reached for Ben too, but her legs gave out, and she crumpled to the ground.

Finn was running for the *Falcon*'s turret stations, Jannah on his heels.

Something rent his very soul, and he staggered, barely catching himself on the wall of the corrider.

"Rey," he whispered.

She was gone. He had just begun to understand how her presence could weigh so strongly in his mind. He should have told her. He'd meant to.

Now he'd never have the chance.

"Finn?" Jannah prompted, as agonized tears streamed down his cheeks.

Chewbacca asked what was wrong.

But Finn's breath had left him completely, and he couldn't respond.

Ben's fall had been caught on a jagged outcropping. His ankle was twisted, and he was pretty sure he'd broken at least two ribs. But he *had* to get back to the throne room.

Because he couldn't sense Rey at all.

The climb up was agonizing. Each time he reached for a handhold, a hot knife of pain stabbed his left side. Dizziness threatened to send him tumbling back into the abyss, but he kept on, one hand over the other, until finally his fingers grasped the top.

He hauled himself over the side. Paused a moment to catch his breath. Dragged himself to his feet.

Ben made it only a few steps before he crumpled, forced himself to his feet yet again, limped forward.

He could see her now, collapsed on the floor, and the pain in his chest was suddenly so much worse than that of a couple of broken ribs.

She seemed at ease, almost as though she were sleeping, except her eyes were wide and staring, lifeless and dull.

He hardly knew what he was doing as he crouched beside her, wrapped his arms around her limp form, yanked her onto his lap. Rey's skin was growing cold. Her barren eyes stared up at him, and he imagined them accusing him. *You* did this. This is *your* fault.

No, Rey would never be that way. Those thoughts were the vestiges of Snoke's conditioning. Rey was good. Kind. No matter what had happened between them, what he'd done, she'd always showed him compassion.

He cast his gaze around the ruined cathedral, as if answers might lie in the shadows. But there was nothing. Just aching emptiness and a sense of loss so sharp and terrible it was like a vise around his gut.

Ben pulled her against his chest and hugged her to himself for a moment. He'd just found her, *really* found her. He'd wasted his life, he knew that now. But anyone who could have shown him the way forward, helped him be Ben again, was gone. Luke. His parents. And now Rey.

He couldn't make himself believe it. Rey was the strongest person he'd ever known. She'd fought off the darkness in a way he never could. She'd saved everyone. She deserved better.

As he held her, he sensed something. The tiniest spark. And he realized: The Force hadn't taken her yet.

He knew exactly what Rey would do, in his place. It was the easiest decision he'd ever made.

He cradled her gently and placed his hand on her abdomen. He closed his eyes. Called on the Force. Ben didn't have much strength left, and he was about to do something he'd never done before. Fortunately, Rey had shown him how to give.

Ben poured everything into her. He found reservoirs he didn't know he had. He gave her his whole self.

Her diaphragm rose with a breath, and her warm hand covered his. Her eyes lit up.

Rey seemed surprised to see him. She sat up, but she didn't draw away.

They stared at each other a moment. He waited for her to understand what had just happened. It would be okay if she left him behind now. Got on with her life without a backward glance at him. It's what she *should* do.

Instead she smiled, and she whispered, "Ben!"

She was *glad* to see him. Glad to be with him in this moment. It was the greatest gift she could have given him.

His heart was full as Rey reached for his face, let her fingers linger against his cheek. And then, wonder of wonders, she leaned forward and kissed him. A kiss of gratitude, acknowledgement of their connection, celebration that they'd found each other at last.

But then she drew back, concern on her face. She could feel him growing cold.

Ben smiled at her.

He had given Rey back to the galaxy. It wouldn't atone for the darkness he'd wrought, but it was what he could do.

Ben Solo had no regrets as he collapsed to the ground. The Force reached for him in welcome. His final awareness was of Rey, clasping his hand with her own.

Rey stood over the place Ben had fallen, staring down at his empty tunic. Tears streamed down her face.

He had sacrificed everything for her.

She did not mourn Kylo Ren. She would never mourn Kylo Ren. But she dearly would have loved the chance to get to know Ben Solo. It felt like half of her was missing, and she supposed it was.

The girl who had felt alone for all those years on Jakku had been part of a dyad the whole time. And just when she'd discovered that precious connection, that incredible oneness, it was ripped away.

A voice came to her through the Force, clear and strong. *I will always be with you,* Ben said.

She smiled. Let the truth of it wash over her. "No one's ever really gone," she whispered.

She retrieved her lightsabers and sprinted from the ruined cathedral.

The moment Rey came back to herself, Finn knew.

He launched himself out of the turrent seat—no one was pursuing them anyway—climbed the ladder and sprinted for the cockpit.

"Chewie, I felt her!" he said.

Chewie roared, something about wishful thinking and shouldn't he be back at the turret station watching their backs?

"I'm certain of it," Finn said, scanning the horizon from the viewport. Debris was falling everywhere. Exegol was going to be a wasteland after this. Not that it had been paradise to begin with. But all those Star Destroyers were going to smolder for years.

There was no sign of Rey.

Neither Chewie nor Lando continued to insist that he leave the cockpit, so he stayed, searching, searching, searching . . .

"There!" he yelled pointing to a battered T-65 X-wing. Then he hollered into his wristlink: "Look. Red Five is in the air. Rey's alive!"

"I see her," Poe acknowledged.

Finn didn't think the moment could get any better, but then a transmission beeped on the comms console. Chewie jabbered with excitement.

"People are rising up all over the galaxy, Poe," Finn informed him. "We did it!"

He heard the smile in the pilot's voice as he said, "We did it."

---

C-3PO couldn't take his photoreceptors off the console. His friends were out there, fighting and dying.

The last transmission he'd received from R2-D2 had been to warn them about a strange electrical storm that was making it hard to keep General Poe's X-wing in the air. "Oh, dear," C-3PO said, over and over again.

Then the tide of battle changed. Now, the same reports were coming in from all over.

"Destroyers!" he exclaimed to anyone who might be listening. He waved his arms in celebration. "They're going down! Everywhere!"

Thirty-one years ago, Wicket had stood in this exact spot on Endor's forest moon, rejoicing in the destruction of the Death Star. He'd been such a cub then, his fur still a youthful brown.

Debris had rained down in the sky for a decade afterward, but life on Endor would never go quietly, and the moon fought back with lush verdancy.

Then the First Order had come.

Wicket pointed toward the sky as a chunk of Star Destroyer fell like a fiery comet. "See that?" he said to his tiny son, Pommet, in Ewokese. "Our friends did that."

"Princess Leia?" Pommet asked wide-eyed, for he'd heard all the stories. "See-Threepio?"

Wicket nodded. "See-Threepio," he agreed. He had no doubt the golden, godlike one was responsible for yet another deliverance.

"Come," he said, leading his son back toward the village. "There will be feasting and fireworks tonight."

# CHAPTER 19

Finn jogged down the *Falcon*'s access ramp into the jungle base of Ajan Kloss. Most of their ally ships had returned to their own systems and planets, but a few had decided to follow the surviving Resistance ships home. Their base was going to be fuller and busier than ever.

The troop lander touched down next, and BB-8 rolled down the ramp followed by a jubilant Rose. Finn grinned ear-to-ear to see that his friend was all right.

D-O scream-babbled with happiness when he spotted BB-8. He plunged toward the larger droid and whipped circles around him, barking with welcome. "H-h-happy!" he said.

Everyone was hugging, rejoicing at being alive. Finn passed Beaumont, who clapped him on the shoulder.

Finn caught sight of Poe stepping away from his X-wing and heading toward Zorii. The two stared at each other a long moment, then exchanged a friendly nod.

Then Poe arched a brow, a question in his eyes, but Zorii shook her head no.

Poe smiled and walked away, resigned but happy.

Everyone around them was reuniting: C-3PO greeted R2-D2 as he was craned out of Poe's fighter, Beaumont and Klaud and Connix were sharing a laugh, D'Acy and Tyce hugged and then indulged in a long kiss. Even the orbaks were celebrating, tossing their manes and stomping on cue for the pilots in exchange for treats.

Chewie was lifting Rose off her feet when Finn saw Maz interrupt. "Chewie!" she called, motioning for the Wookiee to bend over. "This is for you." He got down on one knee, and when they were of a height, she placed Han's Medal of Bravery in Chewie's hand and closed his huge fingers around it. "He'd want you to have it," she added.

Poe found him next, and though the pilot had been celebrating along with everyone else, Finn sensed some hesitation.

"General Leia thought they'd destroyed the Emperor at the Battle of Endor," Poe said. "But he came back. More powerful than ever."

"You think he might come back again," Finn said.

"Maybe," Poe said, staring off in Zorii's direction. Of course Poe would worry about that. He was acting general now, and like any good general he was anticipating what fight still lay ahead. "Or some other evil will rise. Evil always rises."

"Naw," said Finn. "Not for a long time, anyway."

Poe gave him a questioning look.

"Don't get me wrong, what General Leia did with Solo and Skywalker was incredible," Finn explained. "Heroic and brave. But it was just one small group against incredible odds."

Poe began to smile. "We're not just one small group," he said, understanding. "The Resistance is a million people, a thousand places."

"General Leia united *a whole galaxy*. This time, it's for real." Poe's grin became huge, and Finn wrapped his friend in a hug.

C-3PO and R2-D2 were coming toward them. "Did you hear that?" C-3PO asked, looking toward the sky.

Lando looked around at the Ajan Kloss base. Everyone knew who he was, but it was different, being known without knowing. Of all his oldest, best friends, only Chewie was left.

He was happy for everyone though. This new galaxy—the *New*

New Republic?—was for the next generation to deal with. He'd get himself back to Pasaana soon. In the meantime, he was just glad to have helped.

"Where are you from, General?" came a voice at his shoulder, and he turned.

It was Jannah, the kid from Kef Bir.

"Gold system," he said. "What about you, kid?"

"I don't know," she said, and her gaze turned distant. "I don't know."

It hit him like a proton torpedo to the gut. He wasn't returning to Pasaana after all. Thousands, maybe millions of kids had been taken by the First Order—like his own little girl. And some of them, a very few, were special. The ones like Finn and Jannah, who had somehow managed to shake their First Order conditioning and make right choices.

Lando and the *Lady Luck* would help these special kids. Find their families, if that's what they wanted. Help them discover their place in the new galaxy. Heck, maybe he'd find his daughter. Probably not; he knew the odds. But that would be a pretty good way to spend his twilight years, right? If the kids were amenable, anyway.

"Well," he said to Jannah. "Let's find out."

The wondrous smile she gave him told him all he needed to know.

Rey landed Luke's X-wing and hopped out of the cockpit. BB-8 rolled toward her, warbling with excitement.

"Beebee-Ate! You made it!" she said, bending down, checking his antennae, his port covers. He'd come out of the battle with hardly a scratch.

She wandered through the base, taking strength and joy in everyone's gaiety, but feeling vaguely alone. People clapped her on the back as she passed—word had already spread that the Emperor was dead. Rey wondered if they'd be so quick to congratulate her if they knew she was his granddaughter.

Or maybe they would. Leia and Luke had been the children of Darth Vader, after all. Maybe the good people of the Resistance didn't care about nonsense like bloodlines and family history.

Finally, she spotted the people she was looking for. Finn and Poe, shouldering through the crowd, looking for her, too. Their gazes caught.

It was all Rey could do not to burst into tears. Her friends. Her family. They had all made it.

Suddenly, they were wrapped in a three-way hug. Rey felt the wetness of Finn's tears against her own cheeks, and Poe squeezed so tight it was hard to breathe.

"Rey," Finn whispered. "I've been meaning to tell you—"

"I know," she said, thinking of the way his presence had become so bright in her mind.

"We all know," Poe said.

A warmth flowed through them, a connection separate from the Force and in its own way just as powerful. Rey didn't care to put a name to it. She only wanted to live in the moment and let it flow over her like water in the desert.

There was so much work to do. Dead to mourn. A galaxy to get up and running. But for now, the celebration continued all around them, and they kept right on hugging.

The *Falcon* touched down on an empty desert plain. The twin suns of Tatooine had yet to show their faces, but early-morning light washed the land in pink and white. Rey and BB-8 descended the ramp and squinted against the reflected brightness. The place was so stark, the ground so bleached, it was almost like the salt flats of Hiila Basin back on Jakku.

Rey stepped forward, toward a domed adobe building jutting from the sand. Only BB-8 accompanied her. All her friends had offered to come with her, but Finn had insisted they stay behind. He understood that she needed to do this alone.

She carried three lightsabers with her. Her own, which she had finally finished, was hooked to her belt.

Rey carried the other two in her haversack.

The adobe building had an arched doorway, but years of wind and sand had half buried it. There'd be no accessing the Lars homestead that way.

Moisture vaporators rose in the distance at irregular intervals, tall spindly towers much like the wind-grain traps on Pasaana. The intervals were irregular, she realized, because some had fallen over.

She stepped past the building and discovered what appeared to be a large sinkhole, half filled with sand. A closer look revealed an arched window and a half-covered door at the base of the sinkhole, built into adobe walls.

At her feet lay a tower panel from one of the fallen vaporators, slightly curved, large enough for one person to sit. She yanked it aside, turned it around, and aimed. A few hours from now, the metal would be too hot to touch. Until then, it would make a perfect sand sled.

She climbed in, drew up her knees, and pushed off. The sled whipped down a sand drift into the heart of the sinkhole, where it gently collided with the base of a broken condenser tower. Rey stepped out and looked around.

So many memories here. She could *feel* them—yearning, loss, worry, desperation, love—and not just Luke's. Two generations of Skywalkers had visited this place.

A cavelike entrance in the wall drew her forward. As she passed into shadow and her eyes adjusted, she noted a long dining table, covered with dust. She ran a finger through the dust, tracing a line of soft blue. Luke had dined here. And also—she reached out, sensing—Anakin?

An adjoining alcove contained some kind of beverage dispenser, but most of the levers and paneling had been scavenged, probably by the local Jawas. A single tall beverage cup made of plastex lay on its side, oddly pristine.

She wandered around for a few more minutes and discovered what used to be a speeder garage, Luke's sleeping loft, and the remains of an electrostatic repeller that had probably kept sand and dust away for years.

Other rooms remained inaccessible to her, their entrances buried in drifts.

Rey stood in the center for a while, taking it all in. Would her life have been different? If she'd been raised in a real home like this, by an aunt and uncle who loved her?

Perhaps not. The family she'd been seeking had been ahead of her the whole time, and she wouldn't change a thing.

The cracked adobe walls and jutting pipes made for an easy climb. She reached the top and pulled Luke's and Leia's lightsabers from her haversack.

Holding them side by side in her hand, she gazed down at them for a long moment. They'd belonged to her teachers. Her family.

She placed them on the ground, wrapped them gently into a small package, using some fabric and a leather tie. Calling on the power of the Force, she pushed, and the lightsabers sank, lower and lower until the ground had fully welcomed them, shrouded them in cool, quiet rest.

Rey stood, pulling out her own lightsaber. She ignited it.

Her lightsaber glowed white-gold, and she gazed at it a long moment. It was single-bladed, with an outer casing and emitter salvaged from her quarterstaff. The final result felt like the exact inverse of the lightsaber held by the dark Rey of her vision, and she *loved* it. It was beautiful, it fit so perfectly in her hand, and she would carry it with her forever.

"Hello!" came a strange voice, and she turned. An old human woman approached, skin wrinkled and sand-blown, hood pulled up against the elements. She held the reins of a tall, gangly etobi, probably on her way to the nearby trading post.

"There's been no one for so long," she said. "Who are you?"

"I'm Rey," she said.

"Rey who?" the old woman asked.

Light snagged Rey's gaze, and she turned her head.

Leia and Luke stood on the edge of the homestead, glowing blue, smiling at her. Rey missed them both so much.

Luke gave her a gentle nod, *It's yours, Rey.*

She turned back to the trader woman. Standing tall, she said, "Rey Skywalker."

"Ah," the woman said, unsurprised. "See you around?" And she hobbled off without sharing her own name.

Rey Skywalker headed toward the *Falcon* to return to her family. People were precious. They were life and *light.* She couldn't have survived the Emperor, couldn't have resisted him, if not for the goodness and strength of her friends, and the generosity of the Jedi who had come before. *And Ben*, she reminded herself.

As she approached, BB-8 warbled that he'd had enough of desert planets. But he gave no complaint when she paused to gaze into the vast desert morning.

Together Rey and BB-8 watched as Tatooine's twin suns rose on a new day.

# ACKNOWLEDGMENTS

Any decent rebellion starts with a plucky team. My plucky team includes but is not limited to editors Tom Hoeler and Jennifer Heddle; my husband, C. C. Finlay; my agent, Holly Root; the Lucasfilm Story Group, but especially Pablo Hidalgo; my fellow novelizer Michael Kogge; J. J. Abrams and Chris Terrio for providing such great material to work with; and, of course, George Lucas, who started it all.

But with this, the final Skywalker Saga novelization, I find I'm most grateful to you, readers and fans of *Star Wars*. Thank you for your enthusiasm, your lightsaber duels, your impeccable costumes, your insatiable appetite for yet more books, your utter devotion to details. Thank you to the fans who dip into the *Star Wars* galaxy only once in a while, have been obsessively following the material for four decades, and everyone in-between. Thank you for engaging with the material both critically and joyfully. Thank you for your passionate vlogs, blogs, and podcasts. This is the best community in any galaxy, and I'm so proud to be part of it.

*The Rise of Skywalker* may be the last of a saga, but the Force will be with us. Always.

## ABOUT THE AUTHOR

RAE CARSON has been inspired to create stories ever since seeing a certain 1977 film. She's the *New York Times* and *USA Today* bestselling author of eight novels, including the acclaimed Girl of Fire and Thorns series, the award-winning *Walk on Earth a Stranger,* and *Star Wars: Most Wanted.* She lives in Arizona with her husband, surrounded by cats and tie-in merchandise.

# ABOUT THE TYPE

This book was set in Minion, a 1990 Adobe Originals typeface by Robert Slimbach (b. 1956). Minion is inspired by classical, old-style typefaces of the late Renaissance, a period of elegant, beautiful, and highly readable type designs. Created primarily for text setting, Minion combines the aesthetic and functional qualities that make text type highly readable with the versatility of digital technology.

EXPLORING MUSIC